D1055098

Dear Reader,

The editors at Harlequin and Silhouette are thrilled to be able to bring you a brand-new featured author program for 2005! Signature Select aims to single out outstanding stories, contemporary themes and oft-requested classics by some of your favorite series authors and present them to you in a variety of formats bound by truly striking covers.

We want to provide several different types of reading experiences in the new Signature Select program. The Spotlight books offer a single "big read" by a talented series author, the Collections present three novellas on a selected theme in one volume, the Sagas contain sprawling, sometimes multi-generational family tales (often related to a favorite family first introduced in series), and the Miniseries feature requested previously published books, with two or, occasionally, three complete stories in one volume. The Signature Select program offers one book in each of these categories per month, and fans of limited continuity series will also find these continuing stories under the Signature Select umbrella.

In addition, these volumes bring you bonus features...different in every single book! You may learn more about the author in an extended interview, more about the setting or inspiration for the book, more about subjects related to the theme and, often, a bonus short read will be included. Authors and editors have been outdoing themselves in originating creative material for our bonus features—we're sure you'll be surprised and pleased with the results!

The Signature Select program strives to bring you a variety of reading experiences by authors you've come to love, as well as by rising stars you'll be glad you've discovered. Watch for new stories from Janelle Denison, Donna Kauffman, Leslie Kelly, Marie Ferrarella, Suzanne Forster, Stephanie Bond, Christine Rimmer and scores more of the brightest talents in romance fiction!

The excitement continues!

Warm wishes for happy reading,

Marsha Zinberg

Marsha Zinberg
Executive Editor
The Signature Select Program

SAGA

DEBRA WEBB

COLBY CONSPIRACY

HARLEQUIN®

TORONTO • NEW YORK • LONDON
AMSTERDAM • PARIS • SYDNEY • HAMBURG
STOCKHOLM • ATHENS • TOKYO • MILAN • MADRID
PRAGUE • WARSAW • BUDAPEST • AUCKLAND

ISBN 0-373-83663-5

COLBY CONSPIRACY

Copyright © 2005 by Debra Webb

This edition published by arrangement with Harlequin Books S.A.

® and TM are trademarks of the publisher. Trademarks indicated with
® are registered in the United States Patent and Trademark Office, the
Canadian Trade Marks Office and in other countries.

www.eHarlequin.com

Printed in U.S.A.

Dear Reader,

Welcome to the world of the Colby Agency. The Colby stories are very dear to my heart and I hope you will enjoy this one.

For five years now I've been fortunate enough to write stories about Victoria Colby and her staff of fine private investigators. I have worked hard to make each and every character as real and true to reader expectation as possible. Last year, Harlequin and I brought you the story of James Colby Jr.'s return (*Striking Distance*). Many, many of you wrote to me to tell me how very much you loved this story. Your letters and e-mails meant a great deal to me. Telling Jim's (aka Seth's) story the way it needed to be told was something I had hoped to be able to do. I have you and Harlequin to thank for that amazing opportunity.

Now I am pleased to bring you *Colby Conspiracy*. This story will give you a close-up insight into the more human side of Victoria and her private world. As always when I write a story, I hope to send you on an edge-of-your-seat ride that will touch every emotion. Oh, and and don't forget the bonus features—I've written something very special for you there!

Best to you,

Deb Webb

This book is dedicated to all the readers who have followed this marvelous journey with me from the beginning with the very first Colby Agency story. Thank you so much for coming back over and over again. I hope that I will never disappoint you and that we will venture into many, many more Colby Agency stories to come. Cheers!

CHAPTER ONE

THE RAIN had stopped. Victoria Colby-Camp stood near the massive window, staring out at the shimmering downtown city lights reflected in the inky black of the Chicago River. This wasn't really the best time for her to be distracted. There were more hands that needed to be shaken, more affirmations of gratitude that should be made. Only an hour ago, she had received her second prestigious award as Chicago's Woman of the Year, but she couldn't help being drawn away from the glitz and the glamour and toward the unknown and the darkness shrouding the city she loved.

No matter that she stood in the mammoth marble lobby of the R. R. Donnelley Building, with its ancient Greek and Roman architecture, or that hundreds of silk- and sequined-clad guests mingled around her. She could feel the subtle shift…the ever-so-slight change in the very atmosphere of her happy but fragile world.

She had every right to be ecstatic. After half a life-time of hoping and praying, she finally had her son back, alive and growing stronger every day. Jim scarcely reflected even a hint of the Seth persona that had rav-aged his life from the age of seven until just one year ago. Great strides had been made with therapy and the love of the woman who had somehow managed to touch his battered heart.

Tears welled in Victoria's eyes when she thought of all that Tasha had done to save Jim, to bring back the man, as well as the boy, who had barely managed to survive behind the ugly mask of a killer named Seth. Victoria smiled and blinked the tears away. Jim and Tasha had set a date for their wedding. All that Victoria had hoped for was finally coming to fruition.

"My dear, this is no place for the guest of honor to be hiding out."

Victoria turned at the sound of the familiar male voice belonging to the man she loved. He was the other long-awaited wish come true in her hard-won battle for happiness. The man she had loved and admired from afar for so very long was now her husband. Emotion tightened her throat. Though a part of her would always love James Colby, the father of her son, her heart now belonged fully to this man...to Lucas Camp.

She smiled, gloried in simply admiring his handsome, however rugged, face for a few seconds before she answered. "I just needed a moment to myself."

The heart-stopping smile that he reserved just for her spread across her husband's face. "This is your night, Victoria. You deserve this honor and more. Come." He folded her arm around his. "Let's have another toast to the Woman of the Year." He leaned down and pressed a gentle kiss to her cheek. "To my lovely wife."

Victoria allowed Lucas to lead her back into the

midst of the festivities. She smiled, offered the expected gestures and comments with all the grace required of a woman in her position, but part of her could not let go of the nagging instinct that everything was about to change.

CHAPTER TWO

THOUGH DANIEL MARKS had had no aspirations about going out tonight, he was glad the rain had stopped. He watched the flow of pedestrians as they ventured from the shops and restaurants on the Magnificent Mile from his vantage point in a luxurious suite on one of the uppermost floors of the historic Allerton Crowne Plaza. He'd never been big on hotels, but he had to admit that even he was impressed by the stately European decor of this one. But what he found most appealing was the location. Close to everything that was anything in the city of Chicago, and one place in particular—the Colby Agency.

Daniel had made this journey to the Gold Coast district of the Windy City by special invitation. After leaving his military career six months ago, he had taken some time to consider what he wanted to do with the rest of his life. Then he'd floated résumés to a few agencies of interest to see what sort of offers he might attract. Victoria Colby-Camp, the esteemed head of the Colby Agency, had invited him to come to her fair city and spend a week or two getting to know the area—at her expense, no less.

He was scheduled to meet with her on Friday. It was

Monday night, and he'd been here two days already. Time enough to get the general lay of the land, and, with one of the city's top real estate agents at his beck and call, to consider possible areas where he might want to live if he accepted a coveted position with the Colby Agency.

Daniel scrubbed a hand over his jaw and laughed at himself. He hadn't been made an offer yet. Maybe he was assuming too much. He'd only been invited to meet with the venerable head of the agency. But he understood from her come-get-to-know-us offer that she was more than a little interested. He didn't find that part surprising, since the Federal Bureau of Investigation and Homeland Security had been interested, as well.

Hell, he wasn't oblivious to what he had to offer. He'd spent ten years in the army as a military strategist and left with the rank of major, knowing he could have been promoted to lieutenant colonel immediately if he'd opted to continue in service. Like most everything else in his life, he'd been on the fast track from the day he'd entered Officer Candidate School.

But he had grown weary of the bureaucracy. Of the political head games that only the military could play with such precision and impact. Not that he'd left the army with a bad taste in his mouth, not at all. Daniel, without question, maintained the deepest respect and admiration for those serving their country in any and all capacities. He simply felt as if he'd done all he could in that world. His momentum had hit a ceiling, and he was going nowhere fast, with more frustration than he cared to tolerate. A mere promotion in rank wasn't enough.

He needed more…something where he could reach his fullest potential without all the political runarounds.

That was the reason he was here in Chicago, rather than in D.C. talking to bigwigs at the Bureau or Homeland Security. With any government agency, he was bound to run into the same thing that had prompted him to move beyond the military. He felt certain that the only way to escape all the bureaucratic crap was to go into the private sector.

So here he was, lounging in a swanky hotel and pondering what the future might hold for a thirty-two-year-old man who'd spent every day of his life since college proudly wearing the prestigious uniform representing the American Armed Forces.

He ran his fingers through his regulation short hair. He couldn't see that changing. It was force of habit. Every other week, he got a haircut. Nor were the physical rigors of his former career going to be left by the wayside. He intended to keep up the physical training for his general well-being, as well as to make him a better investigator—wherever he went to work. Keeping in shape served a dual purpose.

He turned away from the window and strode across to the minibar. The only thing he'd had any trouble getting used to was wearing civvies, civilian clothes. Twisting off the cap of a bottle of beer, he peered down at his stonewashed jeans and cotton cargo shirt. It wasn't any hardship, really; it just took a little more planning. He'd worn the same assortment of uniforms for ten years; he'd never had to worry if anything matched or looked right together; army regulation had dictated his wardrobe, from the cap on his head to the shoes on his feet.

After a long draw from his beer, he dropped onto the foot of the bed and clicked on the local news. Might as well learn the bad with the good. If offered a position with the Colby Agency, he anticipated no reason why he would not be readily accepting. So far, he liked the city. Couldn't see any problems with fitting in.

A frown nudged its way across his brow and he wondered, if he stayed here, would he finally move on to the next logical level of his life. His military career had proved too unpredictable for putting down any sort of permanent roots. He'd been involved in several short-term relationships, but nothing even remotely permanent or serious. His savings were quite adequate—he could afford to buy a home and finally put down those kinds of roots. Not that he'd actually known that sort of lifestyle even before joining the military. He was the quintessential military brat, moving from post to post his entire life, with the exception of the four years he'd spent at Columbia, studying political science with an emphasis on prelaw. Rather than going on to law school, he'd opted for the military, just like his father. He'd felt the need to do his duty. He did not regret that decision now.

His own parents had retired to Florida five years ago. Needless to say, his father was not happy about Daniel's decision to return to civilian life, but he was man enough to restrain himself on the issue. Daniel's mother simply wanted her one and only son—only offspring, for that matter—to be happy. She wanted grandchildren.

Daniel didn't know if he was ready to do the whole wife-and-kids thing just yet, but he couldn't say he didn't feel the need to find something more stable, more long-standing, in a relationship.

He turned up his beer once more and downed a deep, satisfying swallow. Maybe he just needed to get laid. He'd steered clear of physical entanglements since officially exiting the military, more to ensure that a sexual relationship didn't influence his objectivity about his future than anything else. He wanted to do this right. This was a big step for him.

The Colby Agency was where he wanted to be.

He'd researched a number of prominent private agencies and not a one could hold a candle to the Colby Agency's sterling reputation. Victoria Colby-Camp selected only the cream of the crop as members of her staff. Daniel liked the idea that he would be working with the best of the best from all walks of life. Some were former military, like him, but others came from the Bureau, from the ranks of various smaller law enforcement agencies or other, more routine occupations.

He eased back onto the mound of pillows and scanned the television channels, studying the faces that represented local media. Faces with which he would become very familiar, since the Colby Agency was a very high-profile part of this city. Whether Victoria knew it or not, he had already made up his mind. This was where he wanted to be.

And whatever it took, he intended to make it happen.

CHAPTER THREE

CHICAGO BOASTED the largest Chinatown in the Midwest. Densely populated with more than 10,000 residents, mostly Chinese, the area south of Cermak Road was chock-full of Asian grocery and herbal shops, bakeries and restaurants. Traditional Chinese architecture filled the colorful streetscape, welcoming new visitors and longtime residents alike.

Amid the terra-cotta ornaments and mosaic murals, bold, sculpted lions guarded street-level doorways. But nothing in this eclectic culture could protect against the events playing out beyond the commercialized places where tourists wandered. Here, in this less-than-desirable section, there was no glamour or glitz, certainly no goodness. There was only fear waiting around every corner, and survival of the most ruthless was the single prevailing law.

The alley was long and narrow, dark and damp from the rain that had fallen earlier that evening.

Homicide Detective Carter Hastings was barely three months from retirement. He'd turned fifty-five a few weeks ago. Most might not consider that milestone old, but it was damned ancient for a cop. He had decided that he would spend the rest of his life making up for all he'd missed or failed to accomplish these past thirty-odd years. In particular, he wanted to rectify his relationship with his only child, his daughter. He'd let the job rule his life for far too long. He wanted to know his daughter the way a father should.

But that wasn't going to happen now.

He stared into the cruel eyes of certain death towering over him. "I won't tell anyone," he pleaded. "I swear I won't." Carter had never considered himself a coward, but tonight, knowing what he knew, he begged for mercy. He needed just one more day to set to rights all he'd failed to follow through on…to say the things he hadn't said to the daughter he loved.

But this kind of evil knew no mercy. He should have realized years ago that this secret would come back to haunt him, that he could never trust a person who clearly had no soul to stand by any sort of promise. He had no one to blame but himself.

He prayed he would be the only one to pay for his error in judgment.

"Stand up and take it like a man, Hastings."

The words hissed out at him as if they'd risen straight from the hottest flames of hell. Funny, Carter mused, in a way they had. Even the grave's unyielding grip couldn't restrain this kind of evil.

"I kept that secret," he urged, a growl of anger roaring up into his throat, sealing his fate once and for all. He would die tonight. Nothing outside an act of God could save him, and with him would go the whole truth. "You don't have to do this. What purpose would it serve? It's over. Do you hear me! It's been over for nearly twenty years. No one has to know it was you."

Diabolical laughter echoed off the cold, damp walls of the dilapidated buildings crowding in on the place and time that now represented the rest of his life.

"You always were a softy," his killer taunted. "I knew that when you fell for the wife of the victim. All that stopped you from being just like me was your so-called principles." Another of those cruel sounds that couldn't really be called a laugh split the eerie quiet. "You brought this on yourself, Hastings. You should have stayed out of it. I will not tolerate your interference. Don't expect me to believe you're finally willing to set aside those fine principles."

Carter closed his eyes and said a final goodbye to the daughter he'd been less than a decent father to. Sent a quick prayer heavenward for the other woman whose life his long-ago actions would forever change. Now he would never have the chance to make up for his past sins.

The sound of the bullet exploded around him an instant before he felt the hot metal sear his brain.

Carter watched his killer walk away without a single backward glance. Then his eyes closed for the last time.

CHAPTER FOUR

THE STICK turned pink.

A surge of giddiness attacked Tasha North.

She was pregnant!

She and Jim were going to have a baby!

The idea of what a grandchild would mean to Victoria sent another thrill through Tasha. She couldn't wait to tell everyone.

"Come on, North, you can't expect me to believe you haven't missed your work at the CIA."

Tasha blinked and lugged her thoughts back to the here and now. "I'm sorry, Martin. What did you say?"

Martin, decked out in his typical uniform—an elegant designer suit—for schmoozing, stared, exasperated, at her from across the linen-draped table. "I fly all the way from D.C. to Chicago, bring you to one of the ritziest restaurants in town and I still don't warrant your full attention."

She smiled, tamped down her excitement and focused her attention on the man who had been her mentor in the CIA and who, as he so bluntly put it, had gone to all of this trouble in an attempt to lure her back to the Agency.

"I apologize, Martin." She sighed. She couldn't tell

him the real reason for her distraction. "I'm just a little preoccupied." Lord, what an understatement. As she'd gotten dressed this evening for his unexpected visit, she'd considered that a new wardrobe would be in order. Her tight little skirts, the ones Jim loved so much, and formfitting blouses would have to be traded in for something more readily expandable.

Another wave of giddiness washed over her.

Okay, she told herself, stay calm. It was all she could do not to float right up out of her chair. She couldn't wait to tell Jim.

She glanced around the crowded restaurant. Martin was right. He'd brought her to Carmine's, a very classy Italian restaurant filled with Chicago's social elite. The last thing she wanted was for him to think that she didn't appreciate the gesture, however wasted it was.

"The CIA misses your talent," he went on, moving past the awkward moment and diving straight into the heart of the matter. "You've only worked part-time for the Colby Agency this past year, desk work at that. Don't you miss doing field work? Getting deep into the game?"

Truth was, she had gone on only one mission into the field, period, and that hadn't even been for the CIA. Apparently Martin had forgotten that little detail. Lucas Camp had recruited her—stolen her from the CIA, actually—and sent her on a mission that would forever change her life.

That's how she'd met her fiancé...the father of her child...the man she loved with her entire being. James Colby, Junior. Jim. The man who'd stolen her heart even before she'd known his true identity.

"Martin," she said with genuine sincerity, "you will

always be very special to me. But I won't be coming back to the CIA." Surely after a year, he should have come to terms with that reality. Her life was here now. She had no intention of giving up one moment of her time with Jim. Happiness bloomed in her chest all over again. She and Jim were pregnant! And in just a few weeks, they would be married. Her heart fluttered.

Her life was perfect. All that she'd dreamed of was coming true.

Martin sat back in his chair and heaved a disgusted sigh. "There's nothing I can do to change your mind?"

She shook her head, feeling too incredibly blissful to be depressed by his blatant discontent with her decision. "Sorry, but this is what I want to do. I hope you can understand that."

He exhaled another of those impatient breaths. "I suppose, deep down, I suspected this would be your answer."

Tasha studied her longtime friend and mentor. Same dark hair and handsome mug that kept the new female recruits mesmerized, but there was something more in his eyes now, something she couldn't quite read. Her gaze narrowed with an abrupt surge of suspicion.

"What're you up to, Martin?" She remembered that final test he'd put her through last year before pronouncing her field worthy, knew exactly what this powerful man was capable of.

A grin slanted across his face. He reached into the interior pocket of his jacket and drew out an envelope. Plain, white. "You're getting cynical on me, North." He offered the envelope to her. "This is for you," he said mysteriously.

Her uneasiness showing, Tasha accepted the envelope. "What's this about?" The size and shape was consistent with that of a typical birthday card, but it wasn't her birthday.

He nodded to the seemingly innocuous envelope. "Just open it."

Dividing her attention between him and the envelope, she pulled loose the flap and reached inside. It was a card. She read the words embellishing the front and her heart leapt. *Congratulations on your upcoming nuptials.*

He'd heard the news.

"Martin, you're such a shit. You really had me thinking you were going to be upset if I didn't come back to the CIA." She clutched the card to her chest and smiled at him, tears burning in her eyes. God, she would not cry in front of him. He'd never let her live it down. "Thank you."

He shrugged. "What can I say? You're very special to me, North." His tone was uncharacteristically soft and genuine. "I want you to be happy, even if it means you won't ever be coming back to the Agency." He gestured to the card once more. "Now, look inside."

Confused, she opened the card and her mouth gaped at what it contained. A voucher for an all-expenses-paid, two-week honeymoon in Europe from a renowned travel agency here in Chicago. When she'd found her voice, she blurted, "Martin, this is too much! I can't accept this."

He winked. "Sure you can. You just tell Lucas Camp that he might have stolen you from me, but you still love me the best." His lips tilted into that lopsided grin again. "Let's see that old bastard top this."

Tasha couldn't help herself. She had to scoot from

her seat and rush around the table to give him a hug. She did love him. He would always hold a special place in her heart, as well as her life.

As THE TAXI traveled east on Division Street, Tasha barely contained the urge to dial Jim right then on her cell phone and give him the news. She shivered at the idea of how deliriously happy she knew he would be. She resisted the impulse. This was too important to do over the phone. It had to be done in person.

Jim had come so far the last few months. He had made great strides in coming to terms with the atrocities that had been done to him after he'd been kidnapped from his family at age seven. He'd progressed to the point of what most people would say was normal. Anyone who met him now would never suspect that just a year ago, he'd been a cold-blooded killer for hire. His primary mission in life had been to assassinate his own mother, whom he thought had abandoned him.

Tasha shuddered at the memories of just how ruthless the alter ego Seth had been. Jim Colby had been buried so deeply under that evil persona that reaching him had been almost impossible. Somehow, she had managed to do just that. Seth had grabbed on to what she'd offered—her heart and soul—and slowly but surely Jim Colby had resurfaced—been reborn.

She would be lying if she didn't admit that there had been some aspects of Seth that had intrigued her—still did—but he was gone for good, and it was for the best. Her life with Jim was worth every moment of pain and uncertainty she'd endured with Seth.

No. There was no way she would ever go back to the

CIA or anywhere else. Jim was her life now. Jim and the baby. She was perfectly content doing research for the Colby Agency on a part-time basis. She no longer felt that burning desire to prove herself or to make her mark among the superspies of the world. This was her life, and she adored every minute of every hour.

Being plain old Tasha North—soon to be Tasha Colby—fulfilled her every desire.

She'd fought the fight of her life and won, had walked away with the kind of love few ever found, and now they were about to move onto the next level…marriage and a family. The latter was a little sooner than expected, but she was definitely up to the challenge. The thought of carrying Jim's child made her tremble with anticipation. She pressed her hand to her flat belly, closed her eyes and took a deep, steadying breath. Jim would be thrilled!

When the taxi reached her street in Old Town, Tasha dug out the fare and a nice tip. She looked up at the Queen Anne row house that she and Jim shared, a present from his mother, Victoria Colby-Camp. She loved the house. It was perfect. But Tasha hadn't mentioned to Martin how she and Jim had gotten their cozy home. As much as she appreciated his wonderful gift, Victoria had cornered the market on gift giving. She had spent the last year trying to make up to her son for all they'd missed since his abduction nearly nineteen years ago.

Tasha hopped out of the cab and strolled up the walk to her door. She inhaled deeply of the night air, enjoying the clean scent of the recent rain that still lingered. She hesitated before unlocking the door and surveyed the sky and the stars that had peeked from behind the clouds. She wanted to remember everything about this night. Wanted it to hold a special place among the memories she and Jim were making together.

Another rush of pulse-tripping anticipation launched her back into gear. She couldn't wait another second. She had to tell him the news.

No sooner had the key turned in the lock than the knob was twisted out of her hand and the door jerked open.

Harsh fingers dug into her forearm and hauled her inside.

Before she had a chance to react to the stab of fear a lethal masculine voice demanded, "Where have you been?"

Even in the dark, even with her heart pounding like a drum, Tasha recognized that voice—felt the malice in it penetrate all the way to the very depths of her soul.

Seth.

"Jim." She reached through the darkness, tried to touch him. What could have brought about this relapse? Something had to have happened to—

He slammed her against the wall. "I said," he snarled, "where the hell have you been?"

Tasha's body started to quake. She struggled to steel herself against the fear and worry running rampant inside her. "I've been to dinner," she said calmly. "You knew—"

"So you just take off?"

His face was pressed so close to hers she could feel the warmth of his breath on her cheek, could smell the liquor. Jim never drank, not anymore. The doctors had warned it might destabilize his condition.

Renewed fear raced through her veins. One doctor in particular had warned that Jim was still vulnerable, that a break from reality could occur unless strict precautions were taken to insulate him from the slightest stress. But he had been okay for months. He was well… happy…he was Jim, the man she loved.

The baby. Oh, God. Hurt knotted inside her. Please, God, not now. Don't let him regress. Her thoughts whirled frantically, futilely. There had to be something she could do to stop this…to bring him back…

"Jim, please, tell me what's happened?" She hated the quiver in her voice, the desperation. He'd been through too much already. It just wasn't fair for him to spiral back into that abyss all over again. Not now, after he'd come so very far.

"Shut up and take off your clothes," he commanded savagely. "I've been waiting for you."

Tasha froze, considered her options. Did she play along and hope he snapped out of whatever the hell this was, or did she fight back? Not now. Not knowing that she was pregnant.

"Jim, let me call your doctor," she pleaded, praying she would somehow get through to him.

"Stop calling me that," he warned, his muscular body pinning her to the wall. "Little Jimmy died a long time ago," he taunted cruelly. "Now stop stalling."

He wanted sex. Okay, she could play along. Surely he would snap out of this.

Drawing in a steadying breath, she reached toward the top button of her blouse. Her fingers shook before she could stem the reaction.

"You're too slow," he growled, then ripped open her blouse.

She bit down on her lower lip to hold back a gasp.

"Hmmm," he breathed. "You smell so sweet." He licked a trail down her throat and across her shoulder. She shivered, couldn't help herself. "You like that?" He breathed the words on her damp skin.

"Please, Jim, let's just talk," she begged, suddenly fearing that he would take this too far... Damn, she didn't know what to expect.

But she had to protect the baby.

His hand closed brutally over her breast and Tasha knew exactly what she had to do.

She went limp in his arms, surrendered completely. His full attention was focused on the breast he'd revealed. His mouth landed there and she made a sound of encouragement. As he kissed his way back up to her throat she rammed her fist into his unsuspecting gut.

He staggered back, doubled over.

Acting on pure instinct now, she landed a kick to the side of his head, forcing him to the floor. Then she made a run for it.

At the same instant that her fingers curled around the doorknob, his manacled around her ankle, closing like a vise.

She screamed, grabbed at the door even as he pulled her away from it.

He was too fast, too strong.

He yanked hard. She fell forward onto the hardwood floor. As he dragged her to him she kicked hard with her free leg and landed a blow to his jaw.

He swore and flung his full weight down on top of her. She grunted at the impact. His right hand clamped around her throat.

"Don't move," he growled between clenched teeth.

Tasha stilled. Her breath raged in and out of her lungs, barely hissing past the hold he had on her throat. Part of her screamed inside, urged her to keep fighting, but another part feared for the baby. She couldn't afford to antagonize him any further. He was too strong.

His fingers all but cut off her airway. He used his right hand to shove her skirt up her thighs. Then he spread her legs and burrowed his way fully between them. His mouth came down on top of hers hard.

She felt him wrench open his jeans. Felt his thick sex spring free and prod against her panties. She closed her eyes and tried to lie still, told herself it would be better this way. Don't give him any reason to hurt you.

He tore away her panties and shoved into her in one brutal plunge.

She caught her breath, winced against the pleasure of feeling the man she loved inside her and at the same time fearing the demon driving him.

"Now that's more like it," he said silkily, tauntingly. He flexed his hips, driving deeper. He kissed her lips, then her jaw. She shivered, afraid to guess what he might do next.

She squeezed her eyes shut and tried to pretend that this was only a nightmare. It couldn't be real…couldn't be happening. Not now. Tears seeped past her tightly clenched lids, but she couldn't hope to stop them.

His lips encountered those salty tears and he stilled.

He drew back from her then and though she couldn't see his eyes in the darkness, she felt the change in his body—the sudden, jagged turn his respiration had taken, the slight tremble of his hands as his grip loosened.

"Oh, God." The words tore out of his throat on a wounded moan of agony.

He scrambled off her, pulled her onto his lap. "What've I done?" He ran his hands over her purposefully, hurriedly, as if searching for injury. "Did I hurt you? God, please tell me I didn't hurt you, Tasha."

"I'm all right," she managed to say, pushing past the emotion lodged in her throat. "I'm okay."

He cradled her in his arms for a long while. Tasha couldn't say how long. He kept telling her over and over how sorry he was. How he hadn't meant to hurt her. And then he carried her to the bathroom and bathed her gently in the deep claw-footed tub. He smoothed the washcloth over her skin lovingly in an attempt to soothe the hurt.

Tasha watched him, her heart too damaged to question the sudden reversal. But her eyes saw clearly the price he'd paid for the lapse.

She only knew that he was behaving like Jim now. Inside, she cried, both thankful and scared out of her mind. Because no matter what her eyes saw, no matter what her ears told her as the man she loved attended to her needs, begged for her forgiveness, nothing he did or said would change the cold, hard truth.

Seth was back.

CHAPTER FIVE

BOUND BY THE CHICAGO RIVER and developed by the industrial working class, Chicago's Lower West Side was as diverse as it was eclectic.

"Stop here."

Upon Emily Hastings's order, the taxi driver braked and eased the cab up to the curb on 18th Street. She paid the fare and got out, lugging the carry-on bag with her. The weight of the hastily packed bag dragged at her shoulder, but she ignored it. She made a quick swipe at her skirt in an attempt to smooth the travel wrinkles.

She was home, for the first time in too long to remember.

She inhaled deeply, drawing in the inviting scents of corn tortillas and spiced peppers from the Mexican restaurants and specialty shops that formed the cultural heart of the neighborhood. She let the sounds of salsa emanating from open windows and doors—and it wasn't even noon yet—seep into her soul.

Her feet guided her; no thought was required. That was good, since her eyes were too busy taking in the changes since she'd last been here...*home*.

Nineteenth-century buildings served as stoic, sophisticated backdrops to the vibrancy of the street vendors.

Emily felt a smile tilt her lips as she surveyed one of her favorites. Walking to the bus stop everyday for school, she'd watched as the dilapidated structure had been overtaken by artists searching for low-rent digs. Over time, the whole district had been brought to life by murals and dotted by funky galleries, all as a result of the influx of those starving artists. Emily had been too young to really understand the change; she'd simply been enthralled with the evolution.

As she took the turn onto her old street, Emily felt the wonder wane a bit. Other memories, ones not so comfortably recalled, filtered through her mind. The sound of weeping at her brother's wake…the constant arguing between her parents after the death of her only sibling. The sharp pain of knowing that life would never be the same.

Emily pushed those old hurts aside and strode more briskly toward the house where she'd lived as a child before fate had taken its heavy toll on a typical lower middle class family, breaking it into pieces that would never again fit together.

She stood on the sidewalk for several seconds before stepping up onto the stoop. It looked just the same, only smaller. She stared up at the bow-shaped window on the second floor of the modest house. Her old room. She'd sat at that window many nights and prayed that her parents would stop fighting, that everything would be okay again.

But her prayers had gone unanswered.

Her brother had died, at age sixteen, of a sudden heart attack. His rare, congenital heart defect had gone undiagnosed. Her mother had blamed her father. As a cop, he hadn't been a good enough provider, in Emily's mother's opinion. The loss and pain, all of it, were her father's fault.

So her mother had left, taking Emily with her. They'd moved all the way to Sacramento, California, in an attempt to escape the memories.

Emily's father had stayed right here. In this house, living with the memories and somehow surviving.

But now he was gone, too.

She blinked out of the trance the past weaved and reached up to the ledge above the door to retrieve the spare key her father had kept there for as long as she could remember. Her bracelet jingled as the numerous charms clinked together. She still wore it every day, had since the day her father had given it to her more than a dozen years ago, back when life had been normal.

On autopilot, she opened the door and stepped inside. A wave of emotion washed over her, as did the scents she'd associated with her father. Old Spice aftershave and gun oil.

For as long as she could remember, her father had been a cop. She'd sat in his lap many a night as he cleaned his service revolver and explained to her the hazards of not showing proper respect for the weapon. Both Emily and her brother had learned early not to play with guns.

An ache pierced her, and Emily fought for control. How could this have happened?

Her father had been murdered only three months from retirement.

She shuddered and closed the door behind her. Her bag dropped to the floor in the narrow entry hall and she moved deeper into the house.

The call she'd received at five this morning had been surreal, like a dream that couldn't possibly be related to reality. But it was. It was all too gut-wrenchingly real.

Her father was dead.

Murdered.

The detective who'd called had assured Emily that it would not be necessary for her to identify the body and that the body wouldn't be released before day after tomorrow, but she'd insisted on coming to Chicago immediately.

How could she not?

It was the least she could do.

Though Emily had been raised by her mother and stepfather since she was twelve, she still loved her father. Maybe they hadn't seen each other often, but he'd gotten out to California when he could. He'd written regularly, had called once in a while.

No matter how much her mother would have preferred that she forget her father and the past altogether, Emily had never done so.

She moved slowly through the house, peeked into the parlor that looked as neat as she'd expected. Her father had always been meticulous about housekeeping. With his busy schedule as a homicide detective, she imagined that he'd hired a cleaning lady for the more tedious routine work, but the small, everyday tasks of keeping things tidy would have been something he naturally did. Emily had inherited that obsession from him. Her friends had always called her a neat freak.

The kitchen and downstairs bedroom her parents had shared looked exactly the same. Every picture, every knickknack sat exactly where it had fourteen years ago. Her mother hadn't taken a single household or personal item when she and Emily had left. To this day, her mother never spoke of the son who'd died, or of her old life in Chicago. It was as if the past had never happened.

Slowly Emily climbed the stairs to the second floor. Her breath caught when she opened the door to her old bedroom. Her father had left it exactly as Emily remembered. She moved about the room and touched the stuffed animals and pictures that told the tale of her childhood. The small canopy bed with its frilly pink coverlet, the poster of her one-time favorite TV heartthrob taped to the wall. She'd sat in the window seat and daydreamed about growing up and marrying her idol someday.

Dizzy with the remembered voices and moments from her old life, Emily made her way to the other bedroom on the second floor. Her brother's room. A small bathroom that the two had shared separated their rooms.

Colton's room took her breath away. The football trophies. The big high school banner. Photos of him armored in sports gear. He had played them all, the epitome of the perfect athlete. Who would have expected him to drop dead on the field running laps?

Emily picked up a framed photograph—the last one taken of her brother—and touched his face. It had been the beginning of the end. Nothing had been the same after that summer.

She took a deep breath and blinked back the emotion burning in her eyes. Memory Lane wasn't all it was cracked up to be, she decided as she closed up the rooms that served as tributes to forgotten childhoods. She wondered if her father had spent time in those rooms, wishing things had turned out differently. She hoped work had kept him too busy for that. Or maybe he'd moved on, as her mother had, and found someone new with which to share his life. But he'd never remarried and not once had he mentioned another woman to Emily. Just another sad truth to add to the growing stack that represented her old life here.

Back downstairs, she took her bag to her father's room, opting to sleep there while she was in town. She picked up his pillow and inhaled deeply of his essence.

He'd been lost to her for so long that the impact of his death hadn't fully sunk in. It was as if he would walk through the door after his shift ended and all would be the same. But that wasn't going to happen. Maybe she should have identified his body in an effort to force the reality past the barrier of natural denial.

She'd come back to Chicago to plan his funeral, to take care of his final arrangements and his estate. Her mother had refused to come. To her, Carter Hastings had died the same year her son had died.

Emily tossed the pillow aside and decided a hot cup of tea would help get her started. She'd called the law office where she worked this morning to tell them she was taking two weeks off to settle her father's estate. Her bosses had understood.

She'd gone to college and gotten a degree in journalism in hopes of becoming a Nobel Prize-winning author, but it hadn't panned out yet. What did a hopeful journalist do when she couldn't get work in her field? She became a secretary. She could type and file and answer the phone; it was a no-brainer.

After a soothing cup of her father's longtime favorite,

Earl Grey, Emily got to work. Her first chore was to go through her father's official papers and determine what insurance policies were in effect. Someone from Chicago PD's human resources department would touch base with her on whatever benefits would be forthcoming.

By the time dusk fell over the neighborhood, she had contacted the funeral home where her brother had been taken all those years ago and made preliminary arrangements. Barring any unforeseen obstacles, a service would be held Thursday afternoon at two. The wife of her father's partner had called and insisted on having Emily for dinner that evening. She'd almost declined but hadn't wanted to hurt any feelings. The partner her father had served with the past several years was not the one he'd had when she was a kid. She didn't really know what had become of his first partner. Emily had vaguely recalled her father mentioning his first partner had died, but she really wasn't sure

With all she could accomplish today done, Emily shuffled the papers and policies back into neat little stacks and prepared to put them back into the briefcase-size fireproof safe box her father had kept them in. He'd mailed her a key and the location of the safe box years ago. Foolishly she'd kept the key on the charm bracelet he'd given her the Christmas before the divorce. And, even more foolishly, she still wore the damned thing. It was the one part of the past she'd clung to…the single part she hadn't been able to give up. Unlike her mother, Emily had still loved her father, still cherished the memories of the family they had once been so very long ago.

In the process of lugging the heavy fireproof box back into the closet to tuck it back into its hiding place behind the shoeboxes of photos and other family mementos, something shifted inside.

Not the papers or policies. This was something heavier, something she hadn't noticed or heard before.

Curious, she hauled the load to the bed and reopened it. Nothing looked out of the ordinary. The papers were no longer in their neat little stacks, but that was to be expected since shifting the box into its hiding place required standing it on end. Then she noticed the difference. One side of the bottom appeared to jut up a little higher than the other.

Emily pressed down on the uneven bottom, but it didn't budge. She removed the papers and set them aside, then hefted the box to an upside-down position and watched the interior floor fall onto the mattress. A bundle of yellow-tinged envelopes flopped onto the metal plate now lying on the covers.

Emily pushed the box upright once more and considered that she'd heard of, even seen, false bottoms. She just hadn't expected to find her father harboring something like this in his bedroom closet.

She picked up the stack of bundled envelopes and read the addressee's name. James Colby. She frowned. Who was James Colby? She looked at the date and was startled again. The envelope was postmarked over eighteen years ago. Strange.

Emily skimmed through the rest of the letters and noted the same names each time—Madelyn Rutland and James Colby. One was even addressed to a Victoria Colby but had never been processed through the post office. Or, at least, she presumed so, since there was no postmark on the envelope. Madelyn Rutland was a name

Emily recognized. Madelyn had been her father's first partner when he'd moved from beat cop to homicide detective. But James Colby was unknown to Emily, as was Victoria Colby.

Why on earth would her father have kept someone else's letters?

Too tired and emotionally drained to ponder the question any longer, Emily replaced the false bottom and stacked all the papers, including the bundle of letters, inside the safe box. There were probably lots more things she would discover among her father's belongings that didn't make sense to her. After all, it had been many years since she'd lived in this house or been a significant part of his life.

Everyone had their secrets, but her father had always been a straightforward kind of guy. She couldn't imagine him having any deep, dark secrets that would hurt anyone or even disrupt anyone's life.

A bunch of old letters addressed to people she didn't even know was the last thing she needed to worry about right now. Her father was dead.

She had to do right by him. Taking care of his affairs was the last thing she could do for him; that task had to be her main focus.

What possible difference could letters nearly two decades old make now?

CHAPTER SIX

FIVE O'CLOCK HAD come and gone before Victoria had found time to review the day's *Tribune*. Some days were like that, one meeting or conference call after the other. She didn't actually mind. The flurry of activity meant that the Colby Agency continued to thrive. Victoria had worked hard for nearly two decades to carry on what her husband had started. Having her son returned to her last year had made all the hard work and sacrifice worth it.

She had kept alive the legacy of Jim's father. Jim would carry on with the same.

Victoria's brow furrowed with remembered worry. Jim hadn't come in today. He usually called when he planned to take a day off. But today he hadn't. She hadn't heard from Tasha, either.

Months and months of therapy had brought a semblance of normalcy to Jim's life. He'd adjusted extremely well, in Victoria's opinion. But it was hard work and there had been times during the past year when failure had loomed. Somehow her son, showing the true strength he'd inherited from his father, had overcome his weaknesses and the extensive brainwashing he'd suffered.

Victoria pressed the intercom button. "Mildred, would you see if you can reach Jim or Tasha for me, please?"

"Certainly, Victoria."

Victoria stared at the silent intercom for a time after she'd instructed her personal secretary to make the call. That was another part of the past that was over now. Mildred and her niece, Angel, had been saved from the evil the Colbys' archnemesis had wielded.

Leberman.

Victoria couldn't recall how many months it had been since she'd thought of that heinous name. The bastard had died last October, but his devilish machinations had continued for months afterward. The ordeal finally culminated in the world being rid of those who'd conspired with Leberman to ruin the Colbys.

Despite having lived through that nineteen-year nightmare, it still seemed impossible to Victoria that one man could harbor such immense hatred toward another.

"Victoria, I'm not getting an answer. Shall I keep trying?" Mildred's voice floated from the intercom, tugging Victoria from the troubling memories.

She pursed her lips thoughtfully for a moment before making a decision. "That's all right, Mildred. I'll try from home later."

Victoria turned her attention back to the newspaper and attempted to put her concerns about her son and his fiancée out of her mind. It was possible that Jim had had an appointment today that Victoria had forgotten. Tuesday was Tasha's usual day off. Perhaps she was overreacting.

She unfolded the paper on her desk and spread it open. A quick scan of the major headlines before turning the page drew her up short. She dropped the page into place and let her gaze zero in on one particular news article.

Local Homicide Detective Murdered.

Victoria read the accompanying story, regret churning in her stomach.

Carter Hastings…

What on earth?

The name swept her back nineteen years as easily as Leberman's had…back to the night she had realized her son would not be found in the woods near their home. He was gone, had vanished, seemingly into thin air.

Homicide Detective Hastings had shown up at her door and Victoria had fallen apart. She had not wanted to believe that her son might be dead, but obviously Chicago PD had considered that possibility.

Hastings and his partner, Madelyn Rutland, had worked hard to prove Victoria's son had merely wandered off or perhaps had been abducted by someone who wanted a son of their own. Everyone at Chicago PD had wanted to help the Colbys overcome their tragedy. The Colby Agency had already earned a respected place amid local law enforcement. No one wanted to see Victoria's family suffer.

But there had been nothing anyone could do. The vile bastard Leberman had been behind little Jimmy's abduction. And it would be eighteen long years before Victoria would know what really had happened.

Just three years after that horrific tragedy, Victoria's husband had been murdered, and Carter Hastings had once more come back into her life. He had insisted on being the lead investigator. She would never forget the way he comforted her and worked diligently to bring James's murderer to justice. But Carter had been searching for a ghost…a man more elusive than he could have imagined. Still, she had appreciated all his hard work and his endless emotional support.

The time between Jim's abduction and James's murder still carried a measure of guilt for Victoria. Hers and James's relationship had not been the same after their son went missing. They'd struggled to hold things together those final three years, but it hadn't been easy. For years after James's death, she had worried that she should have done more to make things right between them, but she just hadn't been able to get past the pain. Living with the reality that she might never see her son again, that he was likely dead, had been too monumental a burden to allow her to contend with anything else—even her beloved husband's needs.

Lucas had helped her to get past those haunting months and years. He'd reminded her over and over how much James had loved her, how very well he had known that she loved him. The loss of a child brought hardship upon even the best marriage. Maybe that's part of what had made Victoria fall in love with Lucas. Or maybe she'd been a little bit in love with him from the very first time she'd ever met him.

A wistful smile tugged at her lips. No matter the harsh realities of her past, her life was wonderful now. She had her son back and the man she loved beside her.

That nagging feeling she'd suffered last night at the gala filtered into her thoughts.

Victoria shoved it aside. She refused to be plagued by worry any longer. She had worried enough in the past for a dozen lifetimes.

This was her time. She deserved this happiness and she would not waste any of it borrowing trouble.

She picked up the phone and put through a call to Chicago PD. Carter Hastings had been incredibly helpful to her all those years ago. The least she could do was offer whatever help her agency might be able to provide for him.

"Chief Holmes, this is Victoria Colby." She listened as the chief of Chicago's homicide division parlayed the usual pleasantries. "Yes, it was good seeing you and Karen at the gala last night."

Chief Marvin Holmes reiterated how no one he knew was more deserving of the honor of Woman of the Year than Victoria. She appreciated the sentiment. "Thank you, Chief. I was actually calling about this terrible news I've just read in today's paper about Detective Hastings."

Victoria's posture stiffened at the abrupt change in the chief's tone. It was as if the call had suddenly been diverted to some other office and some other man.

She tried to make another inroad, offering her condolences and suggesting that certainly all of Chicago PD was shocked and determined to bring this killer to justice. But the chief wasn't biting. The change in the whole tone of the conversation was so extreme that Victoria felt uncomfortable continuing to attempt to discuss the topic.

"Don't hesitate to let my agency know if there is anything at all we can do to facilitate this investigation."

Chief Holmes hurried to end the call after that, insisting that he had a meeting. Victoria dropped the receiver back into its cradle, her mind reeling with questions and mounting confusion.

Why in the world would the chief be so evasive, so

downright uncooperative about a case? She understood that this one was particularly sensitive because one of their own had been murdered, but why would her help— at the very least her condolences—not be welcome?

Before she could dwell upon the puzzling questions, her door opened and Tasha appeared. Victoria instantly set aside her troubling thoughts and offered her future daughter-in-law a warm smile.

"Tasha, what brings you to the office on your day off?"

Jim's fiancé didn't have to answer. As the younger woman quickly closed the door behind her and strode straight up to Victoria's desk without pause, Victoria could see that something was wrong.

"We have to talk."

It wasn't so much the words, or even the expression on her face, but something Victoria saw in Tasha's eyes sent her apprehension rocketing to the next level.

Every instinct Victoria possessed, had honed over the last decade and a half, warned that the shift in her world had just occurred.

CHAPTER SEVEN

TASHA HADN'T WANTED TO COME TO Victoria this way.
She had hoped to work out the situation on her own, just
her and Jim. But when she'd awakened this morning, Jim
had been missing and last night's incident had morphed
into a whole other dimension. She'd spent the entire day
searching for him with no luck. Every place he liked to
go, the clinic where he still received therapy, even the
Colby offices. She'd looked everywhere and no Jim.

"Tasha, sit down," Victoria urged, no doubt noticing
the paleness that fear and exhaustion had painted on her
skin. "Tell me what's happened."

Tasha had always known her future mother-in-law
had uncanny instincts; she only prayed that she could
keep being pregnant a secret from her. Not that she
wanted to hurt Victoria or to keep things from her, but she
didn't want to tell anyone else until after she'd told Jim.

She couldn't tell him last night.

Not even after he'd begged her to forgive him for the
slip back into the darkness of his alter ego. He'd bathed
her, made her hot chocolate and hovered over her for
hours afterward in an attempt to make up for his slip.
He'd promised it wouldn't happen again.

But he'd been wrong.

Eventually, his sweet coddling had turned sensual and they'd made love. It was then that she'd felt Seth again. Just little glimpses…but he had been there, as real as if she'd been making love with two different men.

Tasha trembled even now, felt guilty for thinking such negative thoughts. It wasn't that she hadn't cared about Seth, loved him on some level, even; she just couldn't live with that ruthless part of who and what Jim had once been. No one could.

"It's Jim," she said, knowing Victoria waited for some kind of explanation. "He's suffered a regression."

The look on Victoria's face said it all.

Regression. The single most dreaded word known to the family members of a therapy patient.

Victoria sank back into the luxurious chair behind her desk. "Please, tell me exactly what happened."

Her fingers twisting together in apprehension, Tasha's knees pretty much gave way on their own, bringing her bottom in contact with the closest chair. Having said it out loud made the whole situation even more real. Tasha swallowed in an attempt to dampen her dry throat. She wasn't sure exactly how to begin. There were parts she simply couldn't share with Victoria. Parts she would be the first to admit that maybe she'd imagined. Tasha closed her eyes. No, she hadn't imagined his ruthless touch, the brutal way he'd taken her even after his drawn-out apology for the way he'd greeted her when she'd come home.

Something was very, very wrong.

What could have happened to trigger this kind of sudden regression? The doctors had insisted from the beginning that any possible regression would be trig-

gered by something. That's why they'd all been so careful and followed every order of the team of psychiatrists
studying Jim's unparalleled case. They kept no liquor
at home, not even wine.

And yet, here she sat, about to tell his mother the
worst news possible.

"Last night when I came home from dinner with
Martin," Tasha began, then hesitated, scarcely able to
utter the rest, "*Seth* was waiting." Vivid images from
their encounters last year—when she'd been working
undercover in an attempt to determine the true identity
of the hired assassin named Seth—fluttered one after the
other through her weary mind.

Please, don't let this destroy Jim, she silently prayed.

Color visibly drained from Victoria's face. "Dear
God, no."

Tasha managed a nod. "I'm afraid so."

Unable to hide as much as she'd like from the per-
ceptive woman, Tasha sat helpless as Victoria surveyed
her closer, no doubt noting the turtleneck sweater she
wore, though the early fall weather hadn't cooled
enough to warrant sweaters just yet.

"Did he hurt you?"

The pain underscoring the question ripped at Tasha's
chest. Victoria had only had her son back for one year;
even the vague idea of losing him again had to be killing her, just as it was Tasha.

"Not really," Tasha allowed, hoping to spare her feelings. But Victoria was not one to be fooled so easily.

"Bruises?"

Tasha nodded. "And a couple of scratches." She
would not, under any circumstances, mention the other

soreness. It was far too intimate. Tears crowded behind her lashes when she considered again how scared she had been for the baby. She quickly pushed aside the memories, couldn't risk Victoria seeing it in her eyes.

Victoria nodded. "Shall I call Dr. Pendelton?"

Tasha shook her head. "I'm all right." Dr. Kyle Pendelton was a longtime client of the Colby Agency. He was also a good friend of Victoria's. "But Jim is missing or hiding."

"You've been looking for Jim," Victoria guessed, her worry visibly mounting.

"Yes. I've looked everywhere I can think of. Checked with the clinic. No sign of him." Tasha swallowed tightly. "I guess this means you haven't heard from him, either."

"Unfortunately, I haven't."

Tasha felt her heart sink further. What could they do now?

"All right," Victoria said, her voice offering hope and the kind of sheer determination that Tasha should not have doubted even for a second. "We have to assume, then, that the situation has progressed into darker territory."

Tasha had to give her full credit—Victoria's strength was incredible. Her ability to hold her own under the circumstances was more than Tasha could say for herself just now. She was crumbling inside. But that wouldn't help Jim.

"What do we do about it?" Tasha asked, feeling hollow and impotent.

"We assume the worst and go from there," Victoria said bluntly, almost—almost—sounding completely objective.

Tasha watched, feeling numb, as Victoria instructed

Mildred, her personal secretary, to convene a staff meeting in the conference room.

Most of the agency's investigators didn't leave until around six, which meant everyone would be there.

Tasha wrung her trembling hands and ordered herself to be calm. She had to deal with this just as Victoria did. She owed it to Jim. Anything less was unacceptable. He needed Tasha right now, more than ever. The beginning had been tough, but coming this far only to fail would be devastating to him. To all of them. Tasha had to be strong for Jim.

For the baby.

Minutes later, as Tasha and Victoria entered the crowded conference room, Tasha had about pulled herself together. She surveyed the room, feeling her nerves settle a bit as she acknowledged the strength in the faces she knew so well. Ian Michaels and his wife, Nicole. Simon Ruhl. Ric Martinez. Zach Ashton. Ethan Delaney. Maxwell Pierce and Doug Cooper-Smith. Amy Benson-Calhoun. Incredibly—or maybe it was pure luck—this was one of the few times that all the investigators were actually in town at the same time.

Her gaze shifted to the plaque that held center stage in the massive room and paid tribute to those who had once served the Colby Agency but had moved on for personal reasons. The names listed included: Katherine Robertson, Nick Foster, Trevor Sloan, Alexandra Preston, Ryan Braxton, Trent Tucker, Heath Murphy. There was a special tribute to the agency's founder, James Colby.

There were others who worked behind the scenes, such as Mildred Parker, and half a dozen other research personnel, including Tasha herself.

But would this hand-selected staff be good enough to find a man like Seth if he didn't want to be found? Tasha refused to refer to his latest actions as something Jim would do, because he wouldn't. Jim loved her, had asked her to marry him. This wasn't him…it was Seth, the lethal alter ego that Leberman had created.

As Victoria explained the situation, the familiar faces in the room grew more solemn.

Tasha knew what they were thinking.

Jim Colby's damage had been too severe, too deeply ingrained. Making him whole again was too much to ask. The past few months had only been the quiet before the storm.

Tasha had even considered as much herself, but she refused to believe the man she loved couldn't be saved. She'd seen his progress, had felt the change. He could do this. Something had to have happened to trigger this unexpected episode.

The idea that with the sort of brainwashing Jim had endured for years could carry some sort of hidden event that would only surface when the right situation occurred was a possibility. The specialist whom Lucas Camp had brought in to research that aspect had suggested as much, but there had been no way to tell for sure. It was more or less a game of wait and see.

And now something had gone wrong.

An *episode* had occurred.

But before they could determine the cause, they had to find Jim. As Seth, he was a danger to himself and almost anyone else he encountered, including the people he loved most. Seth had no conscience and was ruthless.

Tasha thought of the baby again and prayed that Leberman would not enjoy one last victory. That bastard was dead and gone. Tasha had watched him die by the hand of the very monster he'd created. Seth had killed his maker. She shuddered at the memories.

She glanced around the room again. They needed Lucas. He was the foremost expert on Leberman, even more so than Victoria.

As if reading her mind, Victoria said, "I'll get in touch with Lucas right away. He's in D.C. and won't be back until Friday but at least he can get in touch with the specialist who evaluated Jim before."

And with that final announcement, the entire Colby Agency set to work to find and rescue one of its own before he crossed a line where even Lucas Camp wouldn't be able to help him.

CHAPTER EIGHT

IT RAINED AGAIN on Thursday, the day Emily said a final goodbye to her father.

Thankfully, by the time those who'd come to pay their last respects to one of Chicago's finest arrived at the church, the sun had poked through the clouds and brightened the somber afternoon.

Emily remembered the church from Sunday mornings as a child, a lifetime ago, it seemed, when her family had been a complete unit. Elaborate carvings and intricate stained-glass windows graced the interior of the limestone-and-brick chapel. With just enough pomp and circumstance, the service had provided a distinguished send-off for the man she had always loved but scarcely knew.

Emily had called her mother last night to give her one last opportunity to change her mind about attending the service, but she'd adamantly refused.

So Emily stood alone as hundreds upon hundreds of those who'd known her father passed, offering their condolences and shaking her hand. She had expressed her gratitude so many times the words now felt empty and forced. She felt numb and more exhausted than she ever had before.

She'd lost count of the police officers who'd assured her that nothing would stop them from solving her father's murder. So many promises of support and offers of assistance had been given that her head was spinning. The whole concept that her father had been murdered still hadn't penetrated as deeply as she knew it eventually would. It felt surreal…impossible. Her father had been one of the good guys…a cop.

But cops lost their lives every day in the line of duty.

"Miss Hastings, your father was a dear man," the woman who took Emily's hand next said. "Please contact me at the Colby Agency if you need anything at all."

Colby.

Emily blinked. She stared in confusion at the woman. Middle-aged, attractive, dark hair tinged with silver. Did she know this woman? Where had she heard that name?

And then it hit her.

The letters.

"Excuse me," Emily said, hanging on to the woman's hand when she would have moved on. "Did you say Colby?"

The woman smiled. "Yes. I'm Victoria Colby-Camp. Your father was a good friend."

"I have—" Emily hesitated. What difference did the letters make? The woman would probably just throw them away. After all, they were more than a decade old—almost two, in fact. But Emily's father had kept them for some reason. Maybe she should have read one or two. "Are you acquainted with or related to a James Colby?"

"Why, yes."

The woman's attention had turned keen now. Emily

moistened her lips, suddenly wondering if maybe she'd made a mistake. What the heck? She'd gone this far. "I have some papers." She gave her head a little shake to clear it, forced herself to focus. "Some letters, actually, that I think might have belonged to you or some of your family."

Dark eyes filled with confusion searched Emily's.

The awkward moment stretched a few seconds more and Emily hastened to add, "Perhaps I could send them to your agency?" She shrugged. "I don't know that they're of any importance, but I found them in my father's papers and…well…"

"How kind of you," Victoria Colby-Camp said, saving Emily from having to find a way to make sense of her offer. "Perhaps I could drop by and pick them up."

There were so many things for Emily to take care of tomorrow that pinning her to a time she might actually be available wouldn't be easy. "I'll be in and out so much. Why don't I drop them by your office?"

The woman nodded. "That would be fine." She smiled. "Please let me know if there's anything you need, Miss Hastings."

Emily watched her walk away. A woman of means, she decided. There was something about the way she spoke and moved. Understated elegance, extreme intelligence.

A shiver raced over Emily's skin as she thought of the bundle of letters. Why had her father kept old letters belonging to another man?

Before she had time to worry about the question, more hands reached out to her, more faces offering their sympathy.

She just wanted this day to be over.

A LONG SOAK in the tub had done Emily a world of good after the exhausting afternoon.

She curled up on her father's well-worn sofa and sipped her tea, glad the worst was behind her.

Last night, she'd lain in his bed and considered the time that had passed since she'd lived here, before she fell into a restless sleep.

It wasn't as if they'd been close the past fourteen years, but that didn't prevent her from feeling sad that he was gone. He had been her father. And though she'd only spent the first twelve years of her life under the same roof with him, those few years were brimming with good memories. Well, all but that last year. When her brother had died, everything had changed.

Before climbing into the tub to relax her tense muscles, she had combed through her father's things yet again. The only pictures he had were those taken when their family had been together.

What kind of life had he lived since then? Had he found any sort of relationship with another woman? Her mother had married barely one year after the divorce, had lived happily since then. Had her father been able to find happiness again?

There certainly was no indication anywhere in his home. All that Emily found were a few articles he'd cut from newspapers about work. A couple of awards he'd received for going above and beyond the call of duty—something he'd always done. But there was nothing of a personal nature, other than clothing and hygiene products.

Not a single item that indicated any hobbies he might have enjoyed or friends he might have had.

Emily remembered her mother arguing that he was

nothing but a workaholic. But that hadn't been entirely true, at least not when she'd been a child. She recalled vividly doing lots of family things with her father—ball games, picnics, even camping trips.

She knew that anything her mother said had to be taken with a grain of salt. Her mother felt intense bitterness and resentment toward that time in her life, but Emily felt certain those harsh feelings had more to do with the loss of her son than the divorce.

She thought about the woman she'd met at the service today, Victoria Colby-Camp. Emily's gaze drifted to the bundle of letters lying on the table near the door.

Maybe she should have thrown them away. Or maybe she should have looked to see what they were about before she passed them on.

No. They weren't addressed to her or her father. She had no business looking at them.

Tomorrow morning, first thing, she would have a courier deliver them to the woman named Victoria at the Colby Agency. There was no need for Emily to go there personally. She already had enough to do tomorrow, and she didn't want to feel that awkward tension again.

A heavy sigh escaped her lips. She just wanted to get her father's business affairs resolved, to do right by him when the woman he'd loved and had children with refused. It was the least Emily could do.

He had been her father, even if he hadn't been a part of her everyday life.

And she would miss him.

CHAPTER NINE

FRIDAY MORNING, Victoria was glad to have Lucas back in Chicago. She'd stayed home an extra thirty minutes just to have a cup of coffee with him.

As the elevator opened into the lobby of the Colby Agency, she had to smile. They had been married almost a year now and she still refused to take a single day for granted. When they were apart due to his work in Washington, he called several times to simply say hello and that he missed her.

Warmth spread through her. It felt so good to have the man she loved in her life.

Victoria greeted Elaine, the receptionist who had taken Amy's place when Amy had moved into the investigative side of the business, as well as several of her investigators as she made her way to her office. Lucas wouldn't come in until later, after he'd made the final arrangements for the conference call with the specialist who'd evaluated the brainwashing technique used on Jim.

Inside her office, Victoria closed the door and leaned against it for a moment. She was glad Mildred hadn't been at her desk so she could escape to the privacy of her office without having to answer too many questions this morning.

Jim had finally showed up at his and Tasha's home last night. He had looked slightly worse for the wear, but he was all in one piece and that was the most important thing. Victoria had called off the massive manhunt for her son, but her relief was short-lived.

Jim remembered nothing about the past four days. His only blip of memory was of the intense encounter with Tasha. Nothing about the time since—not where he'd stayed, not what he'd done.

At least he was safe. That was something. Tasha would take him to the clinic today where he would be fully evaluated by the team of doctors who had been working with him for the past year. Perhaps they would find some reason for his abrupt regression.

Victoria's gaze lit on the package on her desk as she crossed the room.

She shrugged off her coat, hung it up and moved behind her desk to see the sender's name.

Emily Hastings.

A chill went through her, but she shook it off. She couldn't say what it was about the idea that bothered her, but she'd felt that same sensation of foreboding at the service yesterday when Emily had first mentioned the letters.

Victoria couldn't imagine what Carter Hastings had been keeping related to the Colby name. Perhaps this was something from the cases he'd worked all those years ago—first her missing son, then James's murder.

But why would he have kept anything at his residence? And Emily had said letters. What sort of letters?

Victoria sat down and reached for the package. Every instinct warned that she should prepare for the worst, though she couldn't understand why.

As she opened the package, she considered that she had seen Carter from time to time since those dark, painful days of so long ago, but she hadn't seen him often. She remembered vividly fourteen years ago when his son had died and then the divorce that had followed. Like hers, Carter's life had not always been pleasant. But, also like her, the fine detective had been a survivor. She'd noted in the *Tribune* the numerous times he'd received one commendation or another. Just another thing they'd had in common—when life took a wrong turn, they had thrown themselves into their work.

Victoria withdrew the bundle of envelopes and her heart stumbled as she read her husband's name penned across the first one. The handwriting was bold but feminine, long, even strokes. The postmark indicated a date six months after her son had gone missing.

Her fingers shaking, she turned over the envelope and withdrew the letter tucked inside.

Dearest James...

Victoria's heart pounded hard once, then sank low in her chest. But she didn't stop. She kept reading no matter that the words tore her apart inside.

...cannot help myself...will always love you...

...I live for those moments we spend together...

Victoria moved through letter after letter until she could not bear to read another. She stared at the woman's name, signed lovingly at the end of each, before allowing the letters to fall from her fingers as her heart shattered into a dozen shards of anguish.

Madelyn Rutland.

How could this be?

DEBRA WEBB   59

How could the man she had loved and trusted…have
cheated on her?

One letter had even been addressed to Victoria, but
the sender had obviously opted not to go through with
mailing it. In the letter, she had warned Victoria that she
could not turn her back on her love for James. That Victoria could not expect to keep him…

"Victoria?"

She jumped at the sound of Mildred's voice on the
intercom. Scrambling, she shuffled the letters back into
a bundle and shoved them into her desk drawer.

"Yes?" Victoria's skin felt hot, but she was freezing
inside. This couldn't be right; there had to be a mistake.
James had been her rock…

"Tasha is on the line," Mildred said hurriedly. "She
says it's an emergency."

Victoria's heart surged back into her throat. Dear God,
what now? She pushed thoughts of the letters out of her
mind and grabbed the phone. "Tasha, what's happened?"

"The police have taken Jim," she said in a rush, her
voice quavering with barely restrained emotion. "He's
a suspect in a murder investigation, Victoria. *Murder.*"

Ice formed in Victoria's veins. "What?" She shook
herself. "For whose murder?"

"That Detective Hastings," Tasha explained, tears
causing her voice to wobble even more. "They think Jim
killed him."

"Don't worry," Victoria told her, but her own fear
made the words feel wrong, "Zach and I are on our way."

Victoria hung up the phone and buzzed for Mildred.
"Tell Zach I need him ASAP."

Mildred didn't ask any questions. She would recog-

nize the desperation in Victoria's voice, had heard it before…far too many times.

Grabbing her coat, Victoria rushed to the door, for-
getting the letters. She didn't have time to worry about
the past right now.

Right now, she had to help her son.

Zach Ashton was the best attorney on staff at the
Colby Agency. She needed him on this. And Ian, she
considered on second thought. She could use Ian
Michaels, as well.

Just then, it didn't enter Victoria's mind; she was too
caught up in the frenzy Tasha's call had set off. But later,
when she'd had time to think, she would wonder what
it was about her old friend Carter Hastings that had suddenly turned her entire existence upside down.

CHAPTER TEN

EMILY SAT IN the stiff chair of the small conference room. Detective Franko, the homicide detective in charge of her father's murder investigation, had called her just before noon and asked her to come in for a meeting.

She had expected to receive an update on her father's case and perhaps answer any final questions as to how they could reach her if need be. Not that she was in a hurry to get back to California. She wasn't, not really. She wanted to close up her father's house and take care of his affairs.

But the moment she had arrived at the homicide division, she had been hustled into this cramped conference room with a cup of stale coffee. And that had been almost an hour ago. She had things to do. Sitting here idly wasting time was not on today's agenda.

She exhaled loudly and tucked her impatience away. Her father's fellow officers were doing all they could to find out what really had happened in that alley on Monday night. She shouldn't be cross about having to wait a few minutes. She wanted her father's killer found, wanted him brought to justice.

The door opened and Detective Franko stepped into

the room. Good. She pushed a polite smile into place. Maybe they could get this over with now. She had things to do for her father, as well. And, the truth was, she couldn't bear to think about his manner of death. If she dwelled on it, she would never be able to maintain her composure and she simply couldn't fall apart. There was no one else to do what needed to be done.

Detective Franko looked to be about thirty-five. Tall, thin, kind, the sort of man who looked as if he would be an animal lover. The weapon that bulged beneath his jacket didn't fit with his persona, she considered as she watched him sit down across the table from her.

"I'm sorry to have kept you waiting, Emily."

"That's all right. Do you have any leads on my father's case?" She prayed his case would be resolved quickly. The people here who cared about him needed that closure as much as she did.

The detective glanced at the file in his hands. "Actually, that's what I wanted to talk to you about."

Her nerves jangled. Had they found her father's murderer already? She'd been in such a daze she'd barely noticed that Chicago PD had a car watching the house—watching her, actually. It followed her everywhere she went. She supposed it was just a precaution, since the police couldn't be sure of the motive behind her father's shooting.

Franko looked from the file to her. "Emily, how would you define your relationship with your father the past year or so?"

To say the question startled her would be a vast understatement. But she'd never been involved with a homicide investigation. Maybe this was part of the routine.

"I don't know," she said, considering the question carefully before answering. The truth made her sound like a bad daughter. But, she reasoned, it made her look no more like a bad daughter than it did her dad as a bad father. "We talked on the phone occasionally, but I didn't get back here often and he was always busy, so we hadn't seen each other in a while."

She didn't see any reason to tell him it had been two years. She'd persecuted herself about that reality since learning of his death; enduring the look she would no doubt get from this detective was more than she could deal with just now.

"So you have no idea about any personal relationships he might have gotten involved in over the past year?"

A frown furrowed across her brow. "No. He never mentioned anything but work when we talked." She shrugged. "And I haven't found anything around the house that would indicate he entertained or kept in contact with anyone in particular." That fact saddened her. She wished her father could have gotten on with his life like her mother had. Well, maybe not exactly as her mother had, but similarly.

"I noticed you speaking with Victoria Colby-Camp at the service yesterday," Franko commented. He made the statement offhandedly, but there was nothing casual about his scrutinizing gaze.

What did her having spoken with Victoria Colby-Camp have to do with anything?

"Yes, she shook my hand and told me how sorry she was my father had died." Emily shrugged. "She mentioned that they were friends."

Her frown deepened. "You'll have to excuse me, Detective, but I'm not following here. What does my talking to someone at the service have to do with my father's murder investigation?"

"You also had a delivery sent to her at the Colby Agency, didn't you? First thing this morning, I believe."

Irritation needled Emily. "What are you trying to get at, Detective Franko?" she demanded. Enough was enough. She was beginning to feel like a suspect rather than the victim's only family.

"We have reason to believe the Colbys were involved with your father's murder," he said bluntly.

"You're saying the woman I met yesterday had something to do with my father's murder?" How was that possible? Had Emily been in such a daze that she had so thoroughly misjudged the woman?

"We found evidence at the scene that implicates her son, James Colby, Jr."

The name echoed inside Emily. She thought of the name on the letters. Surely he couldn't be the same James Colby...

"I'd like you to tell me what you sent to the Colby Agency this morning. It may be relevant to your father's case."

This didn't make sense. The letters were old. She hadn't read the contents of any of them. There had been no reason to.

"I'm sorry, Detective," she said, confusion and uncertainty reigning supreme. "I don't understand what a handful of old letters has to do with my father's murder."

"Tell me about the letters," he pressed.

Why hadn't she looked at the letters? It had seemed

like nothing at the time. How could it be significant to the investigation?

"I didn't read them," she explained, exasperated. "The postmark was nearly twenty years ago and they weren't addressed to my father."

"Who were they addressed to?"

"James Colby."

Franko leaned back in his chair. "We're going to need to execute a search warrant of your father's home, Miss Hastings. Is that going to be a problem? Just so you know, we'll be executing several."

A search warrant? What would they expect to find in her father's home? Would he be doing this same thing at the Colby Agency, too? No doubt.

"Of course it's not a problem," she said, her thoughts fragmenting as she tried to make sense of what all Franko's questions meant. "But I don't understand. You're telling me that you have evidence that James Colby, Jr., had something to do with my father, and I get the impression that I'm a suspect, as well. What's going on, Detective Franko?"

His gaze fixed on hers. "Right now, Miss Hastings, anyone connected to your father is a suspect."

This was insane. She hadn't even been to Chicago in years.

"As difficult as it is to say that to you, Emily," Franko went on, "this is standard procedure. It's not personal."

She blinked, unable to rally a response. Her father was dead, for God's sake. There was no way it could be anything but personal.

Her father had been murdered and she was suddenly a suspect. This couldn't be right.

CHAPTER ELEVEN

VICTORIA SAT perfectly still, uncertain she could bear to hear what Lucas had to say. But it was, unfortunately, necessary. She couldn't let this fester. The hurt twisted inside her, tearing apart all she'd ever believed in...all she'd managed to rebuild.

Lucas sat down in front of Victoria's desk and heaved a weary sigh.

He'd wanted to discuss this at home, but she'd refused. She felt stronger here at the Agency. She needed that strength right now, that and more.

"Yes, I knew about Madelyn."

Victoria's eyes closed as the hurt squeezed her heart.

"But it wasn't what you think—"

Her eyes snapped open. "Don't even try to pardon what he did." The words roared out of her with more strength than she could have imagined she possessed just now.

Lucas leaned forward, settling those caring gray eyes on her. "Victoria, I'm not pardoning anything. The truth is, I'm not certain there is anything to pardon."

"I read the letters, Lucas!" How could he tiptoe around the issue? James Colby had had an affair. Pain stabbed deep all over again.

"That was a tough time for both of you," Lucas reminded her, as if he'd needed to. "The strain on your marriage was immense. James needed someone to talk to. To my knowledge, that's as far as the relationship went."

"She was in love with him," Victoria countered, the word *relationship* making her seethe.

Lucas nodded. "She probably was, but that doesn't mean he was in love with her."

Victoria held up her hands in an act of self-protection. "I can't talk about this anymore."

"Why don't you let me have a look at the letters and I'll try and get to the bottom of what really happened, if you're certain that's what you want."

"No," she said sharply. "I'll do that myself. But there's no time now. Our full attention has to be on Jim. It's going to take both of us working together to get him through this." Victoria closed her eyes again and tried to find a place of calm in her mind where she could think straight.

"We have to assume that they have some sort of evidence against Jim or they wouldn't have been prepared to make an arrest," Lucas offered.

That much was true. Thank God Zach had been able to get a jump on the detective in charge of the case, Detective Franko. Apparently under Zach's legal eagle scrutiny, whatever Franko had hadn't been sufficient to proceed against Jim just yet. But Jim's arrest was imminent. They'd taken him in with the intent of pressing formal charges. After tangoing with Zach, the district attorney, rather than risk running into a double-jeopardy wall, had suggested that Franko hold off until his facts were further substantiated. But that had only bought Victoria a little time; it hadn't actually changed anything.

She had seen the way the very men who just a few days ago had respected her agency had looked at her son. One of their own was dead, and they believed they had his killer. She knew exactly how hard they would work to prove their theory.

Jim was at the clinic undergoing a full evaluation. He would not be allowed to return home unless the doctors were confident that Tasha could keep him under control and under constant supervision.

Tears burned in Victoria's eyes. She didn't want to believe that any of the men or women she knew and respected in Chicago PD would harm her son. But right now, considering the current circumstances, she wasn't sure she could say that.

When a cop died, the whole law enforcement community wanted justice. She could understand how they felt. She wanted justice for Carter Hastings, as well. But not if it meant railroading her son for a crime he surely could not have committed. Her son hadn't even known Carter Hastings.

"We need to know what they've got," Victoria agreed.

"Ashton will get that for us," Lucas voiced his certainty on the matter.

He would, in time. But did they have time? That was the question. Could they sit around here like this and assume that the police—who were obviously less than objective on the matter since one of their own had been murdered—would conduct a thorough investigation? Or would the boys in blue simply go after what they considered the sure thing?

Victoria knew human nature, and human nature would scream for vengeance.

None of this made sense.

Carter had been murdered. Then his daughter had mentioned the letters at his funeral service. What did his murder and those old love letters have to do with each other? And why now? After all this time?

Another wave of hurt washed over Victoria. How could her husband have turned to another woman when Victoria had needed him so very badly?

James had always been like a rock, unshakable. He'd survived being a prisoner of war, had stood fast by her side when Jimmy had gone missing. How could she not have known that there was someone else?

Someone involved in the investigation, for God's sake.

Carter had known. A new kind of ache welled inside her. He'd been so kind to Victoria. Somehow, he must have found out after James's murder and hidden the letters to keep Victoria from finding them. To protect her. Her gaze moved to her new husband. Just as Lucas had protected her from what he had known.

He would do the same thing now. Lucas loved her, would do anything to save her from further devastation. That's why she had to do this herself.

Victoria thought of her faithful staff and, without doubt, knew that any or all of them would do whatever it took to clear Jim's name, ultimately protecting her.

No one wanted Jim cleared more than Victoria. But more importantly, she wanted the truth.

There was only one way to be sure she had the whole truth when all was said and done.

She would oversee this investigation personally. She

would allow no one whose first priority was to protect her to be involved.

That left her with only one option.

CHAPTER TWELVE

AT FIVE MINUTES BEFORE two on Friday afternoon, Daniel Marks stepped off the elevator in the lobby of the revered Colby Agency.

The receptionist greeted him immediately and promptly called Victoria Colby-Camp's personal secretary to come and escort him to his appointment.

Victoria met him just inside her office.

When the initial formalities were out of the way, she suggested they sit. He took a seat at the small conference table and she did the same. He'd declined any coffee, but two bottles of chilled water with accompanying glasses sat on a tray in the center of the table.

"What do you think of the Windy City?"

Daniel came prepared to answer that question. He'd all but made an offer on a loft less than ten minutes from the Colby Agency. "I'm impressed."

Victoria nodded. "You found the information packet we sent you informative?"

"Absolutely." He didn't mention that he'd already scouted out his permanent residence. He didn't have the job yet, though he fully suspected that's what this meeting was about. Since his arrival, he'd decided that this was what he wanted. He felt comfortable here, liked the pace of the city. Its location midway meant that either coast was a simple two-hour flight away.

"Mr. Marks," she began, "I thought I'd learned everything there was to know about this business. I've been operating under the assumption that I'd seen the worst it had to offer. But then, just today, I learned something new."

It was more the expression on her face than her words that made him uneasy. The meeting had definitely taken a different turn than what he'd anticipated.

"How's that?"

"Trust has always been a major foundation of my life," she explained. "As long as I had trust, I had no fears where anything else was concerned, but it seems I was wrong."

Daniel tried to reason how her recent revelations tied in with his consideration for a position within her agency but found no connection. Obviously, he would have to let her lay it on the table for him.

"I've reviewed your record thoroughly and checked your references. I'm fully convinced that you would fit in perfectly here," she told him bluntly.

There was a *but* coming, one he couldn't quite nail the motivation for.

"I appreciate your confidence, Mrs. Colby-Camp. I have to tell you that I've done the same. I'm confident your agency is where I'd like to begin my new career."

Victoria opened a bottle of water and poured herself half a glass. She sipped it a moment before continuing.

Daniel couldn't help wondering if this was a test of some sort. His work and personal history were impeccable, as were his references. Whatever was going on wasn't about his qualifications.

"Mr. Marks," she eventually went on, "I need your help."

Now she'd lost him again. "Excuse me?" He studied her face, saw the lines of worry he hadn't noticed at first. Had he arrived at a bad time? Though they hadn't met before, they had spoken several times by phone. What he saw definitely didn't mesh with what he'd heard in her voice previously.

"Not so very long ago, a very cunning man named Cole Danes taught me that things are not always what they seem and that at times human emotion can be a considerable weakness."

Daniel flared his hands. "That's true in a military setting, as well. There are times when one must set aside human emotion and react on basic instinct, much as an animal does when going after prey or making any other survival decision."

She nodded. "Then you know what I mean when I say that I'm certain the most thorough investigations are conducted by those who have no personal stake in a matter."

"Of course." No question there.

The strength he'd sensed absent in her tone this afternoon was suddenly there, in her eyes. "Mr. Marks, there is no question that I will be offering you a position at this agency. Coming to terms on salary is only a technicality."

Daniel relaxed marginally. "Excellent." Now this is what he'd thought he was coming here for today.

"But first, an unexpected necessity dictates that I hire you as a private contractor to conduct an investigation outside the realm of this agency."

His gaze narrowed as he attempted to read what he saw in her eyes now. She was too good. Whatever fear or uncertainty she felt, she kept it hidden. Was this some sort of test? "What kind of investigation?"

"My son is a suspect in a murder investigation," she told him without elaborating. "I need you to find the truth."

He found the way she summed up her needs rather interesting. "Do you have reason to believe he's guilty?"

She moved her head from side to side. "To my knowledge, he doesn't even know the victim."

"But..." he prompted.

Visibly bracing herself, she responded to his prod, "But there are extenuating circumstances. A lapse in his memory has left him without an alibi."

Daniel felt certain there was more related to the lapse, but he didn't pursue that avenue just now. There was another, more crucial question to be asked.

"What makes you believe the police won't conduct a proper investigation?" There had to be a reason she didn't trust the cops. For that matter, it seemed, she didn't even trust her own staff of investigators. None of which fit with what he'd learned about her or this agency.

"The victim is one of their own," she said somberly. "They want revenge, Mr. Marks. I'm certain most of them won't be thinking clearly or pursuing all the possible avenues. They're not going to be satisfied until someone takes the fall for this. The sooner, the better."

According to his research, the Colby Agency maintained an outstanding relationship with local law enforcement. This couldn't be an easy dilemma.

"All right," he told her. "You give me the facts you know, make whatever assets you have available to me and I'll do what I can to clear your son."

For three beats, she held his gaze, hers unblinking. "You misunderstand me, Mr. Marks," she said, something in her eyes turning bleak for a mere second before sheer determination defeated it. "I don't want you to simply clear my son of guilt. I want you to find the truth, whatever it is."

Daniel had known the moment he'd walked into the lobby of this agency that there was something different about it. The very air was charged with something beyond the usual energy of bustling activity. It felt alive and vibrant on a level that transcended the norm. It seemed like the kind of place where things happened, where lives were changed.

He wanted to be a part of that, couldn't imagine taking a position anywhere else now that he'd met this woman. She, he understood with complete certainty, was the heart and soul of this place.

The challenge she had tossed out before him said all that needed to be said. This woman, the one who'd made the Colby Agency what it was, was desperate and yet she knew exactly what had to be done.

"I'll find the truth for you."

She nodded. "Thank you."

Raised voices sounded outside the door, postponing whatever she might have said next.

The door burst open and both Victoria and Daniel turned to see who'd barged in.

"...in a meeting," Mildred Parker, Victoria's secretary, was saying.

"I don't care! I have to see her now."

A young woman, long dark hair bouncing around her shoulders, stormed into the office, Mildred trailing right behind her. Daniel allowed his gaze to take a tour of the intruder's form. Even though she was as mad as hell, she was a looker—tall, slender, a brunette with hazel eyes flashing with fire.

Apparently he was about to witness one of the less gracious Colby Agency moments.

"I'm sorry, Victoria, I couldn't stop her."

"It's all right, Mildred."

His curiosity piqued, Daniel's gaze slid from the woman who would be his boss to the younger, clearly furious woman who'd strode across the room and planted herself directly in front of Victoria.

"Miss Hastings," Victoria said, "I'm sure you're distraught—"

"I'm more than that, Mrs. Colby-Camp. I'm confused and hurt," she snapped. "Your son killed my father. I want to know why."

CHAPTER THIRTEEN

EMILY HADN'T CONSIDERED what she would say to Victoria Colby-Camp before she'd barged into her office. The fact was, she hadn't thought at all. One thing kept playing over and over in her mind—her father, alone in that alley while a man less than half his age took his life.

"Miss Hastings, this is a difficult time for you and I realize that—"

"My father is dead," Emily interrupted, not the least bit interested in whatever compassionate ploys the woman intended to utilize. "I want to know why." Emily blinked back the sting of tears. She'd made it this far without breaking down, she wasn't about to now. "You showed up at my father's funeral and claimed to be his friend, took advantage of my vulnerability."

"Perhaps I should come back later."

Emily's gaze swung to the man she hadn't even noticed until he stood and spoke. He'd been sitting right there at the conference table. It startled her that she'd looked right over him. But her emotions were raw, her attention focused on one thing only.

"That won't be necessary, Daniel," Victoria said. "Daniel Marks, this is Emily Hastings."

Her confusion momentarily overriding her fury,

Emily looked from Victoria to the man and back. Did she not get it? How could she sit there and offer polite small talk?

"Miss Hastings," Victoria went on before Emily could lodge another demand, "is the daughter of Detective Carter Hastings, the victim in the homicide investigation I was in the process of telling you about."

Victim. Emily's outrage roared again. "I want to know why you didn't tell me the truth."

Victoria's gaze settled on Emily's then. It was the first time Emily had really looked into the woman's eyes since storming her office. She looked as weary and disheartened as Emily felt, maybe even a little angry. But she had no right. No right at all.

"Miss Hastings, I had no idea until this morning that my son was in any way implicated in your father's case."

Emily was about to argue, but Victoria held up a hand.

"To my knowledge my son never even knew your father. However, the police seem to think differently and I intend to find out how and why. That's where Mr. Marks comes in."

Of course she would want to protect her son, but if he was a murderer…

"I can't help but feel like you've taken advantage of me," Emily said bluntly. "I gave you those letters."

She didn't care what the man in the room had to do with anything. This concerned Victoria Colby-Camp and her son. An ache speared through Emily. Not now. She didn't want to feel any of this until she'd finished what had to be done.

Victoria took a deep breath. Her struggle with her emotions was evident but gave Emily no comfort.

"There's nothing I can say to make this any easier, Miss Hastings. But if it helps at all, I want the truth as badly as you do. If my son was involved with your father's murder, I will know it. I won't give up until I have all the answers for myself, as well as for you."

Emily was taken aback. Could she really mean that? No. That was impossible. Any mother would first and foremost want to protect her child, even if that child was a grown man. "Talk is cheap, Mrs. Colby-Camp."

"That's why I'm here," the man spoke up, reminding Emily of how Victoria had referred to him. He moved a step in Emily's direction and offered his hand. "I'm Daniel Marks. Victoria has hired me to investigate this case. I'm not employed by the Colby Agency. Victoria and I have never met before today. I have no reason not to be objective. You have my word on that."

Emily looked from his sincere expression to his hand. "As I said," she responded with no intention of being polite, "talk is cheap."

He smiled and something about that smile made her feel a little less manic, a little less certain that somehow the Colby Agency would find a way to clear a killer.

"You're welcome to call and get an update at any time, Miss Hastings. I'll be happy to share my findings with you."

Later, when she thought back to that moment, she wouldn't be able to put her finger on what made her say what she said next.

"That won't be necessary, Mr. Marks. What I will require, however," Emily turned to the head of the Colby Agency, "is full cooperation. I want to be a part of this investigation. To protect my father's interests, so to speak. In my opinion, that's the only way any of it will be fair or objective."

Victoria and the man named Marks exchanged a look.

"I'm not sure that's a good idea, Miss Hastings," he said. "I have certain training—"

Emily turned her full attention to Victoria, woman to woman. "If you really were my father's friend, if what you're actually looking for is the truth, then you won't have anything to hide. You'll let me in on this investigation. You'll understand that I'm right."

A full ten seconds passed before Victoria responded, but Emily saw that she'd touched a place deep inside the other woman.

"You're absolutely right, Miss Hastings," Victoria said. "I won't leave you out of this investigation. You have a right to the truth every bit, perhaps more so, than I do. I appreciate your candor."

"Victoria—" Marks began, clearly planning to object.

"Is there any reason you can't conduct this investigation under these circumstances?" Victoria inquired with a frankness Emily had to admire, despite her emotional state at the moment.

The question was not a query as to his ability; it was spoken with the same challenge in her tone as if she'd just thrown down a gauntlet. Emily held her breath as she waited for Daniel Marks's response. Would he accept this challenge…or had she vastly overrated her persuasive ability?

Another of those tension-filled moments passed, with Victoria Colby-Camp and the gentleman engaged in a visual standoff. Daniel Marks relented first.

"No reason at all," he said unequivocally. He shifted his gaze, dark, dark brown and very intense, she instantly noticed, to Emily. "As long as we both understand who is in charge. It's my reputation on the line. You may not like my style or my attitude at times, but if we're working together you will follow my lead."

"Not a problem," Emily tossed back, undeterred. Already she was mentally ticking off the list of things she would need to do in order to facilitate an even longer stay.

"I believe we have an agreement, then," Victoria suggested, obviously relieved. She stood, looked from Daniel Marks to Emily and back.

"I'd like to get started right away," Marks said. "We will need to talk about whatever connections, past or present, there are between the Colbys and Mr. Hastings. I'll need a complete understanding of your son's current condition."

"The letters," Emily interjected. "Did you read them?" she asked Victoria.

If the pained look on the woman's face was any indication, the issue was not one she wanted to discuss. "Yes, I've read a few of them."

"Letters?" Marks asked, looking from one woman to the other.

"I found a bundle of letters addressed to a James Colby among my father's things," Emily explained quickly. "I didn't see any need to keep them, so I sent them over." She gestured to Victoria. "The police wanted to know what was in the package I'd had delivered here." She looked directly at Victoria then. "What did you find in the letters?"

"The letters don't have anything to do with your father's death," Victoria said, her voice strained. "They were personal."

A new jolt of anger and uncertainty went through Emily. "I want them back." God, she sounded like a child. But she couldn't risk that those letters contained something relevant, even if Victoria didn't realize it or didn't want to admit it.

"Miss Hastings," Victoria said wearily, "the letters were written to my first husband by a woman with whom he had an affair. He's been dead for nearly twenty years. I can't see how his indiscretion would have any bearing on this case. I assure you if I did, I would be the first to say so."

Her husband? Emily had assumed that James Colby was her brother. Her hand went to her chest. How horrifying it must have been for her to read those letters and learn that ugly secret about the man she'd loved. Still, could they take that risk? What if there was some obscure connection to the present?

Before Emily could launch a rebuttal, Daniel Marks said, "We can't be certain of that." Victoria's gaze moved to him. "Right now, we need to consider any and all connections between your family and the Hastings, however seemingly irrelevant."

Victoria's eyes closed for a moment and Emily suddenly felt the wind go out of her determination. Forcing the issue of the letters was clearly painful for this woman.

Maybe Victoria was right. Emily couldn't see what a decades-old infidelity had to do with her father's murder.

But then, Daniel Marks made sense, too. All connections had to be explored.

Maybe she was the one not thinking straight right now.

"All right," Victoria surrendered. "You may take the letters with you," she said to Daniel Marks. "I would like you to get started right away and I will require a report daily."

He nodded. "Not a problem."

Emily shuddered inside at the idea that she was about to dive into a murder investigation, her father's at that. Was she putting off the eventual emotional breakdown by staying distracted? She and her father hadn't been close since she was twelve, but she had loved him.

Maybe his death hadn't fully sunk in yet.

"Have the police searched your father's personal residence?"

Emily hauled her attention from the worrisome thoughts. "No." She sifted through the conversation with Detective Franko. "The detective in charge of the case did mention they would want to take a look."

"I'd like to have a look first," Marks said, "if you have no objections."

A reason not to allow him to take a look around her father's home didn't immediately come to mind. They were supposed to be on the same team here.

"How will this investigation play into the one the police are conducting?" Emily asked, the question only then occurring to her.

"Miss Hastings," Victoria offered, "our investigation will be totally separate from the one Chicago PD has launched. To be honest," she added, "the reason for my requesting that Mr. Marks look into this case is because I'm concerned that the police won't be objective when it comes to solving the murder of one of their own."

Emily studied the woman a long moment before she

countered, "Can you say that yours will be any more objective? It is your son they suspect."

Victoria nodded to the man standing next to Emily. "That's why I've deferred to an outside investigator. I don't want any mistakes. I want the truth, Miss Hastings, whatever it may be."

CHAPTER FOURTEEN

EMILY DIDN'T ARGUE with Daniel Marks when he suggested they use his personal vehicle to go to her father's home. She had considered picking up a rental car but hadn't as yet.

Mr. Marks drove exactly the kind of vehicle she expected a man such as him would drive—overlarge with lots of muscle under the hood, black and sleek-looking. She imagined that it used enough gasoline in a drive across the city to fuel her small economy car for an entire month as she buzzed up and down the freeways back home. But she wouldn't hold that against him.

So far, she had no reason to dislike him. She did, however, reserve judgment as to whether she could trust him to be as objective as Victoria Colby-Camp wanted Emily to believe he would be.

That was a sizable portion of her motivation behind seeing this through. It was the least she could do for her father. As much as she wanted to believe that Chicago PD would see that justice was done, Mrs. Colby-Camp had made a valid point on that issue. The police had lost one of their own; vengeance would likely be their prime motivation. Certainly not because they were bad cops or inept at their jobs, but because they were human.

As was Emily.

And, yes, she had loved her father…still did. But the distance in their lives for the past several years allowed a certain objectivity. She sighed. Or maybe she was simply fooling herself. Right now, she was functioning on adrenaline and even she recognized a certain level of denial.

None of that would stop her; she intended to see this through. Her father would have done the same for her. It was true that, for the most part, he'd stayed out of her life, but that had more to do with respecting her mother's wishes than serving his own. Emily recognized precisely what her father had done. On some level, she couldn't help resenting that he'd given in so easily to her mother.

On the other hand, as an adult, she understood that he'd done much of what he did to protect her…to prevent even more tension and drama in her life. He'd given up a lot to ensure her life stayed on an even keel. How could she not sacrifice a bit for him now?

She stole a glance in the driver's direction. What motivation drove this man? Was it the money Victoria would pay him for services rendered? What else could it be? she mused. And maybe that was for the best.

He had a nice face, chiseled profile. His dark hair was really short. A good look on him. She recalled that his eyes were very dark brown, almost black, but not unpleasantly so. He dressed like a businessman—navy slacks and jacket, crisp white shirt. And yet, he looked a little heavily muscled for a guy who spent all his time behind a desk.

"You have something on your mind?"

The sound of his deep voice startled her. She shifted her attention straight ahead, but not before he'd glanced her way and caught her looking directly at him.

"I was just thinking," she said, staring at the oncoming traffic. Getting so caught up in her thoughts like that while in his presence might not be a good thing. If her goal was ensuring that this investigation was conducted with complete objectivity, she needed to be on her toes at all times.

"About whether or not you can trust me," he suggested, making the turn onto her old street.

Well, now that just made their new partnership perfect. The man could read her mind.

"Actually," she allowed, seeing no reason to pretend, "I wondered why you'd agreed to take this case, other than for the money, of course."

He considered her question for several moments, long enough to reach the house she'd once called home. When he'd parked at the curb a block beyond her father's front door, he shut off the engine and turned his analyzing gaze on her.

"It's not about the money," he said. That reply didn't surprise her. Most people didn't like admitting they could be bought, even when they clearly could be.

"Really?" The word came out a bit more crisply than she'd intended. "What sets you apart from the rest of us?" She said that exactly as she'd meant to—with utter disbelief. Who did this guy think he was fooling? Most people had their price.

"I agreed to conduct this investigation because Victoria wants the truth." He faced forward a moment, as if gathering his thoughts. It was during that lapse in the

conversation that she noticed something about Daniel
Marks that she hadn't before. A thin, jagged scar made
a path from the top of his freshly starched shirt collar
at the side of his neck and disappeared into his hairline
immediately behind his right ear.

Emily frowned, wondered what sort of injury he'd
survived. She realized abruptly that she knew nothing
at all about this man. Here she sat in his vehicle, alone
with him, and she actually didn't know him at all. She
only knew that Victoria Colby-Camp somehow trusted
him, otherwise she certainly wouldn't have hired him.

Was that the reason Emily felt comfortable in Daniel Marks's presence?

When his gaze landed on her once more, her breath
caught before she could stop it. She wondered vaguely
if her last thought was as transparent as it felt. Having
him read her so effortlessly was entirely disconcerting.

"There aren't that many people who want the truth,
Miss Hastings. Their reasons run the gamut from self-
ishness to fear. Victoria is scared to death of what I'll
find, but she isn't about to let that stop her. I respect that.
I'll find the truth for her."

By the time he'd finished his statement, Emily's heart
had started to pound. Could she say the same? Was her
reason for insisting on being a part of this investigation
as honorable as that? Did she really want the truth, no
matter what that entailed?

Emily closed her eyes and fought to slow the spinning that had begun in her head. Maybe this wasn't
such a good idea. How could she have thought that all
the distance in the world would make her objective
enough to look into own her father's murder? Her

mother would pitch a fit when she learned what Emily was up to. Why put herself through the grief? Her father had been a cop, and he'd died at the hand of a murderer; it happened far too often. Why let herself be dragged through the painful, dirty details?

"Are you certain you want to do this?"

She opened her eyes and hoped he couldn't see the surprise his question elicited. How the heck did he read her every thought? Or was he just good at the guessing game?

"Like Victoria," he added when her silence dragged out, "you may not like what I find."

There were lots of things Daniel Marks might have said that would, perhaps, have made her consider changing her mind about being a part of this. But that statement was not one of them.

"You can't scare me off, Mr. Marks, so don't even try." She shoved her door open and climbed out. No way would she back off. That he obviously wanted her to only made her more determined to be involved.

She strode up the sidewalk to her father's stoop without looking back to see if he was following. It really wasn't necessary. She knew he was, could feel him watching her every move.

Thankfully, she had the presence of mind to glance up and down the street before opening the door. She remembered that Detective Franko had someone watching her. Sure enough, there was another of those nondescript sedans. The cops should rethink their surveillance techniques, especially if they were going for anonymity.

"You'll have to be quick," she said over her shoulder to Marks. "The police have someone watching me. I'm sure they'll let the detective in charge of the case know I've brought someone to the house."

"In that case," Marks said as he came up behind her, "maybe we'd better throw 'em a curve."

Before Emily could hazard a guess as to what he meant, he'd turned her around and closed his mouth over hers. She froze the instant his lips landed on hers. This wasn't some quick little peck; Mr. Marks threw himself into the act. He kissed her long and deep, hugged his arms around her as if he would die before letting her go.

She felt herself melting against him, felt the heat stirring deep inside her, while confusion still reigned in her brain. The reaction was automatic and occurred before she could think of what she should do.

The sound of a horn blaring somewhere up the street made her jump, allowed reality to intrude.

She pushed against his chest, pulled her mouth from the assault of his. "What're you doing?" she blurted between his insistent kisses.

He drew back and smiled down at her. "Just making it look good," he assured her before ushering her across the threshold. Her legs had gone boneless, so she had no choice but to be dragged along by his powerful arms.

The moment the door closed, leaving them alone in her father's entry hall, she regained immediate and full use of her limbs. She wheeled around and slapped Daniel Marks as hard as she could. Her palm stung with the force of it, but she didn't give a damn. Fury had obliterated reason.

"Are you out of your mind?" she demanded. "How dare you take advantage of me!"

He rubbed his jaw, but didn't look the slightest bit contrite. "You said the police were watching you. We don't want them suspecting that we're here conducting our own investigation. They don't generally like interference like that, especially if it's in anyway connected to someone related to a suspect."

Emily's anger waned in light of his undeniably valid observation. She straightened her jacket. "I suppose that makes sense." She resisted the urge to lick her lips. His taste clung there and she didn't want to experience it all over again. She shivered at the thought. He'd surprised her, that's all. Any woman would have reacted the same way. "I would prefer you be a little less invasive next time," she told him bluntly. She'd felt his tongue glide along the seam of her lips. Another little shiver stole through her. That part hadn't been necessary. He could have kissed her without *kissing* her.

"Whatever you say, Miss Hastings."

His look of amusement sent a new rush of irritation through her. There wasn't anything funny about this. She could understand that he'd wanted to throw whoever was watching her off track, but there had been no need to make the move so real. Next time...

And then it hit her. What was she thinking? There wasn't going to be a next time. The heat he'd stirred so easily deep in her belly now surged straight to her cheeks to punctuate her humiliation.

"Where do you want to start?" she said brusquely, determined to get past the embarrassing moment. If Daniel Marks was good enough to impress Victoria Colby-Camp, surely he wasn't one she'd have to prod every step of the way. Besides, the sooner they put the episode behind them, the better.

"How about I just take a general look around first and then we'll go through his papers once more."

Emily nodded—that sounded reasonable to her. She waved her arms in welcome. "Make yourself at home."

She watched as he moved up the staircase. Emily had no desire to follow. There was nothing up there except her and her brother's bedrooms. She could do without confronting those memories again.

Instead, she went into the parlor and considered that this was one room where she hadn't really looked around that much. The framed photographs that called the mantle home now sat there acquiring dust. She thought about each one, remembering the events that had led up to that frozen moment in time.

Her brother's last regional championship had been captured in one. The whole Hastings clan looked ecstatic. Her mother smiled widely, as did her father.

Emily's goofy grin reminded her that she'd been in the throes of puberty. God, she'd hated that time. Probably all adolescents did. The braces and pimples. She shuddered at the memories of acne scrubs, broken orthodontic wires and, worst of all, the overwhelming need to fit in.

After moving to Sacramento, that particular problem had only gotten worse. She'd been too skinny, had bony knees and pigtails, and was still wearing the braces. Making new friends had been the most harrowing experience of her life…well, outside of losing her brother. But she'd survived. During those dark days, the only light had come in the mail—her father's letters.

How had she forgotten that? Maybe she hadn't actually forgotten. More likely, she'd blocked the painful recollections. For the first three or four years, the letters had come two or three times a week. Then the frequency had lessened to once a week or maybe every other week. Eventually, the only written communication had been in the form of birthday or holiday greeting cards.

Emily pushed away the hurt that tried to distract her and moved from frame to frame, taking time to recall each day represented by the images behind the glass. It troubled her that her father didn't appear to have a single photograph related to his life since the family breakup.

Why hadn't he found someone new?

She couldn't be absolutely certain he hadn't. After all, what did she really know about the man he had become? That his work was his whole life? That he was too busy for a personal relationship of any sort, even with his only daughter?

Part of her wondered if she'd been more involved in his life, would things have been different? But she'd had to walk a fine line to keep the peace. Her mother hadn't even wanted her to take her father's occasional calls. Thankfully, her father understood that the situation wasn't Emily's fault. She would have visited more had her mother allowed it. That her father hadn't gotten out to the West Coast often wasn't really a surprise. Her mother had likely made it so difficult that he'd finally stopped bothering.

Forcing her mind beyond the hurtful thoughts, Emily moved methodically through the room. She inspected each table and drawer. She also looked beneath the sofa cushions and inside each book and magazine stored in the single bookcase.

She didn't know what she expected to find, but if there was anything she wanted to find it first. Detective Franko and his team of investigators would go through everything. She didn't mind that they did; she wanted her father's killer found, the sooner the better. Maybe the Colby Agency's investigation had her paranoid. She couldn't help wondering if the police would hide anything from her. The best way, in her opinion, to head off that possibility was to find whatever there was to find first.

There was nothing out of the ordinary or that seemed unexpected in her father's living room. So she moved on to the kitchen. Daniel Marks had already come down the stairs and started going through her father's things in his bedroom. She didn't go in the room or say anything to him. She'd been through the bedroom already, since that's where her father had kept his files. Besides, for her to sort through her father's things was acceptable, but watching someone else do it felt wrong. Though she understood the necessity, it somehow still felt offensive.

Working on autopilot, Emily picked through the contents of each kitchen cabinet and sifted through the drawers, but didn't find a single thing out of the ordinary. No false bottoms, no secret compartments in the wood floor. Nothing.

Not that she'd expected to.

When she'd checked out the hall closet and the drawers of the table that sat near the bottom of the staircase, she had no choice but to join Daniel Marks in her father's bedroom. There wasn't anywhere else to look.

"Do you know anything about this?" Marks asked as she entered the room.

Emily moved closer to see what he'd discovered. It wasn't the safe box, though it sat on the bed next to him. This was a plain old shoebox. She'd noticed the stack of shoeboxes taking up space on the floor of her father's closet but hadn't bothered to look in any of them. The one or two with missing lids had contained family photographs. Apparently she should have checked them all.

Marks showed her a number of articles clipped from the *Tribune*—Shooting Deemed Righteous, Teenager's Death Under Investigation.

Emily accepted one of the clippings and quickly read the article. It was about the shooting of a teenager nearly twenty years ago. Her father's former partner, Madelyn, was the officer involved. Internal Affairs had cleared her of wrongdoing, and some elements of the community had rebelled against the decision.

Emily couldn't remember anything about the incident, but then she'd been very young at the time. According to another of the articles, Detective Madelyn Rutland had been allowed to keep her position in homicide.

"She would have been your father's partner when he investigated the missing Colby child and then the murder of James Colby, correct?"

Emily had dropped on the edge of the bed near Marks. She hadn't meant to, but in reading the articles she'd done so without actually thinking.

"Yes." She looked from the clippings she held to the dark eyes studying her so intently. "What could that possibly have to do with my father's murder? Madelyn left the force years ago. Even before my parents divorced."

"This is the same Madelyn as in the letters to James Colby?"

Emily blinked, abruptly seeing the indisputable connection. "Yes." Was this the true connection between her father and the Colbys? His partner's affair with Victoria's husband? Had he somehow encouraged or hidden the inappropriate behavior of his partner? Surely that hadn't gotten him killed all these years later. For God's sake, Victoria had remarried. What did a nineteen-year-old affair have to do with the here and now?

"We're going to set aside what we feel is relevant," Marks said aloud. "We can always turn it over to the police when we're finished with it."

Emily watched silently as he made a pile of papers that he intended to take from her father's house. Part of her wondered if, by including the letters, he was protecting the Colbys. Victoria had gotten a call from the lobby informing her that the police were on their way up. Probably with that search warrant. So she had given the letters to Daniel Marks. Marks had locked the bundle in the glove compartment of his vehicle the moment he and Emily escaped the building. Emily didn't ask just now if he eventually intended to turn over the letters to the police, but definitely would later. Victoria obviously wasn't worried about handling the police.

Following his lead, Emily went through her father's things, every drawer, every shoebox. As thorough as she attempted to be, Marks proved to be more so. He had a way of moving that went well beyond methodical. She decided he'd been in the investigative business a very long time, knew all the most efficient ways to conduct himself. More surprising was his knack for ensuring that every single item left behind was placed exactly as it had been. Amazing.

When they'd finished, they had amassed quite a collection of papers and clippings Marks wanted to take for further consideration.

"How do we get this stuff out of the house without the police seeing us?"

"Pack your bag," Marks said to her.

"Won't they search my bag?" Even she could see the problem in that tactic.

"*That's* what we want."

Rather than sound dumb by asking more questions, she hurriedly did as he asked. While she hastily shoved her things back into her overnight bag, he removed his jacket and placed it on the bed.

By the time she had completed her packing, Marks had opened a section of the seam holding the lining inside his jacket and started to store page after page, clipping after clipping, between the silky lining and the exterior fabric. When he was satisfied that there were no lumps or bumps, he slipped the jacket back on.

He turned his attention to her then. "Let me have your jacket."

She hesitated, though she knew his intent. Somehow, using her jacket made it more personal. To her knowledge she'd never broken a law.

"We should hurry, Emily. I'm surprised we haven't been interrupted already."

Emily. He called her Emily. Did he do that to further unnerve her?

He held out his hand and somehow she found the wherewithal to remove her jacket and pass it to him. He quickly made the slit in the lining and then stored the rest of the papers inside. When he'd finished he handed it back to her. She slipped it on once more, noting there was no real difference in the weight or bulk. He'd been too careful about how he'd placed the papers for that to happen.

Then he executed another of those unexpected moves. He put his arms around her and hugged her. She stiffened, wasn't sure she could deal with him kissing her again. Not that it hadn't been enjoyable in some ways, but…

"Good." He drew away. "No crinkling."

She blinked, confused.

He held out his arms. "Now you hug me. See if I make any telltale sounds."

Then she understood.

Taking a deep breath for courage she reached around him, did as he'd asked. Incredibly, the thickness of the fabric somehow prevented the papers from making any distinguishable sound.

She dropped her arms and stepped back. "I guess we're safe."

He smiled. "Guess so."

She suddenly felt a little lightheaded. She hadn't noticed before how really handsome he was. She'd noticed the individual features but hadn't let herself analyze the whole package. Nice smile, too. Good kisser, she added before she could stop the thought. She shook off the foolish distractions.

None of those characteristics made him trustworthy. "Is this…" She swallowed tightly. "Is this illegal?" She tugged at the lapels of her jacket for emphasis. It was seriously too late to ask the question, but she needed to know.

He glanced at her navy jacket but didn't stop there. His gaze drifted down the matching blue skirt and then over her bare calves. Her pulse skipped and she resisted the urge to shift from foot to foot. She'd pulled a run in her last pair of panty hose, but that hadn't bothered her until now. She supposed she had no right to complain since she'd certainly scrutinized him twice already.

Just now, silly as it seemed, she wished she'd chosen to wear something a little less bland. But she hadn't been thinking about fashion when she'd packed. The classic navy suit, a couple of skirts and blouses, as well as the black dress she'd worn to her father's funeral, were all she'd brought with her. She would need more casual clothes for her extended stay in Chicago but hadn't had time to think about that just yet.

When his gaze bumped into hers once more, he said, "Yes. I believe what we're doing would be tampering with evidence or perhaps obstructing justice."

She nodded, another feeling of light-headedness making her sway slightly.

Marks steadied her. "Are you all right, Miss Hastings?"

"Yes. I'm fine." She wasn't, obviously, but she had no intention of telling him. He would surely jump on any excuse to exclude her from his investigation. She hadn't considered it until now, but that was probably what the kiss had been about, if the truth be known.

He didn't give up with that flimsy answer.

"Have you eaten today?"

She told herself that she couldn't possibly see concern in his eyes, though it looked exactly like that. They barely knew each other. He couldn't possibly care how she felt one way or the other.

"I…" Had she eaten? No. "I can't remember," she fibbed.

"Come on." He picked up her overnight bag and ushered her into the hall. "Dinner is next on our agenda."

Emily hadn't been aware how much time had passed. It was already dark outside. She could eat, needed to, apparently.

Before they reached the front door a thundering knock rattled the hinges.

Marks turned to her. "That'll be the police. Are you sure you're up to this?"

She knew he meant: could she lie to the cops? Certainly she'd never done anything like that before…but there was only one way to find out.

CHAPTER FIFTEEN

DANIEL WASN'T SO SURE Emily Hastings was as ready as she thought she was, but there was no putting off answering the door. The second knock was louder and more persistent. No member of law enforcement, local or otherwise, liked to be kept waiting. Chicago PD was already on the defensive; no point adding insult to injury. The detective in charge of the case would eventually figure out Daniel's connection to the Colby Agency.

Emily pulled open her father's front door and three gentlemen waited on the stoop.

To her credit, she managed a polite smile. "Detective Franko," she said to the one who stood slightly in front of the other two.

"Miss Hastings." Franko glanced past Emily to where Daniel waited in the hall behind her. "I believe I mentioned," he said, shifting his attention back to her, "that I would want to execute a search warrant today."

She stepped back and opened the door wider. "Of course. Please come in."

Franko flicked another glance in Daniel's direction as he entered the Hastings' home. Tall, gangly, with thinning hair cut regulation short, Franko looked to be about Daniel's age. The two detectives who followed on his heels were younger, most likely with less seniority, the grunts.

"Daniel Marks," Daniel said as he thrust out his hand. Might as well get past the preliminaries.

Franko shook Daniel's hand. "Friend of the family?"

He uttered the question without much inflection in his tone, but Daniel suspected he'd already run the plates on his SUV. Any good detective would get all the facts from available databases before entering the premises and confronting the unknown. That step was likely what had bought Daniel and Emily a little extra time to conduct their own hasty search.

"A friend of Emily's," Daniel said in response, putting his left arm around her waist as he did. He felt her stiffen slightly, but, to her credit, she didn't let her discomfort show. She didn't like it much when he made those sudden overtures, but keeping Franko oblivious to Daniel's investigation as long as possible was the optimum scenario.

That Emily had responded to Daniel's kiss surprised him. But it was his own reaction that startled him the most. But there was no time to dwell on that just now.

Franko nodded, but didn't bother hiding the suspicion in his eyes. Then, he turned his attention to Emily. "We'll be a while, Miss Hastings."

She moistened her lips. Daniel watched the tip of her pink tongue slide over those smooth lips. He told himself he was merely curious about her, but his conclusion lacked real conviction. She showed great strength but seemed so fragile...so vulnerable. Of course, she had just lost her father, but he sensed that her fragility went beyond this most recent loss. This was a woman who'd known loss before and carefully protected herself from future possibilities. Her determination to distance herself emotionally intrigued him. No amount of discipline had ever given him the proper armor for resisting a damsel in distress, whether real or imagined on his part. That Emily Hastings was so easy on the eyes did nothing to allay his curiosity.

He liked her long hair and the intriguing gold flecks in her hazel eyes. Her skirt fell to a conservative length and her blouse, though formfitting, revealed no cleavage whatsoever.

"Is there any reason I need to stay while you…" She inhaled an uncomfortable breath. "I'd like to go if you don't need me to stay."

"I understand," the detective assured her with a kindness that spoke of his respect and/or admiration for her deceased father. "There's no need for you to stay. I'll keep you posted on our investigation."

Franko's gaze moved to Daniel once more. He didn't bother attempting to hide the suspicion in his eyes. "When did you say you arrived, Mr. Marks? I don't remember seeing you at the funeral."

Daniel adopted a deeply remorseful expression, didn't bother correcting the detective as to what he'd said and what he hadn't. "Unfortunately, I missed the funeral," he replied, sidestepping the answer, then stared down at Emily, pumping up the regret another notch. "But I'm here now."

Franko wasn't satisfied, but he let it go at that.

Daniel kept one had at the small of Emily's back as they moved toward the door. That the detective hadn't asked to check her bag surprised Daniel, but he couldn't say he wasn't relieved. The sooner he got her out of here, the better. The tremulous smile she'd managed to keep in place during the final exchange between Daniel and Franko signaled her proximity to losing her composure.

"Excuse me, Miss Hastings," Franko said, overriding Daniel's hopes for a clean escape. Franko moved toward where they waited at the door. "Those are your personal belongings only, correct?" He indicated the bag Daniel carried.

The slightest tinge of red showed on Emily's cheeks, but, again, she surprised Daniel. "Yes, Detective Franko, but if you'd like to check for your own peace of mind, I fully understand."

For three seconds, Franko simply stood there as if he'd rather do anything than ask the daughter of his murdered brother in blue to hand over her bag.

"Please." Emily took the bag from Daniel and moved toward Franko. "I insist that you check." She shouldered off her purse. "My purse, too."

Startled but obviously thankful, Franko took the bag as well as her purse and moved into the parlor to look through them.

Emily waited with Daniel near the door. One glance at her wide hazel eyes warned that she didn't feel nearly as confident in what she'd done as she'd sounded.

Daniel smiled for her benefit, wanted her to know she'd done well. She averted her gaze without any visual acknowledgement of his assurance.

During the two minutes that it took the detective to pilfer through her belongings, Daniel studied the woman waiting next to him. He wondered again at that deep vulnerability hiding under the bravado. He needed more information on her. He'd have to check with Victoria to see what she had on Emily Hastings. He would also need anything she had on Carter, Emily's father. Emily's abrupt appearance in Victoria's office this afternoon had preempted a number of questions Daniel had intended to ask. He would need to amend that situation as soon as possible. The more information he had, the clearer his assessment would be. Information was power. Facts were the building blocks of every defense.

Daniel also intended to question Victoria's son.

"Thank you, Miss Hastings," Franko said as he returned to the hall and offered the bags to Emily.

Daniel stepped forward and took the heavier overnight bag before she could heft it onto her shoulder.

"Let me know if there is anything else I can do," she told the detective as she took her purse.

"I'll definitely be in touch."

Though Franko said this to Emily, Daniel didn't miss his direct glance at him.

Daniel followed Emily out of her father's home and back to his SUV. He'd just been put on notice. His appearance was considered suspect, despite his attempt at putting the detective off the scent. Daniel would be hearing from Franko in the very near future.

Not a problem. He'd spent more than a decade outmaneuvering the enemy; he didn't foresee a problem this time. Not that Chicago PD was the enemy but, at present, they were definitely an opposing team. Opposing to a degree, at any rate.

"What do we do now?" Emily wanted to know when she'd settled into the passenger seat and snapped her safety belt into place.

"Now we take a look at what we have." Daniel pulled away from the curb and merged into traffic. "I ask you a lot of questions," he added, tossing her an assessing look. "You get annoyed and possibly slap me again."

She blushed.

He braked at a traffic light and took the time to enjoy the reaction.

"I won't slap you again as long as you don't kiss me again without permission," she returned with a surprising surge of sass.

"I'll be sure to ask first next time," he teased, hoping to keep the mood light.

Apparently she realized her mistake then. The blush on her otherwise pale cheeks deepened and she wouldn't allow her gaze to meet his.

Emily didn't say a lot on the trip from Chicago's diverse Chinatown to the corner of Michigan and Huron in the elegant Gold Coast District. She appeared lost in her thoughts and Daniel couldn't help wondering if the full weight of her father's murder had begun to sink in fully.

So far, she'd been a pretty busy lady, taking care of the funeral arrangements, as well as the grueling funeral itself, and then settling her father's affairs. There had most likely been accounts to close and notifications to make. And now she had the investigation on which to focus. Staying busy could be a good thing, but it could also delay the inevitable, necessary emotions.

Emily Hastings had lost her father to a violent death. Escaping the grief would be impossible.

Rather than turn his SUV over to the valet, Daniel decided to park it himself. At this point, he needed to be able to move at a moment's notice. The dark sedan that

had followed them to the hotel drove on past where
Daniel had parked, but it wouldn't go far. Daniel had
noted the tail as soon as they'd left the Hastings residence. He'd expected Franko to keep them under surveillance. Before getting out of the vehicle, he unlocked
the glove compartment and removed the bundle of letters Victoria had given him.

Midway from the parking area to the hotel entrance,
Emily abruptly stopped and turned to him. "Why did
you bring me to a hotel?" She glanced around, looking
confused and uncertain. "I plan to stay at my father's as
long as I'm in town."

"This is where I'm staying," he explained, taking a
last look at the cop who pretended to be occupied with
retrieving something from his trunk before continuing
to the entrance. "I want them to think you're staying
with me."

She nodded, though her expression still looked confused. "Oh."

Daniel opened the door leading to the hotel lobby and
waited for Emily to pass. She managed a tight smile and
stepped through the door.

Neither of them spoke as they took the elevator to his
floor. Like any good soldier, he'd left his room in immaculate condition. No discarded clothes on the floor
or cluttered hygiene products.

Emily surveyed the room, looking as if she felt completely out of place. It wasn't a lack of space that made
her uncomfortable; Daniel's host had sprung for nothing
less than the best. The size was generous, the decor luxurious. No, he imagined that her discomfort was more about
being alone in such an intimate space with a stranger.

"Why don't we get started," he suggested in an effort to break the tension. He tossed the bundle of letters onto the desk near the bed.

Her gaze swung from the bundle to his eyes, and she managed a nod. "All right."

He reached to assist her with the removal of her jacket. She didn't exactly flinch but she stiffened.

"Don't hesitate to ask questions, Miss Hastings. I want you to feel comfortable in my presence."

Emily studied the man, Daniel Marks, several seconds before responding to his suggestion. He very much wanted her to trust him, that much was crystal clear.

But would that be a mistake?

"Why did she pick you?" It wasn't necessary to explain that by *she,* Emily meant the head of the Colby Agency. The woman's son was a murder suspect. To Emily's way of thinking, this Daniel Marks must be very good if a mother trusted him enough to put her son's future in his hands.

Marks shouldered out of his own jacket and laid it across the end of the bed alongside hers. Emily suffered a quiver of sorts. Being alone with him in his hotel room made even that simple gesture of partially disrobing feel far too intimate.

"Would you like something to drink?" He indicated the bar across the room. "I have water, soft drinks, coffee, wine, beer and a number of offerings a bit stronger."

He said the last with a hint of a smile influencing the corners of his mouth. Somehow, the idea that he didn't take himself too seriously set Emily at ease. He'd kissed her. Arrogantly put his arm around her in Detective Franko's presence to give the illusion of an ongoing relationship to explain his presence. And yet, that arrogance didn't follow him into other settings.

Oddly, in timing at least considering the circumstances that had brought them together, she liked that.

"A glass of wine would be good," she admitted.

He gave her a nod and strode toward the bar to take care of her request. As she watched him, a number of questions popped into her mind. Where did Daniel Marks come from? Where did he call home? Was he a private investigator like those at the Colby Agency? The only things she really knew about him was that he certainly had broad enough shoulders to support the needs of his clients. The idea of crying on those strong shoulders filtered through her mind, but she promptly booted it out.

Her father was dead. Yes, there was a part of her that wanted to cry. But she wouldn't. She'd emotionally disengaged a long time ago to end the pain of separation. Or maybe reality hadn't set in fully. Whatever the case, she had no intention of crying on Daniel Marks's shoulder or anyone else's. She could take care of herself. That was why she was here. Whether she'd been close to her father the past decade didn't matter. It was her responsibility to help settle any matters related to his death, including finding his murderer.

Her father had no other family. She was it.

"Where's home for you, Mr. Marks?" she asked as he turned, two glasses of wine in his hands along with two bags of mixed nuts, to move back in her direction.

He held out his right hand. She accepted the stemmed glass.

"For now," he said, "this is home."

Emily frowned as she accepted a bag of nuts. She didn't want him to start playing games with her this early in the relationship. The term *relationship* gave her pause, but then she analyzed it in light of the cold, hard facts. They were working on this investigation together. That made for a relationship of sorts.

"I mean usually. Where were you born? Where did you go to school?"

He considered her questions a moment after taking a sip of his wine. Emily used the time to examine his face. A person could learn a lot by watching another's expressions. She did that often at work. It was amazing how much people gave away when they didn't realize anyone was watching so closely. Of course, Mr. Marks wouldn't give away quite so much since he was aware of her scrutiny.

"I was born in San Antonio. I attended school in three different states and one European country." He grinned at her surprise. "I was a military brat."

Now who was giving away their every feeling? Emily blushed, felt like kicking herself for being so transparent.

"I guess you could say home was wherever the military sent us."

"College?"

"Columbia."

"Since then?" She wanted it all.

That grin flashed again. "Wherever the U.S. Army saw fit to plant me."

There was a teasing quality about his voice that somehow niggled its way under her skin and made her feel relaxed in his presence, even though she wasn't fully prepared to just yet.

"You're not old enough to be retired," she pointed out instantly, wondering if something went wrong with his military career. Had he been injured? Her gaze took a quick excursion of his tall frame. He certainly didn't look physically challenged in any way.

"No," he said succinctly. "Ten years was long enough for me." He took a drink from his wine, reminding her that she hadn't touched hers yet. She followed his example, though her attention was keenly focused on what he would say next.

"I felt I'd achieved all I could." He shrugged. "I'd moved up the ranks in record time, but the work no longer offered a challenge for me. I decided to move on."

"So now you do this," she observed.

Daniel hesitated before replying. She was digging. Needed to understand who he was and what he was about. Telling her that he'd only left the military six months ago and that after a hiatus from the decision, he'd decided to go for a position at the Colby Agency might put off earning her trust. But he was a firm believer of honesty being the best policy.

"This is actually my first foray into private sector investigative work," he admitted. "But I'm hopeful that it won't be my last."

She nodded hesitantly. "Have you ever investigated a murder case before?"

Now there was a tougher question, one not so easily answered. He had spent ten years as a military strategist. It was his job to determine the best way to avoid casualties, not to discern the reasons for loss after the fact.

"What I did in the military was not so different from this, Miss Hastings," he explained. "I analyzed the facts of a situation, put together scenarios. Most of my work related to the preventive side of those scenarios. That said, your father's case can't be called typical when his occupation is tied in. We have to assume certain things, considering he'd spent a lifetime dealing with murder as a homicide detective."

"What sort of things?" she wanted to know.

Daniel moved over to the bed and sat down next to the jackets he'd left there. As he explained his theories about her father, he started to remove the papers he'd stored inside the linings.

"First and foremost, we need to bear in mind that he would not be so easily tricked or lured into a dark alley where he would ultimately lose his life."

She blinked but didn't retreat. "Right. My father would never have been so naive." Her gaze zeroed in on Daniel's then. "So he must have known whoever it was that he followed into that alley."

"That's quite possible," he agreed. Either that or he'd been forced there at gunpoint.

"Then there must have been a connection between him and his killer," Emily said. Her smooth brow furrowed with worry or confusion, maybe both, as her gaze moved to the desk and the letters he'd left there.

"My thoughts keep going back to those letters," she admitted. "But I just can't see what old love letters have to do with anything. They weren't to or about my father."

Daniel moved to the desk and picked up the bundle. "Why don't we start with these?"

At her look of eager anticipation, he decided she liked that plan of action. Daniel took his glass of wine and the letters to the table on the other side of the room.

Emily joined him there. When she'd taken a seat, he did the same, choosing to sit directly across from her.

He allowed her to read each letter first, then he accepted it from her and took his turn. There were a dozen; all had been written by a woman named Madelyn Rutland.

The letters appeared to indicate that the woman, Madelyn, had carried on an affair with James Colby some eighteen years ago. The affair had apparently evolved from the investigation into the Colbys' missing son.

The tone of the letters grew in intensity and desperation, culminating in the final one where the author, Madelyn, insisted life would not be worth living without James at her side. She had pressed him for a decision. Madelyn wanted James to desert Victoria. If he had indicated his feelings one way or the other, there was no way to tell from her increasingly urgent written ramblings.

One letter had been written to Victoria but obviously not mailed. In the letter, the author had warned Victoria that James belonged to her and that he had only stayed with Victoria because of their child.

Emily Hastings sighed loudly. "I can't see how any of this relates to my father, other than the fact that Madelyn was his partner back then."

Daniel considered the content of the letters and the devastation he'd seen on Victoria's face when she spoke of the past and Carter Hastings. These letters had obviously come as a shock to her. From what he knew of the Colby reputation, there was no room for this sort of skeleton in the Colby closet. James Colby had been a revered man. That he would cheat on his wife just didn't fit with the world's perception of the man's past. But, then, it happened with high-profile figures all the time.

"Maybe your father wanted to protect Victoria," Daniel offered for lack of any other probable motive. There was, of course, the possibility that Carter Hastings had had deeper feelings for Victoria, as well. Perhaps in working the investigation related to her missing child, as well as the one, three years later, revolving around her husband's murder, Carter had developed stronger feelings for her. If he discovered the letters upon James Colby's murder, he might have hidden them to protect Victoria. Made sense.

Emily considered his suggestion for a time, then said, "He was like that. My mother always said that he took his work too seriously and let it interfere with what he should be paying attention to."

Just another reason to suspect that the man's feelings had moved into personal territory where Victoria was concerned. Hastings's own wife was jealous of his work.

Daniel shuffled back through the letters. "There is also the possibility that Madelyn was nothing but a stalker, attempting to lure James Colby into a relationship. Where would we find her now?" His gaze rested on Emily's. She looked tired, but he wasn't so sure taking her back to her father's place was the right thing to do when the police had finished there.

"I'm not completely positive, but I think maybe she died," Emily said thoughtfully. "I think it was after that shooting involving the teenager." She glanced toward the bed where their jackets lay. "The article mentioned that Madelyn was cleared of responsibility, but she resigned not long after that. Moved away and died, I think."

Her brow lost its smoothness as she concentrated

harder, searching for more details from the past. The transition made him want to reach up and smooth the wrinkles away. He dismissed that dangerous line of thinking, considered that maybe veering away from physical relationships this past six months might have been a mistake.

"I think I remember my father being sad because he'd heard she died all alone some place far away." She chewed on her lower lip as if that would help her to remember, when, in fact, the only thing it did was make him want to soothe it as badly as he'd wanted to caress away the lines on her forehead. "Maybe I can ask my mother. She might recall something about Madelyn that I've forgotten."

Daniel levered his attention back to the case and away from the partner he'd been saddled with. He was supposed to be annoyed at her participation, impatient at the very least. Being mildly attracted to her wasn't in the plan. Kissing her had evidently been a serious miscalculation on his part.

"Your mother could be a source of invaluable information," he commented. Any facts he could learn about Carter Hastings's past could prove useful.

"Maybe." Emily said this with little conviction.

That she had abruptly closed up emotionally made him wonder. "Your mother would resist discussing the past?"

Another of those heavy exhalations. She should stop doing that. Her vulnerability aroused his protective instincts far more than it should. He reasoned that she'd just lost her father and sympathy was at play here, but he had a bad feeling that he was merely kidding himself.

"My mother won't discuss anything about our life in

Chicago," she admitted. "She lives her life as if this part never happened." Emily's gaze settled on his and she couldn't hide the emotion there. "After my brother died, nothing was ever the same. My mom blamed my dad and she left. Took me with her and never looked back. End of story."

Daniel listened as Emily told him how her brother had died. He could see how devastating that would be for any mother or father. But, beyond that, he could also see that the tragedy gave the Hastings one more connection to the Colbys. Victoria had lost her son. Of course, Jim Colby was back now, but years ago, when Carter Hastings lost his son, Jim had been considered gone for good.

When Emily had finished her painful story, her emotions had taken quite a bruising. As a trained strategist, Daniel recognized that moving beyond that part would be beneficial at this point. For both of them.

"We should go through the rest of these papers." He gestured to the bed where their jackets lay. "Maybe we'll find something here."

She looked at him, her eyes still far too bright for his comfort. He definitely did not want to have to contend with tears. Not because he was heartless, but because he felt certain touching her again would be a mistake.

"And if we don't find anything there, what do we do then? We can't just keep digging around in the past. We have to find out what happened this week." She shrugged. "Last week. I want to know why my father was murdered." The emotion in her eyes hardened with determination. "I want to know who did this."

If he'd had any question as to whether this seemingly

vulnerable woman would see this investigation through, he had none now.

Emily Hastings was in for the long haul.

CHAPTER SIXTEEN

EMILY SET ASIDE the final page from the last stack of her father's papers. From the corner of her eye, she stole a peek at Daniel Marks. His profile was lined with concentration. She doubted he'd found anything; she certainly hadn't.

The pages she'd viewed had retold a lifetime of notes on various cases, along with dozens upon dozens of newspaper clippings that reported similar incidents sans the full details. Nothing, not a single line on any of the pages, offered any connection between the Colby Agency and her father. She had read one or two articles that praised the esteemed agency's excellent work with Chicago PD.

When Marks set aside the last page he'd picked up to read, she said, "Anything?"

He shook his head. "I did find one article." He shuffled through a stack. "That recognized the—"

"Colby Agency's great work with Chicago PD," she finished for him. He nodded. "I found a couple of those myself."

"That nails it, then," Marks said. He pushed back his chair and strode over to the coffeemaker. He'd made the first pot three hours ago.

Emily rubbed at her eyes and looked again. Just after

ten. That meant they'd been at this for more than four hours. She felt exhausted. Marks had to be, as well.

"Nails what?" she asked, having no idea what he meant. He had a decade of experience analyzing data and situations; she had basically none. Maybe that was why fate had taken her to the Colby Agency offices today. She'd needed help and she'd found it…in the most unlikely place, considering Jim Colby was suspected of her father's murder.

He poured himself a cup of coffee from pot number three and gestured to her cup. She shook her head. She was already jittery enough. One, maybe two cups per day had always been her limit.

"The only connection we have is Madelyn Rutland."

He was right. "But if Madelyn is—"

Her cell phone rang, interrupting her. She glanced around quickly, trying to remember where she'd left it.

"Here you go." Marks picked up her purse from the chair near the door and brought it to her.

By the time she'd fished out the phone, it had rung three times. She hoped it wasn't her mother. Explaining her decision to stay a couple more weeks wasn't something she looked forward to. She'd left her a message this afternoon at a time when Emily had been certain her mother would be out.

"Hello." Dread had knotted in her tummy by the time she managed the greeting.

"Miss Hastings, this is Detective Franko."

Relief rushed through her, but it didn't last long. Had the detective found something in her father's home? Tension cranked up. What if he'd discovered that she and Mr. Daniels had removed certain items?

She moistened her lips. "Detective Franko." She allowed her eyes to meet that of the man in the room, her partner in crime. "Have you finished?" She'd actually completely forgotten about the search warrant until now.

"Yes. We're done here. You can return if you'd like, but bear in mind that we might need to have a second look. Unfortunately, we won't be able to release your father's car for a while. Is that going to be a problem? When did you plan to return to California?"

Not once since Detective Franko had told her that her father's car had been impounded had she asked about it. She'd come prepared to use public transportation. His bringing it up now sounded curiously like an effort at ferreting out her plans.

"Don't worry, Detective. I'm in no hurry to have the car back. As far as my plans go—" she didn't miss the warning in Daniel Marks's eyes "—I still have a few things to tie up here. I haven't made any firm plans about leaving just yet."

The man watching her so intently flashed an approving smile.

"Well, keep me informed," Detective Franko said, "and I'll do the same."

Emily thanked him and punched the Off button on her phone. "They're finished," she said as she dropped the phone back into her purse.

She should be glad. Exhaustion clawed at her. But, in truth, a part of her didn't want to go back.

Three nights in that empty house was more than enough.

A hotel would be all right. After all, she'd brought her bag. A frown scrunched her brow. Why had she done that? Oh, yeah, it had been his idea.

"I should go…home," she said to him.

He glanced at his watch. "Yeah, it is late." He glanced toward her bag. "We can follow up on the Madelyn connection tomorrow."

Emily nodded. "Okay." She stood, swayed a little before she steadied herself. "I guess I'm more tired than I realized."

"You've had a tough week."

She shouldn't let the gentleness of his voice affect her, but somehow she just couldn't help herself. She'd felt so alone all week; it was nice to have someone, even a stranger, pretend to care.

Grabbing her purse, she considered that that wasn't exactly fair. Her father's friends and coworkers from Chicago PD had certainly shown a tremendous amount of support. But this was different…this felt like it was meant for her, not Carter Hastings's daughter.

Marks started to grab her bag, then hesitated. "You know, we didn't have dinner." He glanced at his watch again. "Why don't I call room service? I've ordered in a couple of times. The menu's pretty good."

Uneasiness slid through her, but her stomach staged a coup and overrode her hesitancy. The peanuts hadn't done the trick. She didn't want to eat in her father's kitchen…not tonight.

"Or we could find a drive-through still open," he suggested at her hesitancy.

Emily couldn't help wondering if Victoria Colby-Camp was paying him extra to be nice to her. She'd spent several hours alone with him in his hotel room; what were a few more minutes? She was starving.

"Room service will be fine." She set her purse aside

and worked up a little more visible enthusiasm. "What do you recommend?"

Daniel felt inordinately pleased. His protective instincts again. After Emily had decided what she would have and he'd placed the order, they were left with nothing but time and silence between them.

He sat on the edge of the bed; she reclaimed her chair at the table.

"So, what is it that you do out in California?" he asked. Might as well cut right through the tension. "Turnabout is fair play," he tossed in when she looked doubtful.

"I—" she clasped her hands on the table "—actually went to college to be a journalist, but it hasn't exactly worked out yet."

He didn't rush her, just let her talk. Instead of prompting her, he watched her, noted the little details he hadn't allowed himself to in the past few hours. Her hair was long, well past her shoulders. Silky. He didn't have to touch it to know.

"Instead, I ended up as a research secretary at a law firm." She lifted, then lowered, her shoulders in a negligible shrug. "I actually like my job—it's just not where I thought I'd be almost five years after university."

"Boyfriend?" As the question he hadn't intended to ask slipped out of his suddenly big mouth, his gaze darted to her left hand. No wedding band. But then, her marital status wasn't actually relevant since this relationship would be a professional one only.

She blinked twice, but kept any other reaction off her face. "I…ah…no." Another blink, but she didn't do such a good job of keeping her expression clean of emotion this time. "You?"

He shook his head and decided to resort to a cliché. "There's a saying," he told her. "If the army wanted a soldier to have a wife, one would be issued."

"You're what…thirty?"

"Thirty-two."

He'd estimated her age to be twenty-five, but she'd said five years had passed since she'd left college. "And you?" he prodded.

"Twenty-six."

Silence elapsed for a time. He couldn't say it was exactly comfortable, but the tension had abated to some degree. He hoped that meant she felt more comfortable with him. Earning her trust would be helpful. The investigation would have been easier if he'd been on his own. But, if she was going to work with him on this one, he needed her to trust him as much as two strangers could trust each other.

"Do you have any brothers or sisters?" she asked, taking her serve and shifting the attention back to him.

"There's no one but me."

"Parents?" When she asked the question, she looked up at him with a kind of sincere innocence that tugged at those damned hero genes again.

"Retired to Florida a few years ago."

Emily had already told him all there was to know about her parents. Well, at least, all that was relevant to this investigation.

She suddenly found herself wondering if Daniel Marks was lonely. Okay, enough with that. Wherever that thought came from, she needed to close that door. Maybe she was the one who was lonely. She worked long hours, was the only one in the office who didn't complain about being asked to stay after hours. Her mother was always busy with her stepfather. And, like Daniel Marks, she had no siblings. Now her father was gone.

Yep, loneliness would be an apt description.

Emily closed her eyes and forced all thought from her mind. She could not be letting her mind go off on these ridiculous tangents. She wasn't lonely; she was grieving.

But the tears wouldn't come.

She had loved her father, still did. Had the loss of her brother and then the subsequent dissolution of her family stolen her ability to let those emotions flow freely? Since all her grandparents had passed away before she turned ten, she'd had no reason to fall apart emotionally since her childhood world had changed.

Concentrating with all her might, she tried to remember a time when she'd cried over some school dilemma or some guy who'd broken her heart.

"Earth to Emily."

Her eyes opened and she tried not to show her surprise at his use of her first name. He'd done that before…sometime during the past few hours. Funny how it felt like so much longer…as if she'd known him for ages rather than only hours, less than a day.

She sat up straight and let out a sharp breath, only then realizing she'd been holding her breath and staring into his eyes. Dark, dark eyes.

A knock on the door kept her from having to explain that she'd drifted off into another dimension.

"Room service," Marks reminded her. Good thing, too, because she'd completely forgotten. She rarely forgot about food.

She watched as he crossed the room. Deliberate,

fluid movements. Calm, confident. But then, he hadn't just lost his father. And he had years of military training. Didn't soldiers learn how to maintain their composure in the most harrowing situations?

What was it like to be a soldier? To ignore one's personal needs and keep driving forward with the mission? It took a special kind of man to follow that path.

"Smells delicious."

Emily snapped back to the present. Marks had already taken care of the tab and rolled the cart into the center of the room.

Maybe staying had been a mistake. She should have gone home hours ago. "I'm not really as hungry as I thought."

Just go, Emily, she told herself. *Go back to your father's and try to get some sleep. Clear your mind.*

"Come on." He pulled her up a chair. "We can talk about Madelyn. You can tell me whatever you remember about her or anything you recall your father having said."

Emily hesitated only a moment. What the heck? He'd ordered the food and had paid for it. Letting it go to waste wouldn't be right.

They ate without speaking for quite some time. She focused on attempting to dredge the recesses of her brain for any memories associated with Madelyn Rutland. There were a few. Madelyn had been a tall woman with dark blond hair and gray eyes.

Her voice had been pleasant, if a little stern. She had been several years younger than her father. If she were still alive, she would perhaps be fifty-one or fifty-two.

Emily shook her head. What could a nearly twenty-year-old affair have to do with her father's murder?

Despite her misgivings, she related what she remembered about the woman. Marks listened intently without comment until she'd finished.

"Do you recall any disagreements between your father and his partner? Any possibility that they might have been lovers?"

Emily had considered why her father had the letters in the first place, and she'd decided that he'd hidden them to protect the Colby family. She could only imagine, based on the postmarks on the envelopes, that he'd done this shortly after James Colby's murder. She fixed her mind on that time but found nothing. The one thing she knew with complete certainty was that her father would never in a million years have had an affair with his partner. She told Marks as much, left no room for further discussion. He left it at that.

"I could ask my mother if she recalled any disagreements between them," she said, but even as she spoke the words, dread welled inside her.

"That might not be necessary," he allowed.

Emily couldn't say whether he'd heard the dread in her voice or seriously thought they could dig up what they needed without talking to anyone from that time. But she was relieved at the possibility of getting off without discussing the case with her mother, even if she had initially suggested it.

Quiet slipped in again and Emily finished off her chicken and rice. She really had been famished, hadn't eaten all day.

"Tomorrow," Marks said after finishing off his steak, "we'll find out whether Madelyn is still alive or not."

Emily sipped her wine thoughtfully. "I do remember

my father saying something about her moving away."
She shook her head, trying her best to snag the elusive
memory. She'd mentioned that possibility already but
couldn't recall the particulars. "And I'm almost certain
we heard that she had died, but I can't remember when
or how my father got the news."

"Confirming her whereabouts won't be a problem,"
Marks assured her. He finished off his water, leaving his
second glass of wine untouched. "I should take you
back to your father's before you fall asleep sitting up."

She was tired. But she did not look forward to going
to her father's house. Still, it was too late to do otherwise.

"Thank you."

Daniel stood, tossed his napkin onto the cart and retrieved her bag. She slung her purse onto her shoulder,
and they were ready.

A familiar silence had fallen over them once more by
the time they reached the parking garage. Daniel let her
keep her thoughts to herself. She was tired. Recharging
would help her recall anything from her past that might
be useful to the case. He didn't see any reason to push
her for information that he could obtain in other ways.
Anything she remembered on her own would be a bonus.

The same sedan that had followed them to his hotel
fell into place behind Daniel's SUV when he reached
the street. He considered that he needed to check in
with Victoria first thing in the morning, to get the information he needed, and then pick up Emily, assuming she
hadn't changed her mind about participating. He didn't
see that happening, but he'd been wrong before.

He glanced in the rearview mirror and noted that the
sedan stayed close. Daniel almost smiled when the idea

of giving them the slip crossed his mind. Not that he knew Chicago that well, but he knew how to lose a tail in any situation. Could make those guys—there were two of them—sweat for a few minutes. But he didn't want to upset Emily. Let the cops do their job.

"Do you know what time tomorrow you'd like to get started?"

As he pulled up in front of her house, she turned to him and, though it was dark, the dim glow from the dash allowed him to see that vulnerability peeking through her mask of bravado again.

"Nine okay?"

"That'll be fine."

She started to get out but he stopped her with a hand on her arm. "I should walk you to the door." He hitched his head toward the rear of the vehicle. "We have an audience."

It took her a moment to get his meaning, then she said, "I'd forgotten."

Daniel climbed out of his SUV, grabbed her bag from the backseat and then rounded the hood. He opened her door and offered his hand to assist her.

With her bag in one hand, he kept the other on her shoulder as they walked the short distance to her father's stoop. "You have my number," he said when they reached the door. "Don't hesitate to call me if you need to." The idea that she might not be safe alone crossed his mind, but the police had her under surveillance. "I don't want you going out alone and if you—"

"My father was a cop, Mr. Marks, I know how to take care of myself," she interjected.

Maybe she wasn't as vulnerable as she looked. One

corner of his mouth lifted in reaction to her no-nonsense declaration. "You're right. You'll have to forgive me for my presumptuousness."

Her lips quirked, just the tiniest flicker of movement, as if she'd intended to smile but hadn't been quite able to manage the feat.

"Make sure it doesn't happen again," she scolded. "Carter Hastings didn't raise a fraidy cat."

The quiver in her voice was unmistakable.

"You sure you're going to be all right?" There he went again, playing the hero.

She took a deep breath. "I'm fine, Mr. Marks. Go back to your hotel. I'm not the only one who needs sleep."

He started to turn away, but decided to make another point clear first. "If we're going to work together, I don't see why we can't be on a first-name basis." He'd already called her Emily a couple of times and she hadn't protested.

She held his gaze for a couple of beats that sent anticipation shooting through his veins. "All right, *Daniel*. We'll skip formality and keep it casual."

He nodded. "I'll see you at nine, *Emily*." He didn't wait for a response. No need. But he didn't get far. He'd made it down one step when her next words stopped him.

"Wait, *Daniel*."

He turned back to her. "Yes?"

"Aren't we supposed to keep up the pretenses?"

Confusion overrode all else. "I'm not sure—"

She kissed him.

Pressed her soft lips to his and draped her arms along his shoulders and around his neck. She didn't even have to tiptoe. With him down one step from her, she just leaned into him…and took his breath away.

She drew back as abruptly as she'd moved in on him. "Good night, Daniel." Instead of drawing away, she leaned close to his ear and whispered, "Now we're even."

She disappeared inside the house before he regained his wits.

"Well, hell," he mumbled as he made his way back to the SUV.

He hoped his move earlier today hadn't been as transparent as hers just now.

Every instinct he'd honed in more than a decade of assessing the threat of his opponent told him that her kiss had been only about revenge.

INSIDE THE DARK HOUSE, Emily sagged against the locked door.

What on earth had she been thinking?

He'd said the police were still watching them. He'd kissed her earlier to make it seem as if they were a couple rather than two people investigating a case currently at the top of Chicago PD's priority list. Wasn't she supposed to keep up the act? Keep the police guessing?

What had she been thinking?

The police were her father's friends. They wanted to catch his killer, just as she did.

She scrubbed her hand over her face and then through her hair. A bath and some sleep. She needed both. Surely he wouldn't hold her momentary lapse into insanity against her. After all, she wasn't thinking straight. Her father had been murdered. She'd had to come back here and do the whole funeral thing alone. Of course she would cling to anyone who showed her the slightest bit of compassion. God knew her mother had failed to be there on too many occasions to count.

Okay. She pushed off the door. Bringing up the past and her mother's, as well as her father's, failures after the divorce would accomplish nothing. She'd kissed Daniel Marks. No harm done. He'd kissed her first. It wasn't as if she'd crossed that line first.

The wine hadn't helped, she mused, as she made her way upstairs. She'd never been much of a drinker and should have known better.

Choosing the stairs, she couldn't bear to sleep in her father's room again. Using his soap would be out of the question. She'd made that mistake already. Getting depressed all over again wasn't something she wanted to do.

Rummaging through the upstairs hall closet, she found a bar of soap that had likely been purchased by her mother a lifetime ago. The towels seemed clean, if not freshly laundered. She discovered an unopened bottle of shampoo under the sink and she was in business.

Emily took a long hot soak, didn't skimp on the hot water or the indulgence of time. Lying there, neck deep in liquid heat, felt incredibly relaxing. Maybe sleep would come quickly when she crawled into bed, hopefully quickly enough to prevent her from lying there obsessing about how she could ever, in a million years, have decorated her bedroom in such a hideous theme.

Dwelling on the insanity of her teenage decor and the sweet heat of the welcoming water did little to fend off reality from her thoughts.

She considered the hurt she'd seen on Victoria Colby-

Camp's face. This investigation wasn't easy for her, either. Emily swallowed against the tightness suddenly squeezing her throat. But if Victoria's son had murdered Emily's father, he had to pay for that horrible crime.

The idea that Victoria had learned of her husband's affair in the same fell swoop that she had been told her son was suspected of being a murderer rubbed at Emily's raw nerves. That had to be a terrifying feeling.

Why was it, she wondered vaguely, that some people had to suffer such horrendous tragedies in their lives? Why did her brother have to die at age sixteen? Why had Victoria lost her son when he was only seven, then her husband three years later? Now, after all those years, she finds her son, only to possibly lose him to a murder charge. How much was one person expected to tolerate in a lifetime?

Emily suddenly felt heavy with regret for what Victoria must be going through. Emily's mother had told her time and again that she'd inherited that fatal flaw from her father. Feeling sorry for someone who'd done harm to you was stupid, her mother had insisted. But Emily couldn't help herself. She was very much like her father on that score.

The saddest part was, even if hers and Daniel Marks's investigation proved that Jim Colby had killed her father, it wouldn't bring him back. Emily's situation wouldn't change; she would still be without her father.

But Victoria Colby-Camp's life would be devastated all over again.

CHAPTER SEVENTEEN

"VICTORIA, WE SHOULD TALK about this at the very least."

She turned to stare at her husband, the man she loved more than life itself. But she could not discuss this with him. He wanted to help. She understood that. Yet, she could not permit his interference.

Lucas Camp wanted to protect her far more than he wanted to find the truth. Of that, she was certain.

Yes, he would do all in his power to prove her son innocent of the suspicions shrouding him. There was no question in that regard. She knew Lucas. He would find a way to make it happen.

Victoria needed the truth, the whole truth.

No matter the cost.

Her hands shook and she clasped them in front of her to prevent her husband from seeing her need to waiver…to fall into his arms and let him take care of the matter. She could not do that. This time, she had to know everything.

She braced herself and plunged forward. "I know you want to help, Lucas, but this time you can't. This time is different."

He moved across their bedroom, his limp barely noticeable with the new prosthesis, and took her hands in his. The feel of his unending strength made her yearn to simply give in.

"Don't let your obsession over what you believe to be an indiscretion on James's part override your instincts, my dear," he urged, his gray eyes pleading. "Jim's life is on the line here. If we don't prove he had nothing to do with Hastings's death, he could end up being charged with capital murder."

She inhaled a painful breath. "Please, Lucas, do you think I don't know that? Why do you suppose I've hired Daniel Marks? I'm counting on him to get to the bottom of what happened that night. Whatever James did or did not do is irrelevant just now."

He didn't believe her. The flash of disappointment in his eyes grabbed hold of her heart and twisted. She didn't want Lucas to be disappointed in her. She wanted their life to return to normal. This last year of happiness wasn't nearly enough. Her son deserved this new life. What evil had swooped down and taken it from him? From her? From her beloved Lucas?

He sighed wearily. They were both tired, should have gone to bed hours ago. Would it really have mattered? Probably not. Sleep would elude her as it had last night…and maybe even the night before that. She couldn't remember now.

"I can see what you're going through, Victoria; and it's tearing me apart inside. Let me help you. Let me help Jim."

She leveled her gaze on his and wished there was another way, but there was not. "You can't help me this time, Lucas. This time, I have to know the full truth."

His hold tightened on her hands when she would

have pulled away. "James Colby was my friend," Lucas said, a gentleness of tone softening the words uttered with such conviction. "We kept each other alive all those years ago. Neither one of us would have made it out of that hellhole without the other."

James and Lucas had served in the military together, had shared a cage as prisoners of war. She knew her husband's words were true, but he'd left out a significant part. Lucas was the one who'd saved James's life, had lost his leg in the process. For more than half his life, he'd worn a prosthesis and never once had he shown regret for what he'd sacrificed. And, yes, James and Lucas had been like brothers. Closer than brothers.

"No amount of letters, *nothing*," he emphasized, "will ever make me believe he would do anything to hurt you. This isn't what you think."

Perhaps not. She closed her eyes and fought the sting of tears. She had loved James with all her heart and soul. Had fallen in love with him the moment they met. She'd never believed in love at first sight until that day. But she'd fallen hard for James. Warmth spread through her at the memories. Truth be told, she'd fallen for Lucas just a little bit, too. The two were a sort of package deal. You didn't get one without the other.

She opened her eyes and looked into the ones filled with such desperation. "Lucas, I recognize how very much you love me. I am also aware of how much James loved me. But I have to know for sure. I've based all that I believe in on what the two of us shared—on what you and I share. I have to know that foundation isn't flawed."

"My only concern," Lucas admitted solemnly, "is that when one goes looking hard enough for trouble, they can usually find it. James Colby was the kind of man most only aspire to be, and still, he was only human. There may have been a crack in his noble veneer, but is there a single one of us who can claim not to have a tiny fracture here or there?"

He was right. On a purely intellectual level, she understood that every word he said made perfect sense. But intellect wasn't at play here. This was about emotions. About her heart. And no matter how she tried to override the ferocity with which she felt the need to learn the truth, she couldn't make it happen. She had to know.

"I'm tired, Lucas," she admitted. "I'd like to go to bed now."

He nodded, squeezed her hands. "Am I still under exile to the guest room?"

Her heart went out to him, made her second-guess her determination…but only for a moment. She, of all people, knew how persuasive Lucas Camp could be. Keeping a certain distance was necessary. She couldn't let him change her mind about seeing this through. This was far too important.

"For a little while longer." Again, that disappointment flashed in his eyes. "I'm sorry, Lucas. I can't help how I feel."

He nodded. "You do what you must."

When he released her and started for the door, worry tightened her throat. "Lucas."

He hesitated, turned back to her. "Yes?"

"I need to be sure you're going to keep your promise about not getting involved." She didn't have to be close to see that the disappointment he felt would have given way to hurt. It wasn't that she didn't trust him; she did. But she also knew that he would go to any lengths to protect her.

"I gave you my word," he said tautly.

He left, closing the door soundly behind him.

Victoria drifted to the foot of the bed and collapsed there, her legs too weak to hold her a moment longer.

God, please let me be doing the right thing, she prayed.

She'd read the file on Daniel Marks. His credentials were impeccable. More importantly, she instinctively felt that he would be a tremendous asset to the agency. He would do this right. She had no doubt.

All that mattered to her was at stake here, and she was betting on Daniel to complete the task.

She peered into the mirror sitting atop her dresser only a few feet away. She looked tired and older than she ever had before. More than anything, she did not want to lose Jim again. She simply could not bear it.

Nor could she endure losing Lucas. Was she alienating him with her uncompromising position on the issue?

Perhaps. But how else could she ever be sure?

She couldn't.

Zach, the agency's top legal counsel, was working on forcing Chicago PD's hand on the matter of evidence. What they had offered up thus far was not sufficient for an arraignment, but they were working 24/7 to find more. Zach suspected they were focusing on proving Jim's guilt rather than finding the real murderer or actual evidence.

Victoria felt the weight of dread creep deep into her stomach. Could she actually be certain that her son hadn't committed this heinous crime?

She had no reason to believe he had. To her knowledge, her son and Carter Hastings had never even met. But did that mean circumstances hadn't brought them together? For what reason? What would Jim's motive have been for killing a stranger? Had he already been under investigation for some other crime? If so, the detective in charge of the case hadn't come across with the information as yet.

That simply couldn't be the case. Tasha kept careful tabs on Jim's activities. She was with him most of the time. But it only took a few minutes to find trouble. She understood that all too well.

Victoria shook her head and pushed to her feet. The only thing she could do was wait. And hope that Daniel Marks was as good as his record claimed him to be.

She changed into her nightgown and washed her face, all the while her mind jumping from scenario to scenario. If Jim had killed Carter—she could scarcely think the words—surely there had been extenuating circumstances. She had watched Jim evolve into the kind of man his father had been. Strong, dependable, loyal. He would not have committed cold-blooded murder.

Victoria recalled the hurt and worry she'd heard in Tasha's voice when Tasha had told her of coming home that night to find Jim in a state of regression.

No, she realized, Jim would never have killed anyone in cold blood.

But Seth would have.

CHAPTER EIGHTEEN

TASHA SENSED SOMETHING, a sound maybe, tugging at her, but she didn't want to wake up. She needed to sleep.

She snuggled deeper into the covers and tried to block the intrusion.

Just sleep.

The pounding grew louder.

Tasha bolted upright. "What the hell?"

Jim's side of the bed was cold.

Fear rammed into her gut. Where was he?

She threw back the covers and dropped her feet to the floor. As she reached for the jeans she'd discarded before going to bed, she hesitated.

There was that sound again.

A heavy thud or splat.

The basement.

She rushed to the door beneath the stairs, but held still for a moment to get a better fix on the sound.

Recognition broadsided her.

The punching bag.

Jim was in the basement working off his tension.

Taking care not to hit any of the spots that creaked she eased down the narrow steps. After Victoria had given them the row house, they'd started the renovations immediately. Not that the lovely home had needed any fixing up, but she and Jim had just wanted to make it their own, add their own special touches.

When his primary therapist had suggested that he join a gym for working out his frustrations, Tasha had thought of the basement they didn't use. Why not turn it into a home gym?

Jim loved it.

When she reached the bottom of the stairs her heart wrenched. Her big strong husband-to-be wore gym shorts and a cutoff T-shirt. He'd worked up a heavy sweat and was still going at it.

She bit back a curse when she noticed the crimson streaking his fingers. There was no way to be sure how long he'd been working on the bag and he'd opted to do so without gloves or taping his hands.

Bad idea.

Her hesitation at walking over to him angered her almost as much as it pained her. How could she suffer trepidation in the presence of the man she loved? They had gotten way past that.

Flashes of memory bombarded her, reminding her of that night, less than a week ago, when she'd come home to find him acting like Seth. She swallowed back the emotion that threatened to close her throat.

He'd scared her. Really, really scared her.

She had to protect the baby, which meant protecting herself.

But since he'd been released into her custody, she had to be responsible for every move he made after his medical observation was completed. Tasha stayed put near

the bottom of the staircase and let the guilt wash over
her. "Jim?"

Apparently in his own world, he kept pounding away
at the bag, each blow enough to knock the strongest man
off his feet. Jim Colby was not only tall and broad-
shouldered, he was incredibly strong. Years of cruel
treatment, including sadistic mercenary training at age
fourteen, had hardened him to pain, to emotion.

The thought took her back to just over a year ago, to
when she'd first met him. She'd been tracking an assassin who called himself Seth. His target had been Victoria Colby. Lucas Camp had commissioned Tasha to
attempt getting close to the assassin to determine who
he was and who had hired him.

She'd done both. Seth had turned out to be James
Colby, Jr., the long-lost son of Victoria. The Colbys'
archnemesis, Errol Leberman, had abducted him at the
age of seven and physically and mentally abused him
beyond the point most humans could tolerate. But Jim
had found a place deep inside himself to hide, and he'd
allowed the Seth persona to take the abuse.

Seth had grown into a totally ruthless, unfeeling man.
No one had ever touched him until Tasha.

She wasn't sure how she had accomplished that feat.
Maybe it had been as clichéd as the idea of falling for
the dangerous man. She settled onto the bottom step and
watched the man she loved pummel the bag to the point
of wearing the skin from his fists.

There was no denying that she had felt something for
him the first time she saw him. She'd wanted to reach
out to him, wanted to touch whatever was left of his cold,

unfeeling heart. Whether she'd merely intrigued him or annoyed him, he'd let her get close, then closer still.

To this day, she couldn't say for sure what had kept him from killing her; God knows, he'd threatened to numerous times. But each time, something had kept him from going that far.

Jim was the man she wanted to marry, to have children with. Seth was far too dangerous. If he came back for good, she would have to leave.

As she watched, Jim peeled off his T-shirt and threw it aside, then resumed beating the hell out of the bag. His muscles flexed with each raging slam of his fist into the well-worn leather. Sweat beaded and rolled down his smooth skin, then was absorbed in the cotton waistband of his shorts.

He went on that way until she couldn't sit there any longer. She didn't know how he endured the pain that had to be radiating up his arms.

"Jim!" She pushed to her feet.

He swiveled to face her, the predatory gleam in his eyes, the hard set of his features sending a new surge of fear through her veins.

"It's late," she said softly in the ensuing silence.

Blood dripped from his fingers, splattering onto the floor. If he noticed, he didn't let on.

He visibly relaxed and Tasha let herself breathe again.

"I couldn't sleep."

His voice was a little huskier than usual, but it was Jim's voice, not the harsh tones of Seth.

"Let me help you with that." She gestured to his hands and started in his direction, careful to keep her movements slow and steady. No sudden moves, nothing to set him on edge.

He stared at his hands.

"Come on." She reached for his arm and ushered him toward the stairs. "I'll patch those up for you," she said softly.

He allowed her to lead him upstairs to the bathroom without protest. She washed his hands and rubbed in some antibiotic ointment. He didn't flinch, just watched stoically.

Please, please, don't let him become Seth again, she prayed once more.

"I can't remember what happened that night," he murmured, his gaze still fixed on his hands and her work there as she bandaged the worst of the tears in his injured flesh.

The possibility that he may have murdered a man tormented him every waking moment. Tasha wished she could relieve him of the guilt and uncertainty, but there was nothing she could do but be here for him.

His therapist had tried a couple of techniques for helping him to remember that night. The specialist Lucas had originally brought in on his case had been stumped. He'd offered only one hope of getting to the truth—deep regression therapy, using a combination of drugs and hypnosis. But the technique carried heavy risks.

They could lose Jim altogether.

All involved recognized just how strong Seth was. If he took over in an effort to protect Jim, sending him back into submission might be impossible.

Tasha put her arms around Jim and hugged him close. "Everything is going to be okay." She held him against her heart, wanting him to feel her life force beating there. "I know you didn't do this, Jim. You'll see. When you remember, and you will remember," she drew back to look into his troubled eyes, "you'll know that I'm right."

His hands moved into her hair. He'd always loved to touch her that way. "I love you, Tasha. No matter what happens, don't ever forget that."

He kissed her softly, let her feel his vulnerability and even the fear, so uncharacteristic of the strong man.

Right then, she made him a silent promise. She would stand by him no matter what the murder investigation revealed. She loved him, loved the child they had created.

She was certain the truth would prove him innocent.

And when that happened, she would tell him about the baby. She couldn't do that now. The last thing he needed was more to worry about.

He lifted her against him, let her feel the hardness of his body before he settled her bottom onto the cool marble counter. She shoved his gym shorts down his hips and pulled him between her spread thighs. The feel of him entering her took her breath. She hugged her legs around his lean waist and held on tightly as he made love to her with an urgency that was palpable.

Grabbing his face, she pulled his mouth to hers and kissed him with the same desperation driving his solid thrusts.

She loved this man.

Losing him was out of the question.

CHAPTER NINETEEN

DANIEL WATCHED AS Emily moved through the electron-
ically filed archives of the *Chicago Tribune*. They'd been
looking for something on Madelyn Rutland for more
than two hours without discovering anything conclusive.

Calling Chicago PD was out of the question. Daniel
had asked Victoria to have one of her staff members,
Simon Ruhl, touch base with some of his old FBI con-
tacts and see what he could find on the former homicide
detective.

It was as if Madelyn had fallen off the face of the earth
about six months after James Colby's murder. She'd
worked with her partner, Carter Hastings, for three months
in an attempt to determine who'd committed the crime, but
the case had gone unsolved. A nasty shooting involving a
teenage boy Madelyn Rutland had insisted had been armed
when she shot him had brought a tremendous amount of
bad publicity down on her head, as well as on Chicago PD.

She'd been cleared, the incident deemed a righteous
shooting, but the stigma had stayed with her. She'd resigned shortly after that and basically disappeared.

Daniel couldn't be sure that Carter Hastings's former
partner had anything to do with his murder. After all, she
was supposed to be dead, but it was the only lead he had.

Zach Ashton, a Colby Agency attorney, had passed along what little information the police had revealed. Jim Colby's prints had been found at the scene, but there was no murder weapon just yet. The only thing the police had was evidence of Jim's presence in a public alley and his lack of an alibi for the time of Hastings's death.

Not enough to formally charge him, but they were working hard to find that murder weapon or anything else that might tie Jim to Hastings.

Daniel had to find another suspect first. Since Chicago PD didn't appear interested in pursuing that avenue, finding Hastings's killer was up to him.

Victoria had given Daniel a complete rundown on Jim's medical history, particularly his mental condition.

Then there was the issue of whether James Colby, Senior, had participated in an illicit affair with Madelyn Rutland.

The two events weren't likely connected, but Daniel had to be certain. Victoria Colby-Camp wanted the truth. Wanted it badly enough that she wouldn't trust the task to her own people for fear one or all would want to protect her from the very truth she sought.

Daniel didn't like hurting people, but he would do the job assigned to him, whatever the consequences to Victoria and her son.

With that thought, his attention refocused on Emily Hastings. Her hasty kiss last night had surprised him. Though it had been a good move, strategically speaking, and would help keep their cover in place, he wondered what had given the seemingly fragile woman the nerve to make such a move. The wine, maybe?

She'd studiously avoided extended eye contact with

him this morning. But he didn't need her to look him dead in the eye to know she hadn't managed to sleep much last night. He hadn't gotten that much sleep himself, but he'd obviously gotten more than her.

Running on empty would only exacerbate her vulnerability, but telling her wouldn't change a thing.

"Here's something," she said, tugging his musings back to the here and now.

She licked her lips and the memory of her taste instantly resurrected in his senses. Shaking off the inappropriate intrusion, he leaned toward the screen to get a better look at the article she'd found.

"Madelyn Rutland passed away in her Fairfield, Indiana, home of unspecified causes. Ms. Rutland served as one of Chicago's finest for more than five years."

"Not much information," he noted. "No mention of family or friends?"

Emily shook her head. "Only what I read to you."

"That appears to confirm that she is, indeed, dead." Daniel considered that finding the facts regarding Madelyn and James's affair might be impossible under the circumstances. Checking with friends or family could prove useful, but would be time-consuming.

Emily continued to survey more archived issues of the *Tribune*. "I thought I remembered something along those lines," she said, more to herself than to Daniel. "I was just a kid, maybe seven or eight, but my father was pretty shaken up by the news. I think he even tried to contact her family, but I'm not sure."

"Do you feel your father's most recent partner would be opposed to talking to us?" He couldn't afford to waste any more time trying to track down a ghost who likely didn't have anything to do with Hastings's murder. What he needed was more up-to-date information from the most readily available source.

Emily shrugged noncommittally. "I don't see why he would." She met Daniel's gaze and this time she didn't immediately look away. "We could give it a try."

Daniel pushed up from his chair. "Let's hope he isn't on duty today. Do you know his address?"

She nodded. "He always sent me a Christmas card."

As they emerged from the *Tribune* building Daniel made a decision about their tail. "I'm going to have to lose our shadow," he said for Emily's ears only. "No point tipping off Franko any sooner than necessary."

He also couldn't help noticing how nicely shaped Emily was. She'd foregone the jacket today. The sweater molded to her upper body in a very distracting manner.

Neither of which had anything to do with his assignment. Keeping that in mind would behoove him. Funny thing was, he'd never had this much trouble before. Maybe the uniform had protected him, worked as a shield between him and his emotions. In any event, he couldn't get sidetracked, especially not with Emily Hastings.

He opened the passenger door and she settled into the seat. "You drive. I'll give you the directions."

Daniel slid behind the steering wheel and started the engine. "Ready when you are." He tossed his passenger a reassuring smile. He would bet this was the first time Emily had considered attempting to lose any sort of surveillance. "Fast and furious would be good."

"You got it." She turned her attention straight ahead without returning the smile. "Stay in the right lane. Go straight for the next three blocks, then make an abrupt left at the fourth traffic light."

He surveyed the fairly heavy traffic and calculated whether staying in the right lane would allow for a sudden left turn. Maybe.

"Don't worry," she said as he eased into the flow of traffic. "Chicagoans are like California drivers. Nudge into their path and they'll let you in. They just won't like it and they'll probably make a fuss." Her hand fluttered dismissively and, if he wasn't mistaken, he saw a smile flirt with her lips. "You know, blowing horns and yelling."

"I can handle that." He was glad to see her smile, even if he'd only gotten a hint of it. The lady had a very nice smile.

Her prediction saw fruition as he merged, too close for comfort, and horns blared, but he managed the move. A quick left and a burst of speed later, he'd temporarily outmaneuvered the sedan.

He glanced at Emily, who appeared to be concentrating hard, chewing on her lower lip as she did so, for further instructions. "Take the next right."

The squeal of tires accompanied his response.

"Take that left up ahead," she said on the heels of that turn, leaning forward like a chess player in anticipation of the next move.

"This one?" he asked as he prepared to turn.

"Wait! No, the next one."

Daniel's foot moved from the brake to the accelerator without hesitation. "You're sure?" he asked with a questioning glance in her direction.

"Yes. That's the one." She leaned back and exhaled a breath of tension. "Sorry. It's been a while."

He surveyed the street behind them via the rearview mirror. Still no more sedan. "Mission accomplished." He shot his navigator an approving smile. "Nice job."

"I can't take credit. When your father's a homicide detective, he's bound to get a call now and then while hauling his kids around. I learned from the best."

The distant quality of her voice told him she was recalling those long-ago, clearly cherished moments. She'd held up so well to this point that he'd started to wonder how her relationship with her father had weathered the divorce.

"Leaving him was tough." Daniel clamped his lips together but it was too late to stop the words. He hadn't meant to venture into that tender territory. Too personal…this investigation wasn't supposed to get personal. Ha! That was a joke.

"Yes." The single word came loaded with restrained emotion.

He cursed himself again for making the statement. "Which way now?" he asked, moving past the topic.

Emily relayed the directions to Detective Norton Morrow's home. He lived in the suburbs on the far north side, well away from the city's heavy traffic and crowded sidewalks. In Daniel's experience, people who tolerated this kind of commute usually did so to escape the hustle and bustle, as well as to land the best schools.

He parked on the street in front of the detective's ranch-style home and turned to his passenger. "We need to play this carefully, Emily."

Emily turned to Daniel Marks and blinked, tried to clear the memories from her thoughts. His question had stirred up half a lifetime of recollections she'd somehow tucked away in a place she rarely looked anymore.

They had been close, she and her father. Closer than she had allowed herself to recall till now. She remembered riding in his car with the window down, the air blowing through her hair, the radio set to her father's favorite classic rock station. He would sing along, winking at her every now and then when he caught her staring at him.

So long ago.

"Emily?"

She snapped her attention back to the present. "Excuse me?" Whatever he'd said, she'd missed it entirely.

"Detective Morrow needs to believe that you're attempting to finalize your father's affairs and that you merely have questions for him related to the murder. He can't know about the investigation."

That was a no-brainer. She tamped down the irritation that surged. Daniel was being careful, that's all. But he needed to comprehend that she wasn't as naive as he obviously thought.

"I know what to do, Daniel."

Emily didn't give him the opportunity to explain or offer excuses. She got out and started up the sidewalk. Norton Morrow was someone she knew as well as anyone else from her life in Chicago. He'd always seemed very nice. Had three children of his own, all grown now. He would understand how she felt. She needed closure on a number of things.

By the time she reached the place where the public sidewalk intersected with the one leading to Mr. Morrow's home, Daniel had caught up with her. To his credit, he didn't say anything. Emily was glad. She felt too confused right now. The memories he'd shaken loose on the way here had tilted her world to some degree.

How could she have forgotten so much?

Or had it been easier not to remember?

After climbing the porch steps, she didn't hesitate at the door. She pushed the doorbell and waited for an answer. She could hear the television. Saturday afternoon football. Another flash of the past zoomed through her mind. Her father had loved college football. The men in the house, her father and her brother Colton, had loved sports, period.

The haunting sound of a telephone ringing echoed inside her head. She remembered clearly when her mother had answered that call. Colton had been taken to the hospital. She should come right away. She should call Colton's father. It was bad. Very bad.

Emily would never forget that trip to the hospital. She hadn't known what was happening. Confused and frightened, she had sat in the car, pressed as far as she could get against the passenger side door, and watched the tears stream down her mother's cheeks.

Emily's brother had died that day. Sixteen years old.

That day, her family had died, as well.

Nothing had ever been the same.

"Emily?"

She hadn't even realized the front door had opened. "Mr. Norton," she said stiffly. She'd called him that for as long as she could remember.

"Come on in here, honey." He hugged her the same way he had at the funeral, then ushered her and Daniel Marks inside. "Let me turn down this ball game."

Her skin felt suddenly cold. Her insides, too. Norton hurried to turn down the volume on the television set. She didn't look at Daniel, didn't want him to see how shaken she was.

"What brings you to see me?" He gestured to the sofa. "Have a seat, darling. Take a load off."

She smiled. The movement felt brittle. "Thank you." She sat down on the sofa, felt the cushion next to her shift as Daniel did the same. He wore khaki pants today, with a navy jacket and white shirt. She wished she could look as calm as he did.

Norton sat down in his leather recliner. Judging by the wear, it was his favorite seat in the house.

"Would you like something to drink?" he asked as he looked from Emily to the man beside her and back.

"No, I'm fine." She turned to Daniel. "Would you like anything?" She stared straight at his forehead, avoiding his eyes at all cost.

"No, thank you."

She shifted her attention back to her father's partner and realized her oversight since he was busy sizing up her companion. "I'm sorry—" she gestured to the older man "—Detective Norton Morrow, this is Daniel Marks, a friend of mine." She almost cringed at the hollowness of her voice.

As if knowing he needed to make a better showing, Daniel got up and went over and shook the detective's hand. Socially polite comments were exchanged and then Daniel resumed his seat. As he did, he draped his arm over the back of the sofa behind Emily. She tried hard to relax, to allow the ruse to appear genuine.

"You know," Norton said, "we were supposed to watch this game together." He exhaled a mighty breath. "Kind of a tradition we had." A shrug lifted his big, beefy shoulders. "I'd send the wife into town shopping and Carter would come over and have a few beers with me while we watched our team get defeated."

Emily blinked back the sting of tears. "I'm sure you must miss him terribly."

His expression hardened. "I should be out there trying to nail his killer," he growled. "The chief won't let me near the case, says I'm too personally involved."

"You were partners," Daniels said, "and friends."

Norton huffed out another burst of frustration. "That we were, but that doesn't mean I'm incapable of doing my job." He thumped his chest. "I'm a damned good detective. Had a good teacher."

Emily knew he meant her father. It was now or never.

"Mr. Norton, maybe you can help me."

His gaze shifted to her, sharpened instantly, as if he hadn't touched the beer in his hand, much less the other three cans now working as a less-than-chic centerpiece on the nearby end table.

Emily moistened her lips and forged onward. "I've found a few items among my father's things that belonged to his first partner, Madelyn Rutland. I'd love to get in touch with her and pass on these things. Do you know how I can reach her now? Did she move away from Chicago?"

He pleated his brow in concentration. "As I recall," he said thoughtfully, "she died a few years back." He nodded. "I believe that's right. But she'd moved away before that."

For several seconds, he stroked his chin as if the stubble there would somehow arouse more of his memories.

"She and your father didn't get along so well in the end. It was that nasty business with that young man she shot. She was cleared, of course," he hastened to add, "but she wasn't the same after that. We all noticed the change."

Emily smoothed her sweat-dampened palms over her skirt and went for broke. "Don't you find it ironic that the last big case Madelyn and my father worked together involved James Colby's murder and now his son is a suspect in my father's murder?" She swallowed the emotion that instantly tightened her throat at having had to utter the words.

Red rose up his neck and Emily recognized that Norton was fighting back his anger. She'd seen him do that before. "Carter did everything he could to help that family and this is the thanks he gets. They should have kept Jim Colby locked away. He's mentally unstable, from what I hear."

Emily hadn't heard that part. She would ask Daniel about that when they left. "Detective Franko hasn't been very forthcoming on the details. Do you really think Jim Colby did this? Did you ever hear my father mention him? Could he have been trying to help Jim Colby remember things about his father or something like that?"

"The only thing I know, Emily," he said somberly, "is that they've got his prints at the crime scene. All they have to do now is connect him to the murder weapon."

"Have they found the murder weapon?" Daniel interjected.

Norton shook his head. "They've found nothing. Just those prints." He looked from one to the other. "You know he doesn't have an alibi."

Emily rubbed her left temple, hoping the ache that had started there would subside before becoming an all-out brain buster. "I just don't understand how he could have murdered my father if he didn't even know him."

"It happens all the time," Norton said. "Carter could have stumbled upon a crime in progress. There's just no way to know since Colby isn't talking."

"Is Detective Franko looking into other possibilities?" she asked, knowing the question wouldn't sit well with her father's old friend. "I mean, what if someone else did it. Are they investigating that possibility, as well?"

Norton set his beer aside and leaned forward to make sure there was no mistake in what she saw in his eyes— sheer determination. "Of course they're looking into other possibilities. Who's been putting ideas like that in your head, Emily?"

Uncertainty held her mute. What did she say to that?

"I think what Emily is asking," Daniel offered smoothly, "is did her father have any enemies who might have wanted him dead? After all, he was a homicide detective. He surely made a number of enemies during his lengthy career."

"We all have enemies," Norton said bluntly. "That avenue has been turned inside out. I spent the first twenty-four hours after your father's murder," he directed this part to Emily, "being interrogated and going over case files, past and present."

Just then, sitting in the living room of her father's partner, Emily wondered if she had allied herself with the enemy. Had she insisted on working with someone who didn't really care who murdered her father, only that he cleared Jim Colby? She'd given herself over to the other side, going so far as to mislead the man who'd been closest to her father. She abruptly felt sick with betrayal.

"So you believe this Jim Colby is guilty? That he killed my father?" The weight of that possibility sank down on her shoulders, crushed her chest.

"I wish I knew the answer, Emily." Emotion glittered in Norton's eyes. "I truly do. The only thing I know for certain is that whoever did this, it was no random act."

Before she could ask for clarification, Daniel spoke up again. "Sir, what do you mean by not random?"

Norton picked up the can of beer and chugged the last of its contents before allowing it to join the rest of his collection. After he'd set it aside and glanced briefly at the television to catch the score, he turned back to Daniel.

"The scene was too clean. That alley felt *swept* clean of evidence. Like someone knew what to watch for, what to take care of and clean up. The slug—" he glanced at Emily and drew in a ragged breath "—the M.E. removed was one of those exploding jobs. Goes to bits on impact. Can't do any kind of decent ballistics on the damned thing."

His words hit Emily like a sucker punch, causing gruesome images to erupt inside her head. She closed her eyes, tried to block the painful pictures.

"Jim Colby was an assassin. He would have known all the right tricks to cover his tracks."

Whatever else was said after that didn't penetrate the shroud of pain and denial around Emily. She didn't want to hear any more. She needed to rethink her position, to look at the facts more closely.

Evidently Daniel sensed her distress. The next thing she knew, he was ushering her out the door and to his SUV. She had the presence of mind to snap her safety belt into place as he started the engine.

Too many emotions to label whirled inside her, making her stomach clench. She needed to think, to process all that she had heard and figure out if she was doing the right thing.

She turned to the man driving, to Daniel Marks. Was he as objective as he wanted her to believe? Could she really trust Victoria Colby-Camp? Jim Colby was her son. Emily would be a fool to believe that the woman wanted the truth more than she wanted to clear her son. No mother wanted to see her child suffer, particularly one who'd lost her only child and missed out on most of his life.

Why hadn't she acknowledged the full import of this before? Apparently, she hadn't considered the whole picture.

"Stop the car," she said raggedly, scarcely able to talk with her chest in the vise of turmoil. She had to have air, had to walk.

Daniel whipped the SUV to the side of the street and she barreled out. She had to move. Her heart pounded, but she couldn't seem to get enough air into her lungs. Her stomach twisted and ached.

Half stumbling in her haste, she hurried toward the narrow alley between the nearest two buildings…had to find a trash can…

She kept hearing Norton's words over and over. The slug had disintegrated. The kind used by a professional or someone who knew how to cover his tracks.

He'd said Jim Colby was a former assassin. Why hadn't anyone told her that? Why hadn't she asked? She'd let Daniel Marks and Victoria Colby-Camp lead her down the path they wanted her to see.

No evidence. A clean scene.

Norton was right. This was no random act. Her father's murder had been planned.

She made it to a Dumpster. Bending over one of the boxes stacked haphazardly next to it, she stopped holding back. Her stomach heaved violently and her throat burned as whatever she'd eaten last was expelled.

When she'd regained control of her body's reaction to the stressful emotions, she straightened and stepped back from the evidence of her lost composure. She swiped the hair back from her face and her hands came away damp.

She touched her cheek, felt the warm wetness of tears. She didn't want to cry. Not now. Not with Daniel standing right behind her...waiting to see if he could help. Why did he do that? What did he care?

She wheeled to face him. "I don't want to talk right now. I just want to go."

He nodded. "I'll take you home."

A wave of emotion hit her so hard her knees almost buckled with the impact of it.

Home.

Nothing about this city would ever feel like home to her again. Maybe it hadn't in more than a dozen years.

But her father had been here and on some level, that had always been her tie to this place. A connection to the past. A past her mother had snatched her away from because she couldn't bear to continue living it.

For the first time in too many years to count, Emily felt the burden of guilt ram down on her.

She should have kept closer contact with her father. Should have known who his friends were, who his enemies were. How he spent his time off. But she didn't know anything. Didn't even know he watched Saturday afternoon football with his partner.

From what she'd seen so far, his work, his fellow detectives and police offers were all he had.

Maybe Carter Hastings hadn't been such a terrific father in recent years, but she hadn't been such a great daughter, either.

She'd let life get in the way. She had allowed her mother's persistent attitude that their life in Chicago had never happened to justify her indifference.

That had been wrong.

The realization shored up her waning determination. She'd made mistakes, all right. Her mother, her father, they were all guilty. No question.

There was nothing she could do about that.

But she could do this.

Whatever motivation prompted Daniel Marks beneath the facade he wanted her to see, she would not leave Chicago until she knew the truth about what had happened to her father.

She was his daughter, all he'd had.

Wherever this investigation led, she would be there.

CHAPTER TWENTY

DANIEL ARRIVED AT the Colby Agency well before regular operating hours on Monday. Victoria had asked him to come before the rest of her staff arrived.

"Good morning, Mr. Marks," Mildred Parker, Victoria's secretary, greeted him. "Would you care for coffee? I've just made the first pot for the day."

"Thank you, Ms. Parker, coffee would be good."

The attractive older woman gestured to her boss's door. "Victoria is waiting for you. I'll bring your coffee in to you. Cream? Sugar?"

"Black." He'd gotten used to it that way in the military. Extended field trips didn't always offer the luxuries taken for granted in everyday life. Daniel couldn't help smiling as Ms. Parker hurried away. Victoria had clearly surrounded herself with the most loyal of employees.

The more he saw of this agency, the better he liked it, he considered as he moved toward the door leading to Victoria's office. He couldn't think of a better place to start his new career. All the more reason to see that nothing got in the way of his current investigation. Though Victoria had promised him the job either way, he couldn't help wondering if this would turn into a test of his skill.

"Good morning, Daniel," Victoria said as he entered her office. Her smile held all the earmarks of a calm, welcoming disposition, but her eyes gave her away. Lack of sleep, intense worry. She feared for her son, and was clearly desperate for this situation to be resolved.

"Good morning, Victoria."

She indicated one of the chairs in front of her desk. "I'm glad you were able to accommodate me at such an unholy hour."

Daniel held back the chuckle that tickled his throat as he settled into the seat. "I'm used to unholy hours, Victoria. Seven o'clock feels pretty tame."

"How is your investigation going so far?" she asked, cutting to the chase. "Have you made any headway in locating Madelyn Rutland or anyone who might have wanted Carter dead?"

The slight tremble in her voice as she mentioned Madelyn's name gave away even more of the vulnerability beneath that seemingly unflappable professional exterior.

"Simon checked with his sources and found nothing. She has either passed away or has simply disappeared," she added, frustration lining her brow.

By Simon, Daniel understood she meant one of her top investigators, Simon Ruhl, formerly of the FBI. If the FBI hadn't found anything on Madelyn Rutland, chances were she was, in fact, deceased.

The door opened and Mildred breezed in with his coffee. She looked to Victoria, who shook her head, declining the unspoken offer.

When the door had closed behind the secretary, Daniel picked up where they had left off.

"How far do you want me to pursue that aspect of the investigation, Victoria?" Her answer would be pivotal to his next move. "At this point I see no reason to believe her relationship with James Colby is related to Carter Hastings's murder."

Daniel paused a moment to allow her to reflect on that statement before he continued. "I guess the bottom line is, how badly do you want to know what happened between your first husband and this woman?"

Victoria's dark eyes clouded with uncertainty as she considered his question. But when she spoke, there was nothing uncertain or indecisive about her words. "I want your focus, first and foremost, on the murder investigation. But I want the truth regarding my first husband's activities, as well. I don't want this hanging over my head for the rest of my days. I need to know. Can you understand that, Daniel?"

"Yes. I understand perfectly."

For the next few minutes he brought Victoria up to speed on the meeting with Norton Morrow, Hastings's partner. They reviewed again what Chicago PD admitted to having in the way of evidence—nothing other than Jim's prints, which only proved he'd been in the alley. They couldn't prove he had been in the alley at the time of the murder. No murder weapon had been located, and there appeared to be no motive for Jim to have committed the crime.

"I feel confident," Victoria said when he'd reported all that he had learned, "that Detective Morrow is correct. I can't imagine that they wouldn't pursue other leads, but the question is, if no other suspects can be found, will they attempt to railroad my son?"

The battle she fought played out dramatically in her eyes, in the weary lines of her face. She didn't want to believe the worst of her longtime friends at Chicago PD, but her need to protect her son overrode all else. Except, Daniel amended, her sense of compassion, her need for truth and justice.

"I've met Detective Franko and I've spoken at length with Detective Morrow. I would be remiss if I didn't express my gut feeling that these men are seeking vengeance. Yes," he admitted, "I do believe the investigation goes beyond your son. The question is, how far beyond?"

Victoria nodded. "I agree."

Daniel wasn't sure how this next suggestion would go over, but he had to make the effort. "How would you feel about my talking to Jim?"

Victoria's guard went up. "I've questioned him at length myself, Daniel," she told him. "Jim has no memory of what happened that night. None at all."

"Have you considered an alternate means for retrieving the memories? Hypnosis? Drug therapy?" He had to know just how far she was willing to go for that truth she wanted.

She didn't answer immediately, but she didn't look away, either. She seemed to search Daniel's eyes for some sense of why he was asking the question.

"We've considered that route, but his primary therapist feels it would be extremely risky. I'm hoping we can avoid that particular risk if the real killer is found."

Real killer. She was assuming her son was innocent. Which wasn't outside the realm of possibility. Jim Colby, to the knowledge of all who knew him, had never even met Carter Hastings. He was not involved with drugs, outside those prescribed by his therapist. Being a Colby ensured that his every need was met financially. There was no reason for him to turn to crime for money or other gratification. Victoria insisted she had never discussed Carter Hastings's involvement with those long-ago investigations with Jim.

There simply was no reason for him to want to harm Carter Hastings.

Just then, as he sat facing the venerable head of the Colby Agency, Daniel decided she needed some reassurances, whether she would ever admit it or not.

"Victoria, if there is anything to find, I will find it. You're right to avoid risking Jim's mental stability until there is no other choice."

As strong as this woman was, as many battles as she had fought and won in her lifetime, Daniel nonetheless saw a flicker of relief flash in her dark eyes. And in that instant, he could feel just how deeply the hurt went, just how badly she needed him to find the answers for her.

He would do his best.

After a few moments more of discussion, Daniel left Victoria's office. He thanked Mildred for the coffee and headed for the elevators. As he moved down the long corridor leading to the lobby, he met a number of the staff members arriving for work. Some greeted him with a smile or a slight nod, while others were already consumed with case files en route to their offices.

Daniel pressed the button to summon the elevator. As he waited, he absorbed the ambience of the place, the distant but building hum of activity…of energy. He thought of the numerous clients who had entered this lobby, whose lives had been touched by this agency. This was a place where people came for help, for answers.

Ironic, he mused as the elevator doors glided open, that even the prevailing spirit of this agency could not protect those within from the ugliness of reality.

Nothing could.

Daniel drove across town to the scene of the crime. His tail appeared to be absent today. He hadn't seen any sign of the unmarked sedan that had followed him and Emily. He couldn't imagine Franko calling off his bloodhounds so quickly. Maybe he'd simply sent someone a little more experienced in the art of stealth.

Daniel parked a few blocks from the alley where Carter Hastings had taken his last breath. He walked back to the entrance and ignored the crime scene tape stretched across it. Taking a final glance from left to right, he stepped over the boundary and moved into the alley.

He studied the place where Hastings had fallen and then, working his way around in a slow, steady pattern, he surveyed the area immediately around it. It wasn't that he actually hoped to find anything the police hadn't, but he wanted a feel for the place. If there was any possibility of discovering new evidence, a guard would still be posted at the scene. Clearly the police were finished here.

Kneeling near the spot where the body had fallen, he estimated the distance to the sidewalk to be about twelve yards. He glanced in the other direction where the alley ended at another, narrower street, about twenty yards away. Neither street was a main thoroughfare so the alley afforded a certain level of anonymity, especially under the cover of darkness.

Daniel stood and looked up in search of exterior lights. There were only two and one had a broken bulb.

He walked the full length of the alley and noted that a number of small windows were boarded up; those that weren't looked dark with decades of grime.

The buildings on either side were warehouses, seemingly abandoned, probably for a better location. Still, he might as well take a look inside, assuming one or both were unlocked. Breaking and entering was something he didn't care to be charged with under the circumstances. Chicago PD would likely use any excuse to interrogate him.

The warehouse to his right was locked tight. Every window was boarded up and the three doors sported heavy-duty chains and robust locks. Warehouse number two, however, proved more welcoming. Several of the windows were broken, and the rear entrance wasn't locked. He doubted it had been for some time. Some faction of the homeless had likely discovered it and taken advantage of the situation.

Daniel braced himself for a defensive maneuver as he moved through the door. He had tucked his .38 into his waistband at the small of his back. He hadn't carried it until now.

Something he did carry on a regular basis was a pocket-sized flashlight. He relaxed his battle-ready stance and reached into his interior jacket pocket to remove the flashlight. Scanning the beam over the floor, he saw where the layer of dust there had been disturbed recently by numerous footprints. The cops and crime scene techs, most likely. He couldn't be the only one who'd felt the need to take a look inside the warehouse.

The lower floor of the warehouse proved to be empty, other than the odd wooden crate and signs of sections having been used as shelter. The tattered remains of discarded clothes indicated the final owner having discovered, via whatever means, a better wardrobe offering.

Daniel cautiously climbed the stairs leading to the second level, which covered only half of the warehouse space. A few more crates and discarded blankets and articles of clothing were the only articles his search yielded.

Just as he was ready to descend the stairs, another broken window captured his attention. Not certain what he hoped to find, he moved in that direction.

The window was not very large, but low enough that he could look out into the alleyway…to the exact spot where Carter Hastings had been murdered.

Daniel moved his flashlight over the metal frame, scrutinizing in particular the areas where dust and cobwebs had been disturbed.

He swore softly as he identified the unmistakable marks of latent prints having been lifted.

Detective Norton Morrow had gone on and on about how clean the scene was. About how nothing had been found.

Daniel couldn't be one hundred percent positive, but every instinct told him that this vantage point was crucial. It provided complete anonymity, as well as a wide-angle view of the crime scene. The perfect place to witness whatever took place below without giving away one's presence. Daniel would wager that Jim Colby's prints had been lifted from right here, inside this warehouse…where he'd watched out the window as *someone else* murdered Carter Hastings.

EMILY PACED the kitchen floor. She'd had three cups of coffee already; another would be caffeine suicide.

She had to do something. Daniel had called her and explained that he had a meeting with Victoria Colby-Camp that morning, to discuss what they'd found—which was absolutely nothing. He'd promised to call or stop by sometime this evening to check on her.

Somehow, Emily had managed to sleep last night. Only after hours and hours of tossing and turning, of course. She should be tired, but instead she felt restless and needed to occupy her time with something. She'd gone through a few more of her father's papers and even made a couple of phone calls to tie up some final loose ends.

That had only been a temporary fix. She wanted to learn more about her father's final days before his death. Norton hadn't really been that much help. There had to be someone who knew whom her father had spoken to or visited or just hung out with that last week or two. She couldn't be sure that information would be useful, but it might.

She exhaled loudly. She should just call Detective Franko and demand to know what he'd found so far. Fury clenched inside her. She hated not knowing. Hated that someone had taken her father's life and, so far, had gotten away with it.

"Okay." She took another deep breath and let it out slowly. No point working herself up. She couldn't accomplish anything that way.

She had to find something constructive to do.

Rubbing at the back of her neck to relieve the tension there, she strode over to the coffeepot and turned it off. If the rest of the pot stayed hot, she would be tempted to have more coffee.

Since she had absolutely no clue where to start, she decided she would go with the one seemingly irrelevant aspect of the case that, at least in her mind, somehow connected the past to the present.

Madelyn Rutland.

Norton thought she'd died. The vague newspaper clipping indicated the same. But Emily needed to know for sure. She also had to find out if Madelyn and her father had parted ways on a sour note. Who knew if it would be significant, but it was all she had.

The best she remembered, Madelyn had never been married. At least not up until the time she'd been partnered with Emily's father. So she could start there.

She went straight to the living room and called information for the city listed in the newspaper death notice. When the operator came on line, Emily asked for a Madelyn Rutland. There was, of course, no listing. That left Emily with only one choice. "Could you give me the numbers listed for all the Rutlands in that area?"

The operator hadn't sounded too pleased but when Emily told her about her father's recent death, the woman softened and obligingly provided the names and numbers.

Since there were twenty-two Rutlands listed, it took a while to go through the numbers. It wasn't until she reached a Doris Rutland that she hit pay dirt. Doris wasn't related to Madelyn, but she did remember her. She also remembered her only sibling, a sister who had married a man named Phipps. Doris even looked up the number for Emily since the couple lived in the same town.

Anticipation making her heart race Emily punched in the number for Maggie Phipps.

"Who did you say this is?"

Emily tensed, twisted her fingers in the phone cord. "I'm Emily Hastings, Carter Hastings's daughter. Madelyn was my father's homicide partner years ago."

"Madelyn's been gone for years," the woman said, her tone suspicious. "Why are you calling me?"

Emily took a wild stab. "My father died last week and I found some things in his belongings that I thought Madelyn might want. I was hoping that you would know how to contact her. You're her sister, right?"

A beat of silence on the other end had Emily holding her breath.

"She's dead."

Emily swallowed, her throat parching as her nerves jangled again. "You took care of the funeral arrangements?" Emily steeled herself for the repercussions of asking such a personal question.

"She didn't want anything to do with us after she took up with her fancy fella."

The breath Emily had been holding dissipated in her lungs. "So she married," she ventured.

"Lady, I have no idea what she did. All I know is she stopped coming home for visits, even stopped calling. She didn't even come to her own mother's funeral, for God's sake. She forgot all about us. We weren't good enough for her after she found *him*."

Emily blinked and chewed her lower lip for a second before asking the question burning on the tip of her tongue. "Did she and Mr. Colby get married?"

The woman on the other end of the line made a harrumphing sound. "That's what she said. Said she didn't have time to bother with us anymore. She had a real life now and no one was going to get in her way."

Emily's fingers were trembling as she unraveled them from the phone cord. "That's too bad, Ms. Phipps."

"Well, my mother had a saying, Miss Hastings, pretty is as pretty does. My sister thought she was pretty and smart. Too much so for what was left of her family. So she deserted us and found herself a rich husband. But one should never get too high and mighty for their family or God'll humble them. I read where her fancy man got himself murdered not long after that. I guess that's why she killed herself."

Emily froze. "She committed suicide?"

"Sure did." The woman snorted indelicately. "Drove all the way back home to do it. Sent me a letter saying how she had no regrets and that by the time I got the letter she would have joined the man she loved by taking a swan dive off Heartbreak Bridge."

"Heartbreak Bridge?" Emily echoed. "What's that?" She would have felt guilty prodding the woman for information had she not sounded so gleeful in giving it.

"It's not really called Heartbreak Bridge. But over the years more than a few brokenhearted lovers have leaped to their deaths from that old bridge. The river's deep and swift-running. The bodies are hardly ever found. Damned fools get all worked up over losing their beloved and climb right over the rail and jump. The coroner told me that most of 'em probably died from the impact. He didn't want me to worry about Madelyn having drowned. He said she probably didn't even know what hit her."

"I guess they found your sister's body if the coroner told you that?" Emily heard herself ask.

"Well, he told me all that, rightly enough, but to answer your question, no they didn't find her. Washed away like a fallen branch from the trees lining that river's bank. Probably hung up God knows where deep under the water."

Emily moistened her lips. Her heart pounded hard in her chest. "How do you know she really jumped?"

"Found her purse and everything she had in it scattered around on the bridge where she'd dropped it."

Emily pressed her hand to her chest. "What a horrible way to die. You must have been devastated when they couldn't recover her body."

The woman made another of those gravelly sounds deep in her throat. "The way I saw it, saved me the cost of a funeral."

CHAPTER TWENTY-ONE

EMILY SLIPPED INTO the deep, hot water and sighed. It felt good to close her eyes and allow the heat to envelop her. She'd spent the whole day going through her father's things, yet again. The effort had proven futile. She hadn't found anything useful or that she hadn't looked at in her last quest.

Her eyes drifted open and she watched the steam billow up from the tub. The day hadn't been entirely a waste of time. She had found Madelyn Rutland's one living relative.

Emily frowned as she considered the woman's insensitive words. All this time, she'd thought her family was the prime example of dysfunction. Who would have thought that one sister could harbor such contempt for the other?

No family who'd cared about her. No husband to lean upon, since she obviously had not married James Colby. No wonder Madelyn had thrown herself from a bridge. The one man she'd cared about had been murdered.

And he'd belonged to another woman.

How sad.

She shook off that last thought. How could she feel

sorry for a woman who would write such beseeching love letters to a married man?

With James Colby's son missing, Emily could see how James and Madelyn might have gotten a little too close. After all, Madelyn had been involved with the investigation. She could even see the two getting involved as a result of the monumental stress.

But even years after the child had gone missing, Madelyn had still written to him. The postmarks on the letters spanned nearly a three-year period. Right up until James Colby's murder.

A relationship that long-lasting couldn't be blamed on a sudden lapse in judgment or a moment of desperation. If, in fact, James Colby had been intimately involved with Madelyn Rutland as much as two to three years after the abduction of his child, the act had been intentional.

Emily moved her head slowly from side to side. How did Victoria Colby-Camp stand not knowing? The possibility that the man she'd loved and held in such high regard had cheated on her had to be killing her inside.

There she went again, feeling sorry for the woman whose son might very well have murdered her father.

Emily squeezed her eyes shut once more as images of her father on his knees and possibly begging for his life flashed one after the other in her mind. Tears stung the backs of her eyes and she fought hard to get her emotions under control once more.

She had to find a way to maintain her objectivity. It was the only way to look at the situation clearly. She couldn't let the pain of her father's brutal death sweep her into an emotional frenzy. Nor could she allow her overactive compassion to have her worrying about Victoria's situation. Her father's murder had to be solved first. All else had to be secondary.

Daniel Marks intruded into her thoughts. His image flickered into focus and she couldn't immediately dismiss it as she'd done the entire day.

Why did she have to feel this silly attraction to him? Now just wasn't the time for personal needs. She knew almost nothing about him. He seemed very nice, was certainly handsome enough. But they had nothing in common except this case, her father's murder.

And they both had totally different reasons for wanting to get to the bottom of what really happened.

She still felt like kicking herself for getting carried away the other night and kissing him. Heat rushed to her cheeks and she suffered those same tingly sensations she had when she'd brushed her lips against his.

At her age, you would think she would have learned how to control her impulses. Apparently, she hadn't.

Forcing the thoughts away she directed her mind into more neutral territory. She hadn't heard from him all day. She couldn't help wondering what he'd been doing. He'd been a little evasive about today. Or maybe it just made the whole situation easier if she looked at it that way.

Still, it would have been nice if he'd called and let her know something about his agenda for the day since he'd left her out.

Then she could have told him about discovering Madelyn's sister. Of course she would, tomorrow for sure. She and Daniel were supposed to meet for breakfast in the morning. He had called and left that message, but nothing else.

Enough with the worry. She needed sleep. No way was she going to get any if she didn't get all the static out of her head.

With that in mind, she ducked under the warm, welcoming water, washed her hair and slowly, taking her time to enjoy the relaxing embrace of the water, cleansed her body.

It didn't take long to complete the rest of her feminine rituals, such as shaving and tweezing her eyebrows. Last, she lathered on her favorite silky lotion. Her charm bracelet jingled as she went about the nightly routine. There was something comforting about the ordinary acts.

A trip to the convenience store at the end of the block had been necessary for her extended stay. She hadn't bothered with anything other than a quick shower since she'd arrived. Today, she'd needed the works.

When she'd dried off and shrugged into the ancient terry-cloth robe she'd found in her old bedroom, she cleaned up after herself in the bathroom and prepared to take the damp towels and her shed clothes down to the laundry.

A high-pitched squeal stopped her cold when she reached for the bathroom door.

The air whooshed out of her lungs in the intervening seconds before she recognized the sound.

Smoke alarm.

Fear shot through her then.

Had she left something turned on in the kitchen? The stove? Coffeepot?

She didn't think so.

Her clothes hit the floor and she flung open the bathroom door. At a wide-open run, she hit the stairs, then took them as fast as she dared.

Smoke wafted into the front hall from the kitchen.

A new gush of fear flooded her.

Did she call 911 or check out the problem first?

Opting for the second choice, she eased as quickly as she dared toward the kitchen, holding the lapel of her robe over her mouth and nose to try to block the smoke.

Flames climbed from a frying pan to the range hood. The once harvest-gold hood was now blackened with soot. Gas flames danced under the frying pan.

"What the hell?"

Her first instinct was to throw water on the flames, but reason took over.

She moved close enough to the stove to switch off the flames beneath the pan. Moving quickly, she snatched up the salt shaker and twisted off the top. Careful not to burn herself, she dashed salt into the pan, dousing the grease-fueled flames.

Her father probably had a fire extinguisher around here somewhere, but there had been no time to look for it.

The salt had done the trick.

A deep breath of relief sent her on a coughing jag. She had to get this smoke out of here.

Her eyes and throat burning, she opened up the back door and a couple of windows. The windows resisted. Paint and disuse had all but rendered them immovable.

The sound of sirens in the distance didn't register until the fierce banging echoed from the front door.

Dazed and utterly confused, she hurried to the door,

wondering if her father's smoke detectors were some-how connected to the fire department.

The second she unlocked and opened the door, no less than six firemen, dressed in full turnout gear, spilled into her father's front hall.

"Ma'am, are you all right?" one asked.

She nodded vaguely. "I didn't call." The words sounded weak and impotent. Her throat still burned as did her eyes. Should she have called?

None of this made sense.

She hadn't called the fire department.

And she sure hadn't left a frying pan on the stove with the flame going under it. In fact, she hadn't cooked a single thing since her arrival. She'd ordered out or gone out.

"One of your neighbors saw the smoke and reported it," the fireman told her. "She thought the place was empty."

Emily hadn't realized that as he spoke he'd been ushering her out the door. She blinked, the fresher air giving her eyes some relief.

"Oh," was all she could think to say—wasn't even sure at this point what he'd said to her.

She felt the heavy weight of a blanket draped around her shoulders. A bottle of water was suddenly in her right hand. She drank to soothe her raw throat while her brain attempted to catch up with all she saw happening around her.

Neighbors from both sides of the block had come out onto the sidewalks to see what the commotion was about. Emily didn't miss the not-so-discreet glances in her direction, and the conversations behind hands that were more than likely related to her. She recognized a few of the faces from the funeral, but she no longer knew any of these people…and they apparently didn't remember her.

The firemen hustled in and out of her father's front door, but she wasn't at all sure what they were doing. The fire was out. At least, she thought it was. But, in truth, she hadn't looked up. The ceiling could very well have been smoldering and she might not have noticed.

Her heart started to hammer even harder, and her entire body quaked uncontrollably. She didn't want her father's home to burn. That was all she had left of him. His clothes…his things.

She glanced around. She'd spent the first years of her life in this house, in this neighborhood. A new kind of sadness settled over her. She didn't know these people anymore. They didn't know her. Probably thought she was some sort of intruder.

This was her father's legacy. A broken home, a wife who'd turned her back on him in every respect and one remaining child that hadn't taken the time to mend fences or to regain lost ground.

And now it was too late.

A sob ripped at her throat.

How had she let this much time elapse? Why hadn't she made more of an effort to spend time with her father?

She hadn't even known what he did on Saturday afternoons, for God's sake. She knew nothing about him except that he was dead…murdered.

The trickle of hot tears on her cheeks had her brushing at her face with the back of her hand. A fine layer of soot was mingled with the salty moisture she swiped away.

"Are you all right, Emily?"

She looked up at the sound of the familiar voice.

Daniel Marks.

What was he doing here? Then she remembered that he'd said he'd call or stop by.

She shook off what was no doubt shock attempting to set in. "I'm all right." Again, her words carried little conviction, so she squared her shoulders and tried to look brave.

He wasn't convinced.

"What happened?"

As he waited for her response, he assessed her eyes carefully, then surveyed what he could see of her. Her face and hands were about all that wasn't completely covered by the blanket.

"I don't really know." She cleared her throat and summoned her courage enough to get some semblance of control over her shaking limbs. "I was upstairs taking a bath and the smoke alarm went off." She took another long sip of water and cleared her throat again. Her throat felt so dry...so raw.

He waited patiently for her to continue.

"When I came downstairs, the smoke was coming from the kitchen."

She shrugged, the blanket slipped. He quickly gathered it back up around her shoulders. Her breath caught just a little at his touch. She ordered herself to focus and went on.

"I don't know how it happened but there was a...a

skillet on the stove. The burner was turned on, and the grease inside the skillet had burst into flames."

That had to be wrong. Why would a skillet or any pan have been on the stove? She hadn't used any. How had the gas burner gotten turned on? Her father's kitchen had been immaculate when she arrived. No dirty pots and pans sitting around, not even soiled dishes in the sink.

"Had you considered starting dinner and perhaps forgotten about it?" Daniel asked gently.

Emily looked into his eyes then. They were nice eyes, caring eyes. She'd noticed that before. She was glad he was here. This just didn't make sense. How had it happened?

"No. I ordered in." She gestured toward the house. "The Thai box is in the trash."

He squeezed her arm reassuringly. "Don't worry. We'll figure this out."

Frustration edged its way into the mix of confusing emotions. Was he only patronizing her? Did he think she had done something so stupid?

Anger seared away the more fragile emotions. "I did not do this! I don't know how it happened, but I was not even in the room when someone…did this."

Okay, now even she had to admit that what she'd just said sounded bizarre. There hadn't been anyone else in the house while she took a bath. The doors had both been locked.

As if she'd spoken the last thought aloud, Marks asked, "You're sure both doors were locked?"

"Yes," she snapped, not caring if he saw her anger. This was insane. She had not set her father's house on fire! She glanced toward the door as several of the firemen exited. All four glanced covertly in her direction.

Oh, God, even the fire department thought she was responsible for this.

"Daniel." She blinked, tried to calm herself, to slow her whirling thoughts. "I don't know how this happened, but you have to believe me, I didn't do this."

"I do believe you."

She searched his eyes, looking for something to back up his words and she found it. The certainty in his gaze went a long way in allaying the fear and frustration twisting through her.

"Let me talk to whoever is in charge," he suggested.

She nodded, too damned exhausted to demand to go with him. Going back inside right now was not something she wanted to do. Instead, she closed her eyes tight to block out the comings and goings of the men in turnout gear and the curious onlookers. She wrapped her arms more tightly around herself and wished she could be anywhere but here.

The sound of car doors slamming jerked her eyes open just in time for her to see Detective Franko and another man emerge from a vehicle. The two didn't bother to look in her direction as they hurried to go inside her father's home.

As they disappeared inside, one of the firemen started to drape yellow tape around the stoop. Why was he doing that? Recognition shook her so hard that staying vertical took every ounce of strength she possessed.

Crime scene tape.

Had they discovered that the back door had been

forced open? She remembered clearly unlocking and opening the front door for the firemen.

Then she remembered.

She'd opened the back door to let the smoke out. It hadn't been locked.

How was that possible? She remembered checking to see that both doors were locked before she went upstairs for her bath. Would she have noticed if the back door or its lock had been damaged by forced entry?

In movies she'd seen locks shimmied open with something as simple as a credit card. But was that possible in the real world?

Waiting out here like a helpless victim wasn't going to answer the question. She stormed up to her father's stoop, leaving the blanket on the street behind her, ducked under the yellow barrier and went inside.

This was *her* home. Whatever had happened here, she had a right to know.

The idea that Franko had arrived signaled that the firemen or Daniel Marks had found something suspicious.

In the front hall, a couple of firemen looked up as she stepped inside, but neither said anything to her.

She heard voices coming from the kitchen. Franko's she recognized, another she didn't. Daniel Marks joined the conversation, as well.

All sounded tense.

Overriding her burst of anger, worry furrowed its way across her brow making her head ache. As she walked slowly toward the kitchen, she wondered if she should call her mother. Emily didn't know why she should bother, but it felt like the right thing to do.

An Important Message from the Editors

Dear Reader,

Because you've chosen to read one of our fine romance novels, we'd like to say "thank you"! And, as a special way to thank you, we're offering you two more of the books you love so well, and a surprise gift to send you — absolutely FREE!

Please enjoy them with our compliments...

Pam Powers

Peel off Seal and Place Inside...

FREE GIFT

How to validate your Editor's
"Thank You"
FREE GIFT

1. Peel off gift seal from front cover. Place it in space provided at right. This automatically entitles you to receive 2 FREE BOOKS and a fabulous mystery gift.

2. Send back this card and you'll get 2 brand-new *Romance* novels. These books have a cover price of $5.99 or more each in the U.S. and $6.99 or more each in Canada, but they are yours to keep absolutely free.

3. There's no catch. You're under no obligation to buy anything. We charge nothing—ZERO—for your first shipment. And you don't have to make any minimum number of purchases— not even one!

4. The fact is, thousands of readers enjoy receiving their books by mail from The Reader Service. They enjoy the convenience of home delivery...they like getting the best new novels at discount prices BEFORE they're available in stores... and they love their Heart to Heart subscriber newsletter featuring author news, special book offers, book reviews and much more!

5. We hope that after receiving your free books you'll want to remain a subscriber. But the choice is yours— to continue or cancel, any time at all! So why not take us up on our invitation, with no risk of any kind. You'll be glad you did!

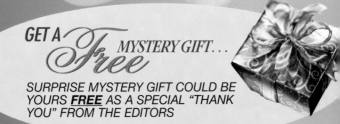

GET A *Free* MYSTERY GIFT...

SURPRISE MYSTERY GIFT COULD BE YOURS **FREE** AS A SPECIAL "THANK YOU" FROM THE EDITORS

THE EDITOR'S "THANK YOU" FREE GIFTS INCLUDE:

▶ Two BRAND-NEW Romance Novels

▶ An exciting surprise gift

YES! I have placed my Editor's "thank you" Free Gifts seal in the space provided at right. Please send me 2 FREE books, and my FREE Mystery Gift. I understand that I am under no obligation to purchase anything further, as explained on the back and opposite page.

PLACE
FREE GIFTS
SEAL
HERE

193 MDL D37Q   393 MDL D37R

FIRST NAME	LAST NAME

ADDRESS

APT.#	CITY

STATE/PROV.	ZIP/POSTAL CODE

Thank You!

The Reader Service — Here's How It Works:

Accepting your 2 free books and gift places you under no obligation to buy anything. You may keep the books and gift and return the shipping statement marked "cancel." If you do not cancel, about a month later we'll send you 3 additional books and bill you just $4.99 each in the U.S., or $5.49 each in Canada, plus 25¢ shipping & handling per book and applicable taxes if any.* That's the complete price and — compared to cover prices starting from $5.99 each in the U.S. and $6.99 each in Canada — it's quite a bargain! You may cancel at any time, but if you choose to continue, every month we'll send you 3 more books, which you may either purchase at the discount price or return to us and cancel your subscription.

*Terms and prices subject to change without notice. Sales tax applicable in N.Y. Canadian residents will be charged applicable provincial taxes and GST.

If offer card is missing write to: The Reader Service, 3010 Walden Ave., P.O. Box 1867, Buffalo, NY 14240-1867

BUSINESS REPLY MAIL
FIRST-CLASS MAIL   PERMIT NO. 717-003   BUFFALO, NY

POSTAGE WILL BE PAID BY ADDRESSEE

THE READER SERVICE
3010 WALDEN AVE
PO BOX 1341
BUFFALO NY 14240-8571

NO POSTAGE
NECESSARY
IF MAILED
IN THE
UNITED STATES

The voices grew louder now. The tension had morphed into outright anger.

She paused in the doorway and surveyed the situation.

Daniel Marks and Detective Franko were squaring off in the middle of the room. Emily blinked, her mind abruptly settling on the old black-and-white tile floor. Her father should have changed that years ago.

The whole house needed an update. The kitchen screamed *fifties,* with its white cabinets that had gone dingy a decade or so ago and its equally antiquated appliances. Maybe the stove was just old—had started itself.

But that still didn't explain the skillet that apparently had contained cooking oil or grease of some sort. Nothing in the kitchen had been out of place when she arrived. Her father likely had breakfast with the guys at some diner. His dinner usually consisted of microwave dinners and sandwiches, if the contents of the fridge and freezer were any indication.

The skillet was the mystery.

The unlocked back door was ample reason to suspect that someone had come into the house while she'd bathed, utterly oblivious, upstairs.

But why?

Did someone mean her harm?

She hadn't lived here in more than a decade. She hardly even remembered anyone. She couldn't possibly have any enemies who wanted some kind of revenge.

The only thing she'd done since her return was bury her father and…look into his murder.

The heated exchange between Marks and Franko jerked her attention back to the here and now.

"You'd better come clean with me, Marks," Franko threatened. "I don't know what the hell you two have been up to, but evidently someone doesn't like it."

Just then, the fireman standing beyond the two arguing men stepped aside, giving Emily a clear view to the stove where the unexplained and blackened skillet sat cold and no longer spewing its dangerous flames.

But it wasn't the skillet that had her heart stumbling in her chest or her blood running cold in her veins.

It was the message written in big, bold letters across the yellowed white tile between the stovetop and the hood.

Back off or die!

CHAPTER TWENTY-TWO

DANIEL STARED AT the warning scrawled across the tiles.

Back off or die!

"What does that mean?"

He whipped around at the sound of Emily's voice, then swore when he saw that all the color had drained from her face as the words penetrated through the shock she'd experienced.

"Emily." He moved to her side. "We can talk about this later. I want you to wait in the other room." There were things he and Franko needed to get clear, things Emily didn't need to hear.

"Who would do this?" She stared up at Daniel then, looking more vulnerable than he could bear.

"We don't know yet."

"This is an official crime scene, Marks," Franko said, barging in before Emily could say more. "I'm going to have to ask the two of you to leave."

Emily stepped forward, anger abruptly flushing her pale cheeks. "This is my father's home. My home," she said firmly. "I'm not leaving until I understand what happened here."

Daniel couldn't entirely hold back his grin. The confusion and frustration playing out on Franko's face was very nearly worth the price of the show.

"Miss Hastings, I can't conduct this investigation properly if the crime scene is contaminated." He held out both hands in a calming gesture, likely as much for him as for her. "I'll give you a full report on what I find, but right now I need to be able to do my job."

Emily shook her head, her attention returning to the blatant warning penned across the wall behind her stove. "I don't understand why anyone would do this."

Franko glanced at Daniel. "That's what I intend to find out," he said, his words a blunt warning. "It appears someone besides Homicide is conducting an investigation of your father's murder."

His remark had the desired effect. Emily's gaze swung back to the detective's, and she looked as guilty as a defendant who'd been pointed out to the jury by an eyewitness.

"Are you accusing me of something, Detective?"

Daniel had to give her credit; she sure sounded properly mortified. The trouble was, she'd already shown her hand with that guilt-ridden reaction to Franko's remark.

Franko split his attention between Daniel and Emily. "Don't play games with me, either of you. I already know that Mr. Marks here is working for the Colby Agency. That I can understand. Victoria Colby-Camp wants to protect her son." His full attention settled on Emily. "What I don't understand is how you can team up with someone working to clear your father's killer."

Again, his words hit home.

"That's enough," Daniel growled, his fingers itching to curl into fists and pound the guy.

Emily drew in a sharp breath and let it go raggedly. "I just want the truth, Detective Franko. I want to know what really happened to my father and I'm not sure any of his colleagues, including you, are looking at this with a truly objective eye."

Franko's gaze narrowed with his mounting suspicion. "You believe you can be more objective?"

Daniel wanted to beat him senseless. Was the guy purposely trying to hurt her?

She looked away for a moment, but only a moment, before she leveled her gaze on his once more. "I don't know, maybe I can't. But I have to try. I owe it to him to see that this is done right."

Franko shook his head, as if his patience had reached an end. "Take my advice, Miss Hastings. Find yourself a partner who's actually on your side."

Daniel clenched his jaw hard to hold back what he really wanted to say to Franko. Something along the lines of if the cops would do their job right he wouldn't even need to be here. But any argument would be futile. Franko, like the rest of Chicago PD, had made up their minds. They had themselves a suspect and that was all that mattered.

"Let's go," he said to Emily. "I don't want you staying here alone any longer." He glanced in Franko's direction. "Not that they're likely to let you, anyway."

Emily nodded in agreement, didn't ask for clarification. She allowed him to escort her out to his vehicle. The press had arrived by the time they exited Carter Hastings's modest home. Daniel did what he could to protect her from the questions and the barrage of camera flashes. But nothing he did would be enough.

She had to understand, though that understanding might not penetrate deeply enough until later, that this incident meant only one thing.

·Someone had been watching them.

Someone with secrets related to her father's murder.

And whoever that someone was, he believed that Daniel and Emily were on to something.

EMILY WASHED her face and dried her hair. She looked a mess and didn't even have any clothes to put on. Why hadn't she thought to go back upstairs for her things?

She hugged the tattered robe more securely around her and stared at her reflection.

Was someone in Chicago PD attempting to warn her and Daniel off the investigation? Were her father's colleagues angry that she would dare work with someone affiliated with the Colby Agency? Franko certainly wasn't happy about it. But she and Daniel hadn't stepped on anyone's toes. Hadn't gotten in the way at all, as far as she could see.

Maybe she'd made a mistake. Maybe Franko or some of the others on the force knew something she didn't. Was Daniel Marks using her?

She thought of the way he'd tried to protect her from Franko's hurtful remarks. But then, had he been, in reality, protecting himself?

She sighed and dropped down onto the closed toilet lid. She just didn't know.

All of this was too much. Her stomach twisted with dread. Her father had been murdered. And the police weren't any closer now to determining who had killed him than they were when she'd first arrived. Not that it had been that long. She understood that these investigations took time.

How much longer could she afford to take off work

and chase after this truth she so valiantly sought? Was this whole team effort just an excuse not to go back home and face her mother?

When she left Chicago, would that be the end of her connection here? Her father was gone. Would there ever be any reason to come back here?

Did she even want to?

A light rap on the door jerked her from her troubling thoughts.

"Emily, I had some things brought over for you."

Things? She frowned. "Just a moment." She pushed to her feet and studied her reflection in the mirror for a moment before exiting the bathroom.

She looked a mess. Dark circles under her eyes. And her skin was so pale. Lifeless.

Heaving a weary sigh, she turned away from the mirror and pulled open the door. She couldn't stay shut up in his bathroom forever.

The explanation for her lengthy stay in the bathroom that had been poised on the tip of her tongue when she opened the door escaped her the instant her gaze landed on Daniel's.

"I wanted you to be comfortable." He thrust a series of large shopping bags at her, four altogether, two clutched in each hand. The pink one she recognized as being from her favorite lingerie chain. The others weren't readily identifiable.

For five more seconds, she couldn't think what to say. Was he being presumptuous or just kind?

"Thank you." A sound of uncertainty whispered past her lips before she could stop it. "You didn't need to go to any trouble."

"But you needed clothes." He grinned. "In a city this large, it's a pretty easy dilemma to take care of. You just call the stores, tell them what you're looking for and they deliver it posthaste."

Wow. She had been in there a long time.

"Okay," she managed, still rattled. "Thanks. I'll…" She reached for the bag. "I'll just get changed, then."

"I hope everything fits." His gaze connected with hers in a way that was wholly unsettling. "I estimated your sizes."

She nodded jerkily. "I'm sure everything will be fine." She couldn't close the door quickly enough.

Dropping back onto the closed toilet lid she stared at the bags for a time before delving inside. The first, a shiny red one, held two pair of high-end designer jeans, in her size, two. Four long-sleeved blouses, all in size small, were wrapped in elegantly embossed paper, also inside the sleek red bag. The price tags had been removed from all the garments.

A white bag with the business name stamped in gold lettering held a pair of black leather flats. A somewhat smaller white bag with no business logo held toiletries, including a toothbrush and toothpaste.

But it was the pink one that did the most damage to her internal defenses. Inside were half a dozen pairs of panties, all in size small, but in several different styles ranging from high-rise briefs to thongs. Staring at the 34B label on the two bras had her mouth dropping open.

How had he guessed her bra size so accurately?

She wasn't sure whether to be flattered or offended. Also in the bag was an exquisite, surprisingly unrevealing, nightgown. That the garment wasn't flimsy or erotic in design made her much more comfortable.

Nope. Presumption hadn't entered into his decision. He'd done just what he'd said—taken care of an essential need. She couldn't very well run around town, or his hotel room, wearing nothing but a ratty robe.

Taking her time, she selected an outfit and pulled it on.

The fit was perfect. She'd never been one to spend lavish amounts on clothing. Her mother had accused her numerous times of being too practical. But Emily saw it as being careful.

Her stepfather being a cardiovascular surgeon had changed her mother's lifestyle considerably. But it just hadn't rubbed off on Emily. Maybe she'd always been stuck in the past. The daughter of a cop.

A tremulous smile spread across her face as she stared at her reflection. Yeah, well, she was proud of being a cop's daughter. Nothing against her stepfather; she cared deeply for him, as well. But, looking at herself just now, she noticed things she'd forgotten to notice in a very long time. She had her father's eyes. Had his nose, or at least a slightly more feminine version of it.

Why, after all these years, did she finally notice those things?

Because he was gone. And it was too late to do anything else.

That deep sadness and regret washed over her again.

She couldn't keep letting those feelings take charge. She had to stay on her toes here, had to make sure Daniel Marks wasn't working against her and that Chicago PD stayed on top of her father's murder investigation.

Emily hung her old robe on the hook on the back of

the closed door and rounded up the bags. She couldn't stay shut up in here forever. As she emerged, she breathed easier as the air in the rest of the room was considerably cooler than that of the bathroom. She sat the bags on the floor near the closet and turned to her host.

"I really appreciate the clothes." She pinned a polite smile into place. "You'll have to tell me how much I owe you." She braced herself for the answer. There was no telling how much he'd spent. A secretary's salary didn't go a long way on luxuries. Not that she was complaining. Her life and her work were as fulfilling as anyone could expect. No one really had the perfect life or the perfect job.

Before he responded to her offer of repayment, he allowed his gaze to take a leisurely tour of her from head to toe and then a slow, thorough return trip. The blatant approval she saw when he'd rested his eyes on hers once more made her feel light-headed.

"You look great. The saleslady wasn't kidding when she said she knew just what to send."

Baffled, Emily confessed, "I'm sorry, I'm not following." She was too tired for this kind of exchange. Too much had happened. She had too many questions that needed answers. And she was starving. She hadn't bothered with lunch, had gotten too caught up in the Madelyn hunt. Then the fire had totally thrown her evening off.

She shuddered when she thought of the message someone had left. The idea that it might be someone from Chicago PD hurt more than she wanted to admit. Were her father's friends that upset with the idea that she was looking into her father's murder? Maybe working with Daniel made it look as if she didn't trust Homicide to do their job.

She should have been up front with Detective Franko in the first place, should have told him exactly what she was doing and why. That would have alleviated most of his misgivings. But she had a good excuse—she hadn't been thinking clearly.

Did that really pardon her sin of omission?

"Let's just call this a business expense," Daniel recommended, dragging her weary mind back to the hotel room and him.

What on earth was she doing in his hotel room?

Business expense?

Again, her responses were slow. "You mean, charge this to the Colby Agency?" That just felt wrong, as if she were taking a bribe from the enemy.

Before she could say as much, he replied, "Look at it this way, Emily. The Colby Agency is the reason for this investigation. Whoever doesn't want us doing what we're doing broke into your house, and now your home is a crime scene and you can't access your essentials. I think that qualifies the purchases as a business expense. For which," he added firmly, "you should feel no guilt."

He made complete sense and still she didn't like it. "I would just feel better if I didn't take advantage of the situation." Surely he could understand that.

He nodded grudgingly. "I can see how you wouldn't want to feel obliged in any way to Victoria under the circumstances."

It amazed her how well he read her. "So, how much?"

He shrugged noncommittally. "Since you've worked so hard to help with an investigation that I'll be paid for conducting," he began, "let's just call it even."

Her jaw sagged. He'd sneaked that one in on her. "Wait just a minute."

He held up both hands. "It's either that or I'm going to have to start paying you a salary."

This was ridiculous. She huffed a sound of impatience and started to demand that he stop this nonsense, but he spoke first. "I don't know about you, but I'm starving. Would you like to have dinner in or out?"

Arguing with him was useless. That was clear. She took stock of the room with its king-size bed and decided that eating out would be in her best interest, though she had no desire to mingle with the public.

"Out."

"You can bring me up to speed on what you discovered today and I'll do the same," he offered.

The memory of talking to Madelyn's sister poked through all the other crazy mixed up events in her head. "Definitely. I found Madelyn Rutland's family."

On the way to the restaurant, which was only a few blocks from the hotel, Emily told him about how she'd tracked down Madelyn Rutland's sister. The conversation confirmed his suspicions about the woman—way off kilter. But the news also brought into question why the Colby Agency hadn't found anything specific on her death. That question would have to wait for another time.

"I did a little checking on Madelyn myself," he said after the waiter had taken their order.

"Really?" Her eyes were wide with anticipation. She had beautiful eyes.

Daniel booted out that line of thinking and refocused on the matter at hand.

"I went looking for anyone who might have been associated with her and who would be willing to talk. I researched former homicide detectives who had left under less-than-optimal circumstances. I found a low-rent private detective on the South Side who worked Homicide during the same period your father and Madelyn were partners. He'd had some dealings with Madelyn and claimed she was a few bricks shy of a load. A real wacko was the way he put it."

Uncertainty disrupted Emily's smooth complexion, causing lines of worry to form. "My father never mentioned anything negative about her."

Daniel sipped his water and purposely kept his tone light. "Why would he? You were a child at the time."

The statement was a bit blunt, but he'd tempered it as best he could.

She considered what he'd said, then replied, "You're right. He likely wouldn't have talked about work problems in front of me and my brother."

During the past few days, Daniel had yet to hear her talk about her mother unless he asked a specific question. He wondered about that. "What about your mother? Would she remember anything like that? Your father may have discussed work with her." Emily had mentioned calling her, but obviously hadn't.

Emily looked away as if he'd touched a nerve. She fidgeted with her napkin, avoided eye contact. "I could ask her. I had even thought about it. She might remember something, but I doubt it."

To take the pressure off her, he took a different direction and told her about his discovery in the warehouse. "It might not be what I think it is," he qualified, "but I'm willing to wager that's why they haven't formally pressed charges just yet."

"So Jim Colby may know who killed my father," she said, more to herself than to Daniel.

"He may indeed," Daniel agreed. "Victoria told me that his therapist is considering all possible ways to uncover what he remembers of that night."

She appeared to ponder that news for a while. As she did, he studied her and noted the gentle yet exquisite angle of her profile. The narrow bridge of her nose anchored by lovely oval eyes. Her lips didn't precisely fit the category of lush, but they were full enough to draw any male spectator's immediate attention. He liked her mouth. Liked her.

Emily Hastings was a genuinely nice woman—still naive enough to be vulnerable and surprisingly devoid of cynicism. But strong enough to stand up for what she believed in and to push forward in an effort to make it happen.

A very nice woman.

The kind a guy wanted to bring home to meet his parents.

Whoa. Obviously his decision to settle in Chicago and perhaps move to the next level of his life had taken root a little too well.

She lifted those pretty eyes up to meet his. "You'll let me know if they decide upon a way to retrieve his memories?"

Daniel couldn't help but smile. "Definitely."

His cell phone vibrated and he reached into his jacket pocket to answer it. Only three people in this city new his number—Victoria, Emily and Detective Franko.

Daniel had left it with him today in case he learned anything on the break-in at Emily's house.

"Marks."

"Mr. Marks, this is Detective Franko."

Tension slid through Daniel. "Detective Franko, I didn't expect to hear from you so quickly." Daniel met Emily's surprised gaze. She would know, as well, that this call meant they had something on the break-in.

"No more surprised than me, Mr. Marks," he said, his tone almost facetious.

Daniel went on alert. This guy was sounding way too cocky. "What did you find?"

"You understand that everything about this case is priority."

Daniel didn't bother responding. Of course he knew.

"We lifted prints from the rear door and ran them immediately. We found several. Some belong to Miss Hastings, to you and, of course, to her father."

"Get to the point, Franko." The detective appeared to be enjoying dragging this out entirely too much.

"You know, Marks, I did a little more checking on you. I found out that you came here for a position at the Colby Agency."

Daniel kept his face devoid of reaction to the statement. The last thing he needed was this guy telling Emily that news in just that tone. Daniel needed her with him, trusting him.

"I'm certain you must have a point, Detective."

"My point is, Marks," Franko said hotly, "I don't know what you people think you're up to, but if you believe for one second that you'll throw me off the scent of that unstable son of Victoria's, you can forget it. I will nail him."

"With what?" Daniel demanded. "The prints you took from inside the warehouse? Well away from the crime scene?"

Detective Franko's abrupt silence confirmed Daniel's conclusion.

"You plant any other misleading evidence, Marks," Franko threatened, "and I'll make sure you're not welcome anywhere in this town."

Daniel shook his head for Emily's benefit, to show the guy hadn't come across with anything just yet. She watched expectantly as the conversation played out.

"What the devil are you talking about?" Daniel demanded. This had gone beyond the ridiculous and into the bizarre.

"The other prints we found in the database belonged to someone you might recognize," he said smugly.

"Really?" Daniel wanted to hang up on the guy, to let him seethe before he called him back. But something in his tone as he'd made that last statement set Daniel on edge. "Who would that be?"

"James Colby," Franko said. "It seems he came back from the dead to issue that warning."

CHAPTER TWENTY-THREE

WEDNESDAY MORNING, Victoria immersed herself in work.

She had scarcely slept in days and her attention span was deplorable, to say the least.

A third cup of coffee hadn't managed to get her adrenaline flowing this morning. She doubted a fourth one would. But she had to try. Anything to keep her mind alert.

Determined to ward off the exhaustion, she pushed out of her chair and strode purposefully to the small conference table in her office, coffee cup in hand. Mildred had brought a fresh pot in not thirty minutes ago. The strong brew steamed as she poured her cup full before settling the carafe back on the tray.

Like the first pot this morning, Mildred had made this one a little stronger than usual. Victoria couldn't help but smile when she considered how long she and Mildred had been together.

A lifetime.

And then some, she added wryly. They had shared each other's every joy and every tragedy.

Other than Lucas, there was not another soul on this earth who knew Victoria better. Not even Jim. But, in all fairness, they had been robbed of all those years. Most of her son's life, in fact.

Leberman, the son of a bitch, was rotting in hell and even that was too good for him.

Errol Leberman had served in the military with James and Lucas. He had later used his military connections and his intensive special operations training for evil and for his own personal gain. James had participated in bringing him down. Leberman's vengeance had been brutal and far-reaching.

He had taken their son, allowed them to suffer unspeakable pain. Then he'd taken James, leaving Victoria to struggle for survival on her own, with not one but two tragedies weighing on her heart and soul.

And somehow, surely by the grace of God, she had managed to survive.

Victoria cradled her warm mug and moved back to her chair. By the grace of God and Lucas Camp, she amended. Lucas had been there for her through it all. He had helped her to go on, to build this agency into one of the finest in the country.

Building this agency had kept her mind off the reality of her life. Her husband was dead and her son was missing, presumed dead.

One would have thought that Leberman would have been through trampling on her heart by then. But he'd simply gotten his second wind. He'd watched Victoria, waited for nearly two decades for the perfect moment. His timing had been so precise that it gave her chills even now.

Leberman had waited for her to fall in love again. Waited for that exact moment when she was ready to give her heart to someone new. Lucas.

Then he'd struck, attempted to kill Lucas. But he'd

walked away, leaving both Lucas and Victoria very much alive when he surely could have killed Lucas, if not her.

But that had only been a preview of things to come. Leberman had wanted to test this new love he'd suspected growing between Victoria and Lucas. Once he'd confirmed his suspicions, the real endgame had begun.

Victoria shuddered, sipped her coffee in an effort to chase away the ice forming around her heart as what happened next filtered into her mind like old horror movie reruns.

For all those years, Leberman had kept one vital secret. He had Victoria's son. Little Jimmy Colby had been raised by that vile monster. He'd been molded into a heartless killing machine. A man who killed for money and cared for nothing or no one, not even himself. A man who called himself Seth.

Leberman had instructed Jim—Seth—to kill his mother. To have his vengeance for the way his family had deserted him.

Lies. The bastard had filled her son's head with lies and hatred.

But Jim had prevailed. He couldn't bring himself to complete the mission for which he had trained most of his life. Instead, he had killed Leberman, ending Leberman's reign of torment once and for all.

For a full year now, Victoria had been allowed to bond with her son, to show him how very much she and his father had loved him. Now this.

Daniel Marks had to prove Jim's innocence.

Any other outcome was unacceptable.

"Victoria."

Surfacing from the agonizing thoughts, she turned her attention to the intercom. "Yes, Mildred."

"Daniel Marks is here to see you. Shall I send him in?"

"Please do." Victoria sat her cup aside and smoothed a hand over her hair. Surely his early morning visit meant he had something to report. Her pulse skipped with anticipation. She needed the part with Jim to be over. She could deal with the rest of the past. As much as she did not want to learn that James had betrayed her, just now that was secondary to her son's situation.

"Daniel." She stood to greet him, then gestured to the chair in front of her desk. "Would you like coffee?"

He managed a polite smile, though she suspected he carried news that offered no reason to smile. The regret in his eyes spoke loudly.

"No, thanks, Victoria. I've had my limit this morning already."

Another one who'd likely had little sleep. "Well, have a seat, then, and tell me what you have to report." Might as well cut to the chase.

When she had resumed her seat and he had taken his, he began. "I followed up on the crime scene. Did a little extra snooping since security was no longer posted."

She nodded, unable to restrain the fluttering in her chest. *Please, please, let some part of this be good news.*

"I suspect Jim's prints were found inside the warehouse at a window overlooking the crime scene. I don't believe he was actually present at the scene. I have no idea why he would have been in that empty warehouse, but that would certainly explain why formal charges have not been pressed. His fingerprints were not within the actual perimeter of the scene. If anything, he was a mere observer."

"But can you prove that?" Victoria had to play devil's advocate here. She couldn't take any chances where her son's future was concerned.

"I tossed the scenario at Detective Franko and he didn't deny it. If he'd had something more, he would have argued the point. Have your legal force apply some more pressure. Considering Franko knows I've sur-mised his secret, he may cave and admit as much."

Victoria nodded. "I'll have Zach see him this morn-ing. Considering this news, he might want to apply a lit-tle pressure to a couple of other public officials, like the chief of police and the mayor. I doubt either of them would want this bit of news to hit the papers."

"Excellent strategy. I had considered the same pos-sibility myself."

Victoria gave herself a mental pat on the back. Oh, yes, Daniel Marks was definitely Colby Agency material.

"How is Emily?" she asked. How could she think only of herself and her son? Emily had lost her father. Despite the geographical challenge of their relationship during the past decade or so, flesh and blood were flesh and blood.

"She's holding up well. There was a bit of a scare last evening."

Victoria frowned. How was it that she didn't know about this? "What happened?"

As she listened, her trepidation building, Daniel ex-plained how someone had come into the Hastings home and started a fire. In addition to the fire, the culprit had left a warning that Emily—and Daniel, no doubt—should back off or die.

"My word!" Victoria pressed a hand to her chest,

horrified that Emily had been alone at Carter's house when such danger struck. "Perhaps you should keep her close at all times, Daniel."

"Already have that under control," he assured her. "She stayed at the hotel with me last night. I took the sofa," he hastened to add. "She was still asleep when I left this morning. That's one of the reasons I wanted to come early and get back to her."

The whole idea made Victoria furious and at the same time had her worried. "Please don't hesitate to ask for resources, Daniel. Any one of my investigators can provide backup or assistance at any time."

"Thank you, but right now I have the situation under control."

She hoped that wasn't going to be his one fatal flaw, a control issue. Victoria didn't take him for the type, but she could be wrong. "As long as you're certain," she allowed.

Daniel considered her statement a moment, then said, "I'll be the first to admit I may need help. But right now, I'm trying to maintain her trust. Bringing a third party into the scenario might prove to be a setback."

Relief lessened the pressure on Victoria's chest. Now there was a rational explanation for his actions. Further indication that her instincts were on target with Daniel Marks. "I see."

"My initial concern," Daniel went on, "with the break-in at the Hastings home and subsequent warning was that someone in Chicago PD had learned of our investigation and decided to prompt us to back off."

"I have difficulty believing that," she said without hesitation.

Victoria considered all that she knew about this case,

including the need for Chicago's finest to find justice for the murder of one of their own. Still she couldn't bring herself to favor that possibility.

"The members of our law enforcement, from the top down, are some of the best in the nation. I cannot see one of them going to that kind of extreme. Not even when the case involves one of their own. These men and women are too good for those kinds of dirty tricks. There has to be another explanation."

Maybe it was instincts honed over two decades in the business of private investigations, or perhaps it was the silence that settled between them after the conclusions she had voiced. Whatever the case, Victoria knew for certain that what Daniel Marks was about to say next was the worst kind of news.

"Detective Franko showed up," Daniel explained. "He let me know in no uncertain terms that he was on to my fishing around in his investigation." Daniel lifted a skeptical eyebrow. "He was not a happy detective."

Victoria restrained her need to demand that he get to the heart of the matter. "I assume they treated the situation like any other crime scene. Called in forensics techs?"

Daniel gave her a confirming nod. "Right away. I can't be certain, but I feel like Franko wanted to rule out the possibility of a cop being the culprit."

She shook her head. "I'm still not buying that one."

"As you can guess, everything about the Hastings case has been put on priority status. The lab work is pushed through ahead of all else."

Her throat had grown dry. She resisted the almost overwhelming urge to snatch up the phone and call Tasha to ask if Jim had been out of the house last night.

Dear God. Here she was already thinking the worst of her son. No wonder Chicago PD thought he was guilty. She was his mother, and even she worried that it might be within the realm of plausibility.

Then came the look. Victoria steeled herself. She knew that look—sympathy, the extreme desire to be anywhere else, to be about to say anything else.

"Victoria, the prints lifted from the door where the intruder gained entrance to the Hastings home were a perfect match to someone in Chicago PD's database."

She could hardly breathe but she had to know. "Who?"

"The prints belonged to your husband, Victoria."

"Lucas?" She shook her head. "That's impossible."

Daniel held up a hand. "I'm sorry. Not Mr. Camp. Your first husband, James Colby."

CHAPTER TWENTY-FOUR

EMILY SAT in the hotel room for a long time after she'd showered and changed. Daniel had said he would meet with Victoria this morning and go over everything with her. Then the two of them, Emily and Daniel, would dive back into the investigation.

Somehow, her father's murder and the letters from Madelyn Rutland to James Colby had gotten all intertwined. It was as if one were a pivotal part of the other, but that was impossible. James Colby had died years ago. Madelyn had supposedly died not so long after that. What did either of those people have to do with her father's murder?

She just didn't know. Not yet anyway.

The pillow and blanket Daniel Marks had used to sleep on the sofa dragged her attention there. He'd been so kind to her. Even though she barely knew him, she felt thankful for his presence. She wasn't sure she could have done this alone. As much as she wanted to believe she could have, she wasn't sure anymore.

She glanced at the clock. He would probably be back soon. Her stomach rumbled, reminding her that she hadn't had breakfast, only a couple of cups of coffee.

The room service was good, according to Daniel.

But she didn't want room service. What she really wanted was some fresh air and maybe a few minutes away from any reminder of him. Part of her wanted to call Detective Franko and demand to know what was going on with her father's investigation. If Jim Colby wasn't actually involved, then who the hell was?

It was so frustrating. No clues. No nothing.

It would be very easy to blame the murder on Jim Colby. She could see that now. The crime scene suggested a killer who knew how to clean up after himself and one who knew the ins and outs of ballistics. Jim Colby would know all those things. But that's where the connection began and ended.

There simply wasn't any evidence to pursue that avenue. She could imagine Victoria Colby-Camp would be ecstatic to learn her son likely didn't commit the murder. But what about her husband…her first husband?

The idea that James Colby's prints were found on her back door made her shiver.

There was that strange connection to the past again. James and Madelyn had apparently been involved. Emily's father had intervened, at least to the point of taking the letters so they wouldn't be discovered…or holding them for some reason.

But why?

And, as if that wasn't strange enough, Madelyn was supposed to be dead but no body had ever been found. And now a dead man's prints show up.

Somehow, as crazy as it sounded, all of it was connected.

Emily shuddered. She had to get out of there, get

some fresh air, take a brisk walk. Daniel had ordered her to stay in the room, but she just couldn't do it.

And maybe the temporary escape would give her the courage to call her mother. God knows, her mother hadn't called her, not even once.

Careful to keep her gaze away from the sofa and the pillow where Daniel had laid his head, Emily left the room and headed for the bank of elevators.

It wasn't that her mother had been a bad parent. To the contrary, she'd been the perfect mother. It was the past—Emily's father and brother—that she had steadfastly ignored. As if none of it had ever happened.

Emily wondered as the elevator doors slid open if there was ever a moment when her mother opened up and let herself remember. Did she close herself up in her room and open those old wounds where no one else would witness her weakness? Did she cry when she recalled those happy days when her son had been a part of her life…when they had been one big happy family?

Probably not.

Maybe it was the better way, the easier way. Living in the past only made one miserable. So her mother had taken it a step further—she didn't even acknowledge the past. What a perfect out. No harm, no foul. Never happened.

As Emily emerged from the lobby, she inhaled deeply of the freshest air the city had to offer, allowed the sun to warm her face. The day had all the signs of getting off to a fabulous start. She might as well enjoy it while she could.

She remembered a small café only a few blocks from the hotel that she'd noticed last night. That would do fine this morning. Meanwhile, maybe she'd call her mother.

It would only be around six on the West Coast, but that was okay. Her mom was an early riser.

Emily punched in the number and waited the two rings her mother always allowed before answering. She didn't like picking up until her caller ID unit had identified the caller.

"Emily, why on earth haven't you come home yet?" No *hello,* no *how are you.*

This might be a bit of a touchy subject. Whom was she kidding? It would be an intensely sore spot.

"I decided to stay for a while and see how the investigation goes," she said, knowing this would only set off her mother but it had to be done. No point in trying to avoid the confrontation.

"Please tell me you're joking." A heavy sigh rattled over the line. "I cannot believe you would put yourself through this."

"Mother, I need to know what happened. I owe him that much."

"Please, you don't owe him a thing."

Emily stopped in the middle of the sidewalk. She didn't care if pedestrians had to go around her. Besides, it was early; there weren't that many people out yet. "Just stop, Mother," she said angrily. She wanted her to hear her anger. She was through pretending.

"I beg your pardon!"

There she went, with the properly mortified tone.

"He was my father. I owe him, whether you want to admit it or not. What kind of daughter would I be if I buried him one day and left the next?"

"I suppose that's some sort of subliminal message as to how you believe I turned my back on your father."

Emily didn't want to do this. Her mother was all she had left. Screaming at each other wouldn't help. "Wait, Mom, I don't want to fight."

Another sigh, this one as weary as Emily felt just now. "Neither do I. I miss you, Emily. I want you to come home."

"I will, as soon as this is resolved."

There was the possibility that it might not ever be resolved. But some aspects of it had to be cleared up. Emily had to help make that happen.

"Mother, I need your help," Emily ventured, hoping her mother had softened on the subject, at least for the moment.

"I don't know how I could help." Ever the cautious one when it came to commitment.

"I need to ask you about Madelyn Rutland, Dad's partner from way back when we still lived here."

"I know who you're talking about."

Maybe it was Emily's imagination, but she was certain her mother's tone had gone colder than she'd ever heard it.

"What can you tell me about her?" Emily held her breath and prayed her mother would be cooperative.

"She was completely off her rocker. She almost ruined your father's career."

Okay. That was a step in the right direction. "How?" Might as well go for the whole enchilada.

"Madelyn always made things up. She wove tall tales about her childhood and her family. Carter knew it was all lies but figured if it made her feel better about herself, what difference did it make, right?"

Emily barely kept her surprise to herself. This was

the first time she'd heard her mother utter her father's name in ages. "Right."

"Anyway, she started work fantasies in addition to her personal fantasies. Her tales grew more and more strange. Carter finally told her she had to rein in her imagination. Things went downhill from there. They didn't get along. Every screwup was blamed on Carter. Then she shot that boy. She left Chicago not long after that. I think she died some time later."

Emily knew there were more questions she should ask, but somehow she couldn't form the necessary queries. Listening to her mother talk about the past had shaken her to the core.

"Sweetie, I really wish you'd leave this alone. Let the police do their job. You don't need to be involved. Nothing but trouble can come of it. Come home, please."

Emily's heart ached. She wanted to hug her mother, to thank her over and over for talking about the past; Emily knew it must have hurt her to do so. But if she overreacted, a moment like this might never come again.

"I'm fine, Mom, really. I'll be home before you know it," she assured, feeling the need more strongly than ever before. "Thanks for your help. If you remember anything else you think I need to know, call me, okay?"

Her mother made a sound that wasn't quite frustration, not quite irritation, but something softer, more nurturing. "Just take care of yourself, Emily. I can't lose you."

Emily realized she was still standing in the middle of the sidewalk, her phone still pressed to her ear even though her mother had already disconnected.

Maybe the adage *absence makes the heart grow*

fonder was true after all. She'd never heard her mother talk so sentimentally.

Dropping the phone back into her purse, she set out for the café with a little more purpose in her step. She hadn't learned much more, but she had a few additional details about Madelyn. Daniel would be proud of her.

Maybe it didn't even matter. The past might have nothing at all to do with the present. But it was the only starting place Emily had.

The sound of an engine being gunned penetrated the haze of distraction, and she turned quickly to look in the direction of the roaring noise.

Her mouth opened, but her scream died in her throat as her heart pounded frantically.

She needed to run!

Fear paralyzed her as the car charged directly at her.

CHAPTER TWENTY-FIVE

DANIEL FOUND EMILY in the hotel room.

She'd called his cell phone and told him what had occurred. He'd already been on his way back from the Colby Agency. Thank God it hadn't taken him long to get back.

"Tell me what happened."

She sat on the end of the bed, her face pale, her body shivering with the receding adrenaline.

Emily swallowed tightly, moistened her lips. "I took a walk. Thought I'd have breakfast at a place I remembered. Get some air." She closed her eyes and he saw her tremble.

Daniel couldn't help himself; he had to touch her, had to reassure her somehow. He placed his hand on her arm. The feel of her skin beneath his palm sent sensations he needed to deny shimmering through him.

"I shouldn't have left you here alone."

She glared up at him then, drew away from his touch. "I'm not a child. I can take care of myself. You're not my guardian, Marks."

At least she still had some fire in her.

"Can you tell me about the car?" he prodded, drawing her back to the subject.

"It was big," she said, "and going fast. I don't remember anything else."

"Was there anyone else around who might have seen it?" He could hope, but it really wouldn't matter now.

She shook her head. "If there was, they took off before I scrambled back to my feet."

He noted the damaged knees of her jeans. "Are you injured?"

"No." She stared down at her knees. "Just ruined the new jeans you bought." She shuddered and hugged herself. "I suppose it could have been someone talking on a cell phone while driving or fidgeting with the radio."

If her tone was any indication, she believed that about as much as he did.

"If you didn't see the car, then you didn't see the driver, right?" he persisted, attempting to stick to the facts.

"I definitely didn't see the driver. I didn't see a damned thing except my life flash before my eyes."

He heaved a heavy breath. "All right, that settles it. I don't let you out of my sight from now on."

Emily gave him another of those taken-aback glares. "You can't be serious."

He shrugged. "We are working on this together. Might as well stick together."

"I'm not helpless," she argued. "Just because some idiot lost control of his car or wasn't watching what he was doing is no reason to panic."

She was in denial. He'd seen it dozens of times in military confrontations.

"Emily," he said gently, "we have to consider the break-in at your house and the warning left behind.

Couple that incident with this one, and it spells trouble. You have to see that."

She looked away. "Of course I see it, but that doesn't mean I'm ready to give in to the pressure. Whoever is doing this isn't going to rule what I do or don't do."

"You're right," he agreed to her obvious surprise. "We're not going to be swayed by whoever is behind these attempts to scare us off. But we are going to be smart and alert."

She shoved a handful of hair behind her ear. "I can live with that."

Considering that someone had just tried to run her down, he was glad to hear it.

Emily looked up at him then. "So where do we go from here?"

Not an easy question to answer. Each event, each clue they uncovered appeared to take them in circles, leading nowhere except to the past…to people supposedly dead and buried.

"We analyze carefully what we know so far and we act accordingly."

"Did you learn anything new from Victoria?"

He shook his head. Watching the shock and then the denial claim Emily's face as his words were absorbed fully had been gut-wrenching. He should never have left her alone.

"I spoke to my mother," Emily said, and this time he was the one who was surprised.

"How is she?"

Emily shrugged. "Okay. It was a rather strange conversation. Usually she won't talk about the past at all.

Well," she amended, "she won't discuss our past here in Chicago. But this morning she did."

Daniel listened as Emily related the conversation. When she got to the part about Madelyn, he interrupted.

"Madelyn had a habit of making up stories about her past?" He needed to be clear on that part.

"That's what she said."

Lines furrowed her brow as she concentrated hard, or maybe her head ached after her harrowing experience. Again, he fought the urge to reach out to her.

"Not just tales about her personal life, either. She told lies about her professional life, too."

The letters immediately came to mind. "I wonder," Daniel said aloud, "if her bent for storytelling would have spilled over into the written word."

"I wondered about that myself," Emily admitted. "How did someone that unstable make it onto the police force? All the way to detective, at that?"

Well, they damned sure couldn't ask Chicago PD.

"There are those who can fool most everyone around them for a time."

Daniel had seen the type during his military days. Most of them would eventually hang themselves, given enough rope and ample time.

"So we have the letters," Emily reiterated. "Jim Colby's prints in the warehouse near the scene. And my father's former partner who was, apparently, a nutcase."

"And let's not forget James Colby's prints on your back door," he added.

Daniel saw only one way to learn more about Madelyn Rutland and perhaps to put that part of this investigation to rest once and for all.

"We need to talk to your father's most recent partner again," he said. "Do you suppose he will agree to meet with us? He'll probably know by now that we're conducting an investigation of our own."

"There's only one way to find out."

Emily fished for her cell phone in her purse and entered Norton Morrow's number. When she didn't get him at home, she called his work number.

"It's Emily," she said after being patched through to him. "I know you're probably busy, but we need to talk."

EMILY HADN'T BEEN SURE what to expect when she called Norton. He could have outright refused to meet with her; he had hesitated, but then he'd agreed to a time and place. She'd selected the café she'd been en route to earlier and ordered the breakfast she'd had her heart set upon.

"We've been ordered not to talk about the case with you, Emily," Norton said. He flicked a fleeting glance in Daniel's direction. "Or with you."

"I can understand the department's need to maintain boundaries," Daniel allowed, with more graciousness than Emily felt at the moment.

"He was my father," she argued, knowing her outrage would grieve her father's old friend. "I have a right to find out what really happened. You guys don't seem to be getting anywhere."

The ten or so seconds of silence that followed were steeped in tension.

"I agree," Norton confessed. "You do have a right to know, but the truth is there's nothing to know yet. We don't have a damned thing."

Emily closed her eyes to block the look of disappointment in his. She didn't want him to see the same reflected in hers.

"We both know Jim Colby wasn't the one who shot Mr. Hastings," Daniel said without preamble. "Not only is there no evidence, there's no motive."

"But he was there," Norton countered.

"You can't be sure he was in that warehouse at that precise moment. You can't be sure of anything."

Emily watched Daniel Marks move in for the kill. He was relentless, wouldn't give an inch. He pressed until the detective visibly surrendered.

"He's all we've got," Norton finally blurted, his face red with frustration.

"Now there's something we can agree on," Daniel stated succinctly.

"Man alive," Norton said, his desperate gaze landing on Emily. "Franko's even going so far as to investigate our own people just to be sure that no one was involved in that break-in at Carter's place."

Emily and Daniel exchanged a glance.

"Does he have reason to suspect so?" Daniel inquired.

Norton shook his head. "He just wants to be sure." He looked straight at Emily then. "He wants to do this right, Emily. We all want your father's killer to pay."

"Norton," Emily said, not sure how to broach the subject, "this may sound a little off-the-wall, but do you think there's a chance Madelyn Rutland could still be alive?"

To his credit, he didn't laugh and he did appear to give the question ample consideration.

"I guess it's possible. She left Chicago. Ended up

who knows where." His face folded into one of confusion. "Why do you ask?"

Emily didn't have a decent answer to throw out, but Daniel came to her rescue.

"There's been some confusion as to how she played into Mr. Hastings's life," he offered. "Did the two get along? Do you think she held him responsible for her professional problems?"

Norton rubbed his chin as he thought about that one. Emily used the time to devour the remainder of her breakfast of blueberry pancakes. She was famished.

"That's possible," Norton allowed. "The two were on the outs most of the time those last few months before she left." He looked from Daniel to Emily and back. "You don't think Madelyn suddenly reappeared and killed Carter?"

When neither of them answered, Norton had himself a deep, however short, belly laugh. "Look, I don't mean to be unkind, but that's pretty far-fetched, you have to admit. Hell, it's almost as bad as finding a dead man's prints on your daddy's back door. There has to be some reasonable explanation. A mix-up of some sort. This is real life. Franko has got the lab analyzing those prints twenty ways to Sunday. He's not going to go with anything that deep in *The Twilight Zone*."

Definitely far-fetched. But right now, it was all they had, and since Chicago's finest had nothing, it seemed like the best route to take.

The conversation pretty much went downhill from there. Norton wasn't about to entertain the idea of Madelyn's returning from the dead, much less James Colby's possible resurrection.

When they parted ways, Norton promised not to mention the meeting to Franko. Emily promised to keep him up to speed on anything she and Daniel discovered.

"Where to now?" Emily asked as she climbed into Daniel's vehicle.

"Now we do a little myth busting."

He'd lost her with that one.

"What kind of myth busting?"

She glanced down at her clothes. She still wore the damaged jeans. She wasn't sure she was dressed appropriately for whatever he had in mind. Her attention meandered over to her chauffer. Daniel Marks was always dressed for the part. Classy, perfectly groomed.

But it was easier for men. Throw on a pair of slacks, a plain white shirt and a jacket, and they were good to go. Not so for women. At least, not for her.

Why in the world would she be worrying about that right now? A distraction, she decided. Her brain needed a handy outlet. Not a good idea in this situation, obviously.

"Madelyn's sister said she was dead, but the Colby Agency didn't find anything on her beyond the fact that she had disappeared and was listed as deceased."

A memory suddenly bobbed to the surface.

"Oh, my God," she said. "Of course they didn't find anything specific. They were looking for results on Madelyn Rutland."

Her gaze collided with Daniel's.

"Madelyn told her sister she had married James Colby. They should be looking for Madelyn Colby."

Daniel shot her a grin that sent electricity sizzling through her.

"Very good, partner. Let's see what our resources at

the Colby Agency can dig up on one Madelyn Colby. Meanwhile, we'll go to the funeral home that interred James Colby and see if the mortician who did the work is still there."

As gruesome as it sounded, it was a good plan.

She relaxed into the seat and let him take the lead. He had the experience. And, so far as she could tell, their goals were the same. They both wanted the truth.

Whatever it might be.

She watched him speak as he called someone named Simon Ruhl at the Colby Agency and requested an all-out investigation on any trace of Madelyn Rutland Colby. Then he just drove. And that was fine. She enjoyed learning the contours of his profile. He looked strong and dependable. Very good-looking and very compassionate.

A good guy.

She liked that about him.

He was a lifesaver.

Funny that she would think that, she mused, for she had the near overwhelming urge to reach out to him and hang on for dear life.

CHAPTER TWENTY-SIX

THE FUNERAL HOME Victoria Colby-Camp had selected all those years ago was as stately as Daniel had expected. The Greek Revival-style structure sat amid a lush landscape that was at once gracious and unnerving.

"Wow," Emily murmured. "This place is really something."

Daniel turned onto the long, winding drive that led to the front entrance. "When a man like James Colby dies, the world sits up and takes notice."

Emily's gaze met his for the briefest of moments.

"Like when your father passed away," he went on. "I understand thousands came to pay their respects for a man who would be greatly missed."

She looked away, but not before he saw the shimmer of tears in her eyes. He wondered if she had grieved the way she needed to. Probably not, considering all that had happened since she'd arrived in Chicago.

When this was over, she would have some catching up to do. If he were lucky, he could be there for her…to hold her hand, if nothing else.

Daniel barely suppressed the need to shake his head as he parked the vehicle. A guy knew he was smitten when he hoped he could hold a woman's hand while she cried.

He used the time it took Emily to unfasten her seat belt to study her profile. Some guys might be threatened by the feelings Emily evoked so easily. But not Daniel. Who knew? Maybe he was simply ready for a deeper commitment. Now wasn't the best of times, but as he'd learned in his military career, life didn't always wait for good timing.

"You spoke to the owner already?" she asked, looking up to find him watching her so intently.

Daniel didn't bother pretending otherwise. She intrigued him, prompted his deepest protective instincts. "Yes. I called him from Victoria's office. Mr. Cortner is expecting us."

"Does he know the subject matter?"

Daniel gifted her with a reassuring smile. "He knows we're here about an old client."

Before she could ask anything else, he exited the vehicle and moved around to her side as she emerged. As they walked toward the entrance, Daniel reviewed his most recent conversation with Victoria. She had Simon Ruhl digging deeper for information on Madelyn Rutland Colby.

Victoria was seriously shaken by the discovery of James's prints at the Hastings' home and the news that Madelyn had claimed to have married James.

Victoria kept reiterating that both were impossible. James was dead. She'd said goodbye to him many years earlier. There was no mistake.

At Daniel's prodding, she'd called Lucas in Washington. He would arrive back in Chicago before dark. As strong as Victoria was, she needed her husband beside her right now. Especially considering the latest turn of events.

The main lobby of the elegant funeral home continued the theme of richness—sleek marble floors and soaring ceilings with intricate architecture. A massive, glittering chandelier reigned above it all.

Very glamorous.

"May I help you?"

A lady, maybe fifty-five or sixty, approached from the right wing. Daniel had already decided that the place was definitely large enough to be divided into wings.

"Good afternoon." He moved forward and offered his hand. "I'm Daniel Marks." He turned to Emily. "This is Emily Hastings and we're here to see Mr. Cortner."

The woman nodded as she shook Daniel's hand, then Emily's. "Freda Watson. Come this way." She gestured toward the hall from which she'd appeared. "Mr. Cortner is expecting you."

When Ms. Watson showed them to Mr. Cortner's office, Daniel recognized that there had been an error in communication.

Once the pleasantries were out of the way, Daniel went to the heart of the matter. "Mr. Cortner, perhaps you misunderstood my request."

The gentleman seated behind the desk designated as belonging to the funeral director was younger than Daniel. No way was he the one who had overseen the care of James Colby considerably more than a ago.

Cortner pushed the black-rimmed glasses a little higher on his nose. "You were expecting my father," he suggested. "I'm Dennis Cortner, Jr."

"Your father served as the mortician for James Colby?"

The younger man nodded. "Yes."

"Is there any chance we could speak with him?" Daniel had a bad feeling deep in his gut that that wasn't going to happen.

"He passed away last year," Cortner explained.

A wasted trip. The man could have told him this on the telephone. "I appreciate your time, Mr. Watson, but—"

"But I was there," Cortner cut in. "I assisted my father from the time I was ten."

Daniel relaxed marginally. "I see. You worked as his apprentice in order to take over the family business."

Cortner nodded. "I'll be training my own son in a few years. These days, few funeral directors actually still do the dirty work, but here we prefer a more hands-on approach. I have numerous assistants, of course, but I'm still closely involved."

Well, someone had to do it, Daniel mused.

"How can I help you?" Cortner looked from Daniel to Emily and back. "Mrs. Colby-Camp called and gave her permission for full disclosure. Anything you need that I can provide is fine by her."

"Excellent." Daniel turned on his interrogation. "You were at your father's side when he prepared the body of James Colby?"

Cortner gave an affirming nod.

"According to Victoria, Lucas Camp identified the body at the morgue."

"That's correct," the funeral director said. "When we picked up the body, the family had provided a recent photograph for our use. There was no question as to the identity of the body we prepared for burial." He moved his head firmly from side to side. "No question at all."

"Do you document your work?" Daniel asked.

A smile broadened on the man's face. "Yes, we most certainly do." He reached for a manila file on his desk. "In fact, I pulled the file before your arrival."

Daniel accepted the file and perused the contents. It contained a detailed report on the procedure as well as photographs documenting the body before and after. James Colby had been shot execution style. He picked up one and showed it to Cortner. "This is the photograph the family provided?"

"Yes, that's it."

Daniel reviewed the report thoroughly before handing the file back to Cortner. He didn't offer it to Emily, nor did she ask to see. He felt certain the loss of her father was far too fresh to view such a closely related scenario.

"I understand the service was closed casket."

"Correct," Cortner said. "That's the way the family wanted it. In fact, that's the most common practice among those in a higher social standing."

Daniel considered the steps involved in providing the sort of service Cortner offered. "When the body has been prepared, I assume the family is allowed one final viewing if they'd like before the casket is closed for good."

"Yes. We really encourage that family members take that last look, especially if they haven't viewed the body at all. We make a special event of it a few hours prior to the public service or the night before, depending upon what the family wishes."

"So the casket isn't opened again after that, not even by the funeral director," Daniel suggested.

"We prefer not to, unless there is a special request for graveside opening. Otherwise there's no reason to reopen it." Cortner's cheeks flushed. "Unless we suspect we've forgotten something, which rarely happens. Or a family member wants to add something, like a rose or other final memento."

"Did either happen in the Colby case?"

Cortner shook his head adamantly. "Absolutely not. My father was meticulous in his work. Generally, the only time mistakes are made here are when clients change their minds. But Mr. Colby's widow didn't make any changes or any last-minute requests."

Cortner sighed. "To be honest, I remember quite well how devastated she was by her husband's murder. She scarcely suffered through the service, much less made a fuss over anything."

"But even after you've closed and sealed the lid there is some time when the body is—" Daniel shrugged in hopes of not having to be specific for Emily's sake "—basically unattended."

Cortner hesitated before responding. "Well, yes, so to speak. We lock the—" he glanced in Emily's direction before continuing "—uh, bodies in the walk-in refrigerator until time for the service."

"May I see the area where your work is done?"

Cortner looked a little nervous at the idea, but agreed since there were no clients awaiting preparation on the premises.

As they stood to take the tour, Daniel tugged Emily to the side. "You don't need to do this part."

She moistened her lips and gave him a hard stare. "I'll be fine. I need to be involved in every step of this investigation."

He didn't argue with her, mainly because Cortner had already disappeared around a corner and peeked back to make sure they were coming.

Cortner showed them around the sales room where display models of caskets and vaults were available for viewing, as well as wardrobe offerings. Then they moved farther down the corridor and through a set of double doors to where the embalming room and the walk-in refrigerator were located.

The door leading to the walk-in refrigerator area stood right next to one accessing the embalming room. But that wasn't what Daniel had wanted to see. What drew his attention was the rear entrance to the building located only a few feet away.

"Is this where you arrive with a delivery?" he asked.

Cortner nodded. "Yes."

"I assume you keep this door locked at all times," Daniel offered.

As if to answer the question, a grounds custodian strolled in through the door just then without hesitation.

So much for security.

Cortner didn't have much to say after that. The flush of embarrassment had claimed his chubby face and he was ready to get Daniel and Emily out of his way.

When Daniel opened the passenger door for Emily, he couldn't help noticing the paleness of her skin. This little field trip had been tough on her.

"You okay?" he asked as she climbed into the seat.

"Sure." She managed a tight smile. "I'd just like to get out of here."

He glanced around. "That makes two of us."

The silence expanded to the point of squeezing all the oxygen from the vehicle as Daniel navigated the truck back down the long, winding drive and to the long stretch of deserted road that would take them back to more acceptable signs of civilization.

"I'm wondering what any of this has to do with my father's murder," she said, her voice sounded fragile in the heavy silence.

"I'm wondering that myself," he admitted. "But clearly someone wants us to believe there's a connection." Finding James Colby's prints on that door had been no coincidence.

Colby had been dead for nearly two decades. A doorknob was touched numerous times each day. No way, even if he had been a frequent visitor to Hastings' home, would the prints have remained all this time. According to Franko, the prints had been fresh, unobscured by time and the elements.

"None of this makes sense," Emily said thoughtfully. "The warning, the prints from two different generations of Colbys—it's like pieces of three different puzzles."

"And then," Daniel said, picking up where she left off, "there's the burning question—what do the letters from Madelyn Rutland have to do with anything?"

"Maybe nothing," Emily said wearily. "I'm the one who found those and opened that can of worms." Her brow lined thoughtfully. "But it was as if Victoria Colby-Camp and I were destined to meet and the letters were the catalyst."

Daniel had always firmly believed that one's fate was determined by one's self, not by the gods or other unseen forces. But this whole thing felt exactly like the kind of fate those who claimed to predict the future touted.

Silence started to crowd in on them again, but this time it was much less smothering.

Emily had gone through a lot in the past week. She needed time to come to terms with each new discovery. Whatever they found at the end of this twisted journey, there would no doubt be surprises and pain.

Glass shattered and Daniel felt a bullet whiz past his ear.

"Get down!" he shouted to Emily.

"What? What's happening?"

"Get down! Now!"

She jerked off her seat belt and dived onto the floor.

Daniel floored the accelerator while checking his mirrors for pursuers.

Nothing.

Another eruption of glass cracked the silence. This time, the bullet lodged in the headrest of the passenger seat.

Daniel swore and started evasive maneuvers. He couldn't see the enemy, which meant whoever it was had hidden in the woods and waited for them to pass. Moving away from the area as quickly as possible was imperative.

But first he had to get past wherever the sniper had stationed himself without getting his head blown off.

"Who's shooting at us?" Emily cried from her protected position.

Daniel didn't answer. He couldn't afford the distraction. He drove like a madman, zigzagging and darting along the highway in an attempt to avoid the shooter's bead.

Another ping. This time, the rear quarter panel took a hit. His diversionary tactics were working.

He kept it up, pushing forward as fast as he dared, considering his abrupt movements.

No one or no vehicle appeared in the rearview mirror or emerged from the wooded area on either side of the road.

When the trees opened up, he relaxed a fraction.

Their shooter had taken his shots from his hiding spot, like a hunter waiting for a deer to walk past his tree stand. At this point, they were out of danger unless the shooter took up pursuit, which would be too risky.

"Cowardly bastard," he muttered.

"Can I get up now?"

He checked his mirrors once more. "It should be okay. Just be prepared to hit the floor again if necessary."

"Okay." She scrambled back into her seat and slipped on her seat belt. "Did you see anyone?"

"No. Whoever took those shots at us had himself a hiding place in the woods." He glanced at Emily then. "He knew we would be coming here."

Daniel's cell phone vibrated and he reached into his pocket, still conscious of the mirrors and any other traffic. "Marks."

It was Victoria. "Daniel, Detective Franko just called."

Daniel frowned. "Does he have news?"

"Yes." Her voice quavered on the one word. "They've decided, under the circumstances, to exhume James's body."

CHAPTER TWENTY-SEVEN

VICTORIA STOOD, Lucas at her side, and watched as the earth covering her first husband's final resting place was removed, one massive scoop at a time. Dennis Cortner, Jr., stood by, ready to do his part. His tense expression indicated just how badly he despised this proceeding, as well.

But no one present had a choice.

"I shouldn't have gone back to Washington," Lucas said, his voice heavy with regret.

Victoria was numb. Tears had eluded her, as had all other emotion. She wanted to find the person responsible for this travesty and...

She pushed away the thought. Why was this happening now? First, the police attempted to blame a murder on her son. Now this! Was there no decency left in the world?

"We'll get through this, Victoria." Lucas squeezed her arm. "We always do."

That much was true. She turned to the man she loved more than life itself. "I'm tired, Lucas," she admitted for the first time in her life. "I am so tired."

Not once had she ever considered giving up, but, just now, as she watched the lid being lifted from the vault containing her husband's casket, she felt defeated.

Completely defeated. As if Leberman had some-how won.

She thought of her son and all that he'd suffered. How could God allow yet another injury to this family?

From the corner of her eye she saw a man moving across the well-manicured landscape of Rosehill Cemetery. She squinted to make out his identity.

Daniel Marks.

She wondered vaguely where Emily was.

After the reality of the call she'd received from De-tective Franko had fully penetrated her disbelief, Vic-toria had called Lucas and then, when she'd regained some of her composure, she'd called Daniel. Two hours later, here she stood.

James was dead. Dear God, Lucas had identified his body. Lucas was the only person who had known James almost as well as she had, perhaps even better in some ways. There was absolutely no way Lucas had made a mistake.

James was dead.

The words echoed hollowly inside her.

"Hello, Daniel," she said woodenly. "Is Emily hold-ing up all right?" That was Victoria's first thought. The past few days had been very stressful for Emily, as well. Perhaps that was why she had chosen not to accompany Daniel now.

"Victoria." Daniel smiled at her and then nodded an ackowledgement in Lucas's direction. "Mr. Camp." Then he turned back to Victoria. "Emily is fine. She's at the agency reviewing what Mr. Ruhl discovered re-garding Madelyn Rutland."

The name sent another stab of hurt deep into Victoria's heart. She swallowed back the emotion that immediately rose into her throat. "Simon will take good care of her. He's one of my top investigators."

Daniel nodded. Victoria felt certain she'd offered Simon's support before. Everything was out of control. She felt as if she were floating freely on a vast ocean, with no way to guide herself or determine her own destiny.

"I didn't bring you up to speed on the phone, considering what you'd just learned regarding this," Daniel explained, with a look to the ongoing work.

The exhumation. Victoria stared at the somber activity a moment before turning back to Daniel. "Have you learned something new?"

The uneasy set of his shoulders answered the question before he spoke. "Someone took a couple of shots at my SUV as we left the funeral home."

"Did you get a make on the car?" Lucas asked, his expression turning flinty with a new kind of fury. He hated this as much as Victoria did.

"Unfortunately not."

Daniel hesitated a moment as the crane lowered back into the grave. Victoria felt her chest tighten. This time, it would come back up with the casket in tow.

"Whoever took those shots," he said, returning his attention to her and Lucas, "had taken up a position in the woods. Like a sniper."

Victoria squeezed her eyes shut a moment. This couldn't be Chicago PD. She refused to believe any member of that esteemed force would stoop to such means, even for revenge.

She opened her eyes and leveled her gaze on Daniel. "Do you have any reason at all to believe local law enforcement is involved with what happened at Carter's home or this shooting? I assume no one was hit. Could this have been nothing more than another warning?"

"That's possible," Daniel offered. "But, like you, I find it difficult to believe that the folks in local law enforcement would go to these extremes. The Colby Agency's relationship with them has been too strong for too long for it to fall apart so completely so quickly."

Victoria agreed. She understood that losing one of their own had caused this rift and had made everyone antsy, but she couldn't see any of them going this far.

"It's time I stepped in, Victoria," Lucas said in no uncertain terms. "This needs to be finished."

Victoria knew all too well that Lucas had resources far beyond hers, but he also had a thousand ways to cover that which proved too unsavory or too inflammatory.

No, she could not allow him to finish this.

She turned her face up to her husband's and hoped he would understand. "Lucas, I have to finish this without you. I'm sorry if you don't understand, but that's the way it has to be."

Lucas sighed heavily. "Very well." He held her hand tightly in his own. "But be warned, I'm not letting you go through much more of this."

His words lit a tiny flame in her heart, chased away just a little of the chill that had descended upon her days ago. Thank God for him. She surely could not survive this without him.

The crane strained and creaked as the mahogany casket she had chosen for James was hefted into the air. Victoria's breath hissed out of her lungs as it was lowered to the ground next to the ripped-open grave.

As much as this task pained her, she would be glad to be finished with it. Maybe then Chicago PD would understand that someone was attempting to frame the Colby Agency.

And she'd thought her worries had ended with Leberman and his evil mercenaries.

No such luck.

Instinctively, she moved closer. Lucas moved with her, as did Daniel Marks.

She remembered well the suit she had selected for her first husband's burial. The tie that had been his favorite. Flashes of memory from that long-ago day flickered one after the other through her mind. The agony. The overwhelming feeling of nothingness.

Lucas had been there for her then, as well. He'd been her buoy in the storm, her one sure thing in this uncertain life. She held on tightly to his arm now as she had then.

As she stepped past the end of the open grave, something shiny winked at her. She hesitated, looked through the clumps of dirt scattered about. Then she saw it.

Gold glinting beneath the sun's glare.

Her wedding band.

Her heart surged into her throat.

She bent down and retrieved it.

Victoria remembered having tucked it into the earth near her husband's headstone a year ago…the day she'd made the final decision to move on with her life and put the past behind her.

"Open it."

The command jerked her attention back to the casket and those gathered around it. Detective Franko had just ordered Mr. Cortner to open the casket.

Victoria held her breath, clung to Lucas as Mr. Cortner performed his grim duty and then stepped back.

Franko moved forward and lifted the lid.

As he stared into the open casket, his face darkened with something like rage. "What the hell is this?"

Instinct driving her, Victoria rushed forward.

She stared into the casket, recognized the blue silk lining.

But James Colby's body was not inside.

CHAPTER TWENTY-EIGHT

TASHA SAT NEXT to her husband, holding his hand.

"You understand, Jim," the therapist said, "that this procedure might very well unleash more of those demons you've worked so hard to drive away?"

"I understand."

Tears welled in Tasha's eyes. She wished she could be as strong as her husband. He totally amazed her, made her love him all the more.

"I'm going to give you something to make you relax," Dr. Cost, his primary therapist, said. "We'll begin in a few minutes."

Tasha held her breath as the needle was introduced into Jim's arm and the sedative it contained unleashed.

She prayed this procedure would not send him hurtling back into the past, back into the only place he'd had to hide. She closed her eyes and told herself to be strong. If he could do this, so could she.

"I'll be fine."

Her eyes opened to find her husband watching her, concern marring the features of the face she had come to love. "I know," she said, her voice shakier than she would have liked. Here he was taking the risk and he was worried about her. "We'll both be fine."

"Now, close your eyes, Jim, and relax."

She shifted her gaze to the doctor as he stood.

He patted her shoulder. "I'll be back in a few minutes, Tasha. Let's give him a few minutes to settle down."

She managed a strained smile and nodded her understanding.

Tasha sat very still, careful not to make a sound that would disturb Jim.

She allowed her eyes to soak in the rough-hewn yet handsome features she loved so dearly. The scar that marred his jaw. The years of physical abuse had left their mark, each scar telling a tale of survival. He'd shared so much with her, made her all the more certain what a very special man Jim Colby was.

It wasn't fair that he had to go through yet another ordeal. Hadn't he been through enough?

Working hard to control her breathing, as well as to hold back the tears crowding into her throat, she focused on the brighter side.

They were going to have a baby. She still hadn't told Jim, for fear the added pressure would make things worse for him. She hadn't told anyone. And she wanted to so badly. She wanted to shout that news to the rooftops!

Victoria needed something to hang on to just now, as well, but Tasha couldn't tell her future mother-in-law until she'd told the baby's father.

Jim deserved to know first.

His respiration grew slow and even and she watched his chest rise and fall rhythmically. She loved the feel of his intensely muscular body. His harsh physical treatment in his former life as Seth had chiseled a form that would make any woman look twice. Jim was stronger than most and built like a male model who'd taken up bodybuilding as a hobby. The sandy colored hair and incredible blue eyes were just icing on the cake.

Tasha prayed their baby would look just like his father. Or *her* father, she amended. The baby could be a girl.

She pressed her hand to her tummy and smiled. In a few months, everyone would know she was pregnant. She needed Jim completely well before then. She needed this to be over so they could start focusing on their baby.

There was so much to do.

A nursery. She'd secretly been clearing out the guest room for that very purpose. But there were so many decisions to be made. Colors. Furniture. And a dozen other little details she couldn't even begin to imagine.

This would be the most important event in their lives. If they were lucky, they might even have another child in a couple of years. A little brother or sister for this baby.

So many decisions. She didn't want to make a single one without Jim's input. He deserved to be just as much a part of this as she was.

But first, they had to get this ugly business behind them.

Whether he ever remembered what happened that night or not, she would never believe that her husband had harmed anyone.

He was the sweetest, gentlest man she had ever known.

She swallowed hard. But Seth, well, that was another matter.

Seth killed without thought.

She squeezed her eyes shut once more. *Please don't let Seth have done anything Jim will have to pay for.*

The door opened and Dr. Cost returned.

"Ready, Jim?"

"Mmm-hmm," he said without opening his eyes.

Tasha took a deep breath and looked up at the doctor. "I guess I'm ready, too."

"Very well. Then we'll begin."

Dr. Cost first introduced a second, more powerful drug into the IV. Then he mentally walked Jim through the hypnosis procedure, taking him back in time to one month ago.

Tasha felt Jim's hand go slack in hers and she knew the technique was working. She placed his hand on the arm of the chair where he sat and then wrung her own in her lap to wait this thing out.

His eyes closed and his body seemingly completely relaxed, Jim answered each question Dr. Cost asked. His voice sounded normal which allowed Tasha to relax a little, too.

Then the doctor guided him back to the night Carter Hastings was murdered.

"What made you go out that night, Jim?"

"A phone call."

Tasha frowned. What call? She would need to mention that to Victoria. Surely someone at the agency, certainly with Homicide, had already checked their phone lines, cellular included, for unidentified calls.

"Who made the call?"

Jim jerked.

Tasha's breath caught.

"I…I don't know." Jim's voice was taut now, and his respiration had grown choppy.

"There's no need to become agitated, Jim," Dr. Cost said calmly. "We're looking at events that have already happened. There is no need to be concerned or fearful. Nothing about that night can hurt you now."

Jim's eyes opened and he turned his head in the direction of the doctor's voice. "Do I look afraid?"

Tasha's heart stalled in her chest.

Seth.

She didn't dare move. Didn't dare speak.

"Actually," Dr. Cost said in that same calm monotone, "no, you don't look afraid at all. Why don't you tell me what you saw that night? We both know you were there."

A low bark of laughter erupted from his throat, sending shivers over Tasha's skin.

"I wasn't there, *he* was."

"I see," Dr. Cost said. "Then perhaps you can tell me what he saw there."

One corner of his mouth lifted in a smirk. "He saw more than he wanted to, that's for damned sure."

"I take it you don't know what he saw," Cost suggested.

Jim's hand snaked out and grabbed the doctor by the shirtfront and jerked him close.

Tasha prepared to jump in if necessary. Her heart slammed so hard against her breastbone that she could hardly breathe.

"That pig got capped and then little Jimmy lost it because he's a coward."

Despite the awkward position, neither Cost's facial expression nor his voice changed in the slightest. "Was it you who killed that detective?"

Jim—not Jim, Tasha reminded, Seth—laughed that unholy sound again. "Can't say that it was," he said silkily. "If you want to know who did, ask the coward.

He witnessed it, not me. I just paid him a little visit afterward since he was too screwed up to hold it together."

He released Dr. Cost. The doctor, being careful not to make any sudden moves, took his time relaxing into his chair once more. Tasha stood down from her battle-ready posture.

"I'm still confused," Cost prompted. "If you weren't there, how do you know *he* didn't harm that detective?"

Seth smiled that killer smile that both drew Tasha and scared her to death. "Because he doesn't have the guts," he snarled. "And he wasn't alone."

Adrenaline rushed through Tasha's veins.

Someone else was there the night Detective Carter Hastings was murdered? Someone Jim saw?

The real killer.

CHAPTER TWENTY-NINE

EMILY SAT ON THE EDGE of the mattress, too exhausted to care that she'd already spent one night alone in this hotel room with Daniel Marks. Going two for two wasn't a good idea, but she didn't have the wherewithal to move forward with some other plan.

Being alone was out of the question.

She watched Daniel pace the room as he spoke with Lucas Camp. Victoria was evidently too distraught to participate in the discussion.

Emily thought of the woman she'd met at her father's funeral and then at the Colby Agency. Strength was the primary outstanding trait she had noted about the woman.

But how could anyone be expected to experience what Victoria had in the past few days and go about her business unscathed?

Her first husband's remains were missing. The casket had been empty except for three bags of sand.

Emily closed her eyes and tried to catch her breath. For days now, she'd felt breathless, as if her heart couldn't keep up with the needs of her body.

She was so tired. So confused.

What did James Colby and Madelyn Rutland have to do with her father's murder?

What if she was chasing all over Chicago with Daniel Marks for nothing?

But then, weren't Detective Franko and Chicago PD doing the same thing?

Apparently Franko considered the Colby connection a viable one. She couldn't be sure about Madelyn, since she hadn't broached that subject with the detective. She'd felt as if he considered her one of the enemy from the first time they met.

That was something else she didn't understand. Was the extreme suspicion and the whole don't-trust-anyone attitude a part of this kind of investigation? Both Victoria and Daniel had warned her that when law enforcement lost one of their own, it changed everything.

Maybe inheriting her father's home and his life insurance made her a suspect, as well. They needn't worry. She wasn't interested in any of that. She wanted justice for her father. Solving his murder was part of his final affairs, as far as Emily was concerned. She had to see this through.

Since Chicago PD wouldn't let her in, she had no choice but to work with the Colby Agency and Daniel.

Her gaze settled on him. She tried to pay attention to his end of the conversation, but she just didn't have the energy to follow it.

Daniel. She still didn't know that much about him, but somehow, in the past seventy-two hours or so, he had become far too important to her.

If she'd had any doubts, lying in this room in the dark with him last night had confirmed her feelings.

No use lying to herself. She had lain here last night and wished she had someone to lean on. Someone like the man Daniel Marks appeared to be. After the fire, she'd felt so alone, more so than ever before.

It would have felt so good to have his strong arms around her, to lose herself in the pleasure his body could no doubt offer hers.

How long had it been since she'd been with a man? Ages. She'd dated occasionally, usually one of those dates a friend or coworker hatched up. Nothing had ever come of it and as soon as the guy had figured out she wasn't into casual sex, well, that had been that.

Watching Daniel now, his jacket long since discarded and his shirt unbuttoned to the middle of his chest, she started to feel abstinence was seriously overrated.

She had no one here. No friends, not really. Sure, there were people she knew from her life as a kid, but most of those were her father's buddies. Her mother couldn't be here for her.

And, God, someone had shot at her today.

She shuddered as she thought of the fire and then the glass shattering in Daniel's vehicle.

The nice folks at the Colby Agency had offered food and drink this afternoon to keep her entertained after Daniel had left her there to join Victoria at the cemetery.

Her heart fluttered as she thought of the way he'd looked when he left. It had been obvious that he didn't want to leave her, but duty had called.

That he appeared to care affected her more than it should have, but she supposed that was to be expected considering she'd been alone, in that man-woman sense, for so long.

He closed his cell phone and turned to face her. "More dead ends."

Couldn't they get a single break? "What now?"

"Mr. Cortner has no explanation for the missing body."

"He was just a kid," she offered, with no idea why she would even waste her time coming up with excuses for him. "We saw how easy it would be for someone to make an unauthorized entry."

"That's true." He rubbed the back of his neck, looked damned exhausted himself. "But you would think that someone would have noticed in the time it surely took to remove Colby's body and put bags of sand in its place."

Emily hadn't thought of that.

"Should we start tracking down the deceased Mr. Cortner's former assistants?"

"Maybe." Daniel picked up the bottle of water he'd abandoned on the table minutes before and took a long, deep drink.

Emily glanced at the barely touched pizza box. Neither of them had had much of an appetite.

Daniel set his bottle aside once more and walked over to sit down beside her.

Her instincts went on alert. Was there more?

"Jim Colby underwent the regression therapy," he said quietly.

Her breath stalled in her chest. "Did they learn anything?"

Daniel settled his gaze on hers. "Jim was there, but he wasn't alone and the therapist is convinced he did not pull the trigger."

Anticipation kicked aside the exhaustion she'd thought would never go away. "Did he see the other person?"

"Apparently they couldn't reach that part. But they'll keep trying."

Her hopes fell. "So we're right back where we started, basically."

He sighed. "Basically."

She shoved a hand through her hair and tried her level best not to let her frustration show. "I'm beginning to think there's no way to unravel this. We just don't have anything to go on. There's nothing to find."

"Look." He took her hand in his and waited for her to meet his gaze. "The police are working all the usual angles, but there's one they haven't considered."

"The Madelyn angle," Emily offered, not so impressed by that piece of investigative work. Madelyn was supposed to be dead.

"I know what you're thinking," he teased. "She's dead, right? Like James Colby."

Realization dawned on her. "Do you think the two of them somehow fooled everyone? That maybe James Colby is alive and well and living it up with his mistress Madelyn?"

Daniel shrugged, but she saw the hint of a smile at the corners of his mouth. "I don't know if I would go that far, but your father kept those letters for some reason. Maybe he knew something and intended to keep them as some sort of proof."

Talk about far-fetched. "But why would one or both come back now and kill my father? What was the motivation?" She'd learned a thing or two in the past few days.

"That I can't answer, but every instinct is screaming at me to follow that lead." He stroked her palm with the pad of his thumb before letting her hand go. "I learned a long time ago that everything happens for a reason. Your father had a reason for keeping the letters. Now, maybe someone has a reason to want to keep what they stand for a secret."

Her brows pulled together into a vee. "But he'd kept their secret all these years. Why kill him now?"

"More questions I can't answer." The smile laid full claim to his mouth now, and the sight lifted her spirits considerably. "But I can tell you that someone doesn't want us doing what we're doing. And if you think about it, what we've been doing is looking into Madelyn Rutland and her connection to your father and James Colby."

He was right about that.

"Whoever set that fire, whoever shot at us, intends to force us to back off," she deduced. Her gaze collided with his. "Madelyn or James Colby himself are the only viable possibilities."

"But they're both dead," he challenged, giving her the same as she gave him.

She was the one smiling this time. "But we don't have a body for either, so who's to say?"

"And that," he nodded, "is why we're going to follow that line of thinking."

At last, their investigation had true purpose. Or maybe she just wanted to believe it did.

Whatever the case, right now she simply enjoyed being here. Sitting so close to Daniel and having him look at her as if he wanted to touch her as much as she wanted to touch him. It was silly, she knew, but she just couldn't help herself. She'd been too needy for too long. How could she not have noticed?

As if he'd read her mind, his gaze dropped to her

mouth and she felt herself making that hopeful lean before her good sense could kick in and stop her.

The first brush of his lips startled her even though she'd anticipated it, sent sensations cascading over her like the heated spill of a shower. Her pulse thumped and her body seemed to melt on the spot.

His kiss was gentle, uninvasive, and it went on and on, giving her time to work up the nerve to touch him. Her palm flattened against his chest, molded to the wonderful contours. He felt so good, so strong. And she needed that strength right now more than she needed her next breath.

The fingers of his right hand slid into her hair and his kiss turned more possessive. His tongue traced the seam of her lips and excitement bombarded her. She opened for him, allowed him full access. Her tongue touched his and she felt a tiny explosion of desire.

Her arms went around his neck and she pressed fully against him. She moaned, uncertain she could bear to feel him against her this way, but she couldn't draw away...couldn't let go.

He drew back abruptly, pressed his forehead against hers. "I seem to have gotten a little carried away," he whispered, his ragged breath fanning her lips, making her shiver.

"Me, too" was all she could manage. She straightened, putting a little distance between them, but her hands couldn't seem to make the transition. She needed that connection, the feel of his warm body.

"I don't want to take advantage of the situation, Emily," he murmured, "but I'd like nothing better than to make love to you right now, tonight. But I won't."

Disappointment flared briefly before common sense

took over. "You're right." She cleared her throat and let her hands fall away from him before quickly wringing them together to make sure they didn't reach for him again. "We should get some sleep."

He nodded. "That's a good idea."

He stood. She watched, struggling with her feelings. She didn't know whether to be mortified or flat-out terrified that this moment would pass and then she would never have the chance to know him that way again.

"Daniel, I—"

He turned back to her and she lost her nerve completely.

Okay, don't be a coward, she chastised. She'd come here alone and taken care of her father's final needs. She'd been shot at. She could damn sure do this.

"I agree," she said, pushing past the lump in her throat, "we shouldn't be too hasty. Shouldn't do anything we might regret later. But…"

She took a deep, bolstering breath. His watching her so intently, waiting for her to continue, almost proved to be too much.

"I need you tonight. Not to make love," Emily hastened to add, though she wasn't so sure she would have said no if he'd been willing. "Could you just hold me? At least until I fall asleep?"

Daniel didn't force her to explain further. Instead, he removed his shirt, kicked off his shoes and moved onto the bed with her. His arms went around her and he held her that way, entertained her with stories about his past life in the military until she fell asleep.

For the first time in days, she slept soundly…like the dead.

CHAPTER THIRTY

DANIEL LEANED FORWARD in his chair, braced his forearms on his spread knees and watched Emily sleep. He should wake her, but he couldn't bring himself to disturb her. She looked so peaceful and innocent.

Holding her last night without taking it further had required every ounce of self-discipline he could muster. He'd managed, but only by the slimmest of margins.

His years in the military had taught him that a man could do without most anything for a time. Food, water, sleep. Each essential carried its limits, as did each man.

He'd almost reached his last night.

Even now, the way her silky hair splayed around her made him yearn to touch it, to feel the softness of it sliding through his fingers. Not once in his life had he wanted so desperately to protect someone…to possess someone as his own.

In his former career, he'd protected his teammates, he'd served his country, risked his life for those very loyalties. But this was different. This need went so deep he wasn't sure where it came from or if it had always been a part of him, waiting to be awakened by the right woman.

The intensity of the yearning went beyond the need

to protect, he reasoned. He wanted to have her, to possess her in every sense of the word.

He shoved his hand through his hair and leaned back in a futile attempt to relax, to shift his attention to anything else.

It was not going to happen.

He'd gotten basically nowhere on this case. Not that his growing preoccupation with his unexpected partner was actually to blame. Personal feelings weren't supposed to enter into the scenario. He knew the rules better than anyone. The army had regulations governing every aspect of a soldier's personal, as well as professional, life.

Somehow he hadn't seen this coming.

He inclined his head and studied the sleeping woman who made him ache to kiss her again.

Nope, this unexpected attraction had definitely sneaked up on him.

For a guy who'd spent most of his adult life outmaneuvering the enemy, he'd damned sure fallen down on the job on this one.

But was it such a bad thing? Emily definitely wasn't the enemy.

And hadn't he decided that he was ready to consider settling down? Buy a house? Start a family?

He laughed softly at that. Talk about letting one's imagination run away. Wasn't the other half of a relationship supposed to be involved in the decision-making?

"I hope it's not me you find so amusing?"

Daniel's gaze settled on wide hazel eyes. "I didn't mean to wake you." He stood. "Would you like to order room service?" He hitched his thumb in the direction of the coffeemaker. "There's coffee. I just made a fresh pot."

She sat up, pushed the covers back and stood. She stretched, making his mouth go intensely dry.

"Thanks," she said on a sigh. "Coffee sounds great."

As she moved across the room, he couldn't help admiring the way her hips swayed ever so slightly. She'd slept in her clothes, but the wrinkles or the disheveled condition of her blouse failed to detract from how feminine she looked.

She moaned as her first sip of coffee slid down her throat. "This is great." She smiled in his direction. "Did you learn to do this in the 3?"

He'd told her a little about himself last night, hadn't been able to hold back. He'd even told her the story about the scar. She'd hesitated at first, but then she'd traced the mark and the rest had been whispers shared between them. She'd learned that he'd had a few close encounters with the enemy on military maneuvers and he'd learned that the very idea of him being hurt had taken her breath away.

That realization had changed something inside him, something he couldn't name. So he'd talked, she'd talked, until she'd fallen asleep. Unfortunately, he hadn't been so lucky. Hours had passed before he'd been able to relax enough to get any sleep at all.

"You learn pretty quick how to make a decent pot of coffee when you spend endless days and weeks in the middle of nowhere with nothing but a tent and a sleeping bag to call home," he said in answer to her question.

"I think I'll jump in the shower."

He managed a smile but what he really wanted to do was follow her. Climb into that shower and run his hands over every square inch of that soft skin.

Time for another cup of coffee. But he doubted even a heavy dose of caffeine was going to do anything for his current condition. He needed to hold her and have her tell him again the story of each and every one of those charms on the bracelet she wore. To feel her body close to his.

Somehow he had to slow this down.

EMILY SHUT AND LOCKED the door. She closed her eyes and sagged against the too-thin divider. What in the world had she been thinking last night? How could she have asked him to hold her like that? He probably thought she was pathetic.

Frustration whooshed out of her and she forced her eyes open. Okay, he was a nice guy. Very handsome. But this whole situation was temporary. Pretty soon, she would be going back to California and he would move on with his life. He would likely be taking a permanent position with the Colby Agency.

Falling in love with him—she recognized this path for what it was—would be a huge mistake.

She was here to see that her father's murder was solved, not to get involved with a man she barely knew.

Then she pushed off the door.

That's what happened when a girl let her social life go. She lost her head over the first nice guy who paid her the least bit of attention.

Once the shower was running, she took care of essentials and stripped off her wrinkled clothes. She climbed into the shower and sighed at the feel of the hot water raining down on her. It felt heavenly.

As she smoothed the soap over her skin, she thought

of Daniel's arms around her, his hands on her body. A blast of internal heat went through her at the memory of him spooned closely behind her as they slept.

She had awakened only once during the night and she'd felt completely safe for the first time in a very long time. How was it she could feel so secure with a virtual stranger when she hadn't felt that way in more years than she could remember…not since her mother had taken her away from her father and away from the only life she'd ever known.

Emily's fingers stilled in the work of washing her hair. How had she so thoroughly blocked all those lonely memories? She'd missed her father so badly, had needed him, especially after losing her brother. But her mother had insisted on behaving as if their whole life had never happened, had only begun after they'd moved to California.

As the water poured over her, washing away the shampoo, Emily felt herself start to shake, felt the sobs rise up inside her so hard she couldn't hope to hold them back. And then the tears came. Hard and fast. She couldn't stop crying, couldn't stop shaking.

Sliding down the tiled wall, she didn't hold back; she let the emotions take control. This had been a long time in coming.

Her father was gone. Murdered. He wouldn't be coming back. Even though they'd been apart all these years, somehow she'd found comfort in knowing that he was still here, at home. But now she would never feel that again. That past her mother had been hiding from all these years was finally gone for good.

The water had turned cold by the time her tears had

given out. Feeling weak but relieved to some extent, Emily climbed out of the shower and toweled dry.

She started at the light rap on the door. She wrapped the towel around her, unlocked and opened the door just far enough to see Daniel standing on the other side.

"Yes?" Her voice sounded rusty. She cleared her throat.

"I thought you could use this." He held out a hand towel full of ice. "Take your time," he said knowing. "I have a few calls to make."

Emily closed the door and braced herself against it once more for support. At every turn, he proved what a thoughtful guy he was. He'd heard her crying and offered ice for her eyes. She had to keep reminding herself of her cynical mother's favorite adage: if something seems too good to be true, it probably is.

How had this unlikely alliance gotten so confusing, so out-of-bounds?

Just another mystery she wasn't sure she could solve.

Abruptly feeling guilty for oversleeping and then taking so long in the shower, she made quick work of drying her hair and making her face presentable. Good thing she carried a few cosmetics in her purse. She looked a fright after her long cry, but she felt better for having let her emotions out.

Felt ready to move forward.

With that in mind, she went in search of her partner. There were answers she needed and she wasn't going to get them loitering around this hotel room alternately swooning over her partner and crying for the father she'd lost more than a decade ago. Her father would want her to be strong. She would do this for him.

"Where do we go from here?" she asked when Daniel looked up from the notes he'd been making.

He smiled and she felt her heart soften, but her determination never faltered.

"I have a plan."

Emily sat down across the table from him. "Tell me," she urged. For the first time since they'd met, she could feel his energy. He was on to something.

"From the moment your father died, his death has kept pointing us back to the past…to the Colbys and to his former partner." He glanced at the notes he'd made and ticked off the items. "The letters, Jim's prints at the scene and then his father's prints after the fire. If you'll think back, the trouble didn't start until we dug more deeply into the Madelyn aspect of that past."

"But Madelyn's supposed to be dead," she reminded. They'd had this discussion last night.

"Right. And, as we know, so is James Colby. Yet we have no bodies. We actually have nothing. It's as if someone killed your father and succeeded in making it impossible to solve the crime. The perfect murder. No evidence, no motive, no nothing. But there has to be motive. No crime is ever committed without a reason. Chicago PD, as well as your father's own current partner, is convinced that the event had nothing to do with a past or ongoing case. That leaves personal. We have to assume this was personal."

She was with him so far. "Madelyn."

"Or someone who wants us to believe it's Madelyn."

"Victoria Colby-Camp?" she suggested, knowing that wasn't the case.

Daniel flashed her a look that said touché. "I'm certain the police would like to believe that. But where is her motive? She didn't know about the supposed affair until you gave her the letters *after* your father's murder."

"And there's no reason to suspect that Jim knew my father," she put in.

"Bottom line," Daniel said flatly, "we don't have a clue who the hell killed your father. We can only assume it's the same person trying to stop our investigation into the past."

"Agreed."

"Since we don't know who or why, we have no choice but to attempt to lure him or her into a trap. We need to force the killer to act."

"Lay some bait," Emily suggested, her heart kicking into a faster rhythm. "Draw him or her out into the open."

"Or, at least, to me."

"To us," she corrected pointedly. She ignored his skeptical look. "How do we do that?"

"Whoever took those shots at us yesterday knew we would be going to the funeral home. He was lying in wait."

Emily nodded. "The only way he, or she, could have known that was to have listened in on our conversation somehow. No one else knew except Victoria and Mr. Cortner."

"Correct. So we lay our trap via the same means. We put through the calls and hope for the desired results."

It sounded like a long shot to Emily, but they had to do something. They had absolutely nothing to move forward on except this one hunch.

"There's one thing," Daniel said, his gaze settling heavily onto hers. "For some reason, Jim Colby was there the night your father died. I think we need him in on this and that puts a volatile spin on the mix. I think you should stay clear of this part. He may be even more unstable after the regression procedure."

She was shaking her head before he completed his sentence. "No way. He was my father. I'm not backing off. I want to be there."

Daniel held her gaze for several beats before relenting. "All right, but if things get too dicey, I want you out. You might feel you owe this to your father, but I would be willing to bet most anything that he would not want you to wager your life for the sake of this investigation."

She couldn't argue that point.

"Let's do it," she told him, accepting his condition.

And just like that, Daniel set the plan in motion.

He called Victoria and made the arrangements, using his cellular phone.

Then Emily called Norton, her father's partner, and told him as much about the plan as she dared. Time and place, but not much else. It wasn't that she didn't trust him, but they had to cover all the bases.

Then, just to make sure they hadn't missed a trick, Daniel called Victoria back using the hotel phone and related a minor change in plan.

Now all they had to do was wait for the appointed time.

And hope like hell that this desperate plan would work.

CHAPTER THIRTY-ONE

DANIEL HAD NOT officially met James Colby, Jr., until about half an hour ago. Daniel glanced at his passenger. He had to admit he was impressed.

Victoria had insisted on going over Jim's history with Daniel once more before she agreed to this plan. For a man who'd been through the kind of hell few could even imagine, much less claim to have experienced, Jim Colby was far more reserved than Daniel had expected.

The guy was smart, observant and looked strong as hell. One would never suspect he'd been mentally and physically abused for most of his life. He was quiet and yet he exuded an energy that left no question as to his keen awareness.

Daniel checked on Emily via the rearview mirror of the car he'd rented before turning his attention back to the street. She'd finally given in to the grief this morning. Allowing her emotions to overflow had given her even more determination to see this through. Daniel would have preferred she not come along on this part but there had been no dissuading her.

Victoria had finally allowed Lucas to get involved. He and three of Victoria's investigators, as well as Tasha North, Jim's fiancé, were already in place in the vicin-

ity of the alley and warehouse where Carter Hastings
had been murdered.

Jim's therapist was to meet them at the warehouse,
supposedly for another round of controlled regression
therapy in hopes of learning more about that night.

In truth, the therapist would only be there in the event
Jim regressed on his own and became unmanageable.
It was the only way Victoria would agree to Jim's participation. The supposed regression session was part of
the bait they had laid.

Daniel saw this plan for what it was, a last-ditch effort
to pull a rabbit out of a hat. They had no clues, no nothing. They needed to force a move. It was the only way.

"You're going the wrong way."

Daniel cut Jim Colby a questioning look, but gave
him the benefit of the doubt. "Perhaps you're thinking
of an alternate route." He braked for a traffic light that
changed to red.

"No," Jim countered, an edge in his tone, "you're
going the wrong way."

Daniel met his gaze and when he did, he knew he'd
just come face-to-face with Jim's alter ego.

Seth.

The quiet, reserved man Daniel had sized up with
such approval was gone. In his place was the ruthless
sort who would shoot first and ask questions later—if
he bothered to ask at all. The lethal look in his eyes
spoke of one thing only—absolutely no fear.

"I know what you're looking for," Jim or Seth said me-
nacingly. "There's only one way you're going to find it."

Daniel let off the brake and rolled forward before
turning his attention back to the street. "How's that?"

"Do exactly as I tell you."

As those icy words split the tension-filled air between them, Daniel was damned glad he was armed. The situation had just moved into an unstable zone over which his only control would be in swift reactions.

Emily held her breath as she waited for Daniel to respond to Jim Colby's ultimatum. She tried to swallow back the lump of fear swelling in her throat, but that wasn't happening.

What was going on here? Was this total about-face the reason her father's partner had called Jim Colby mentally unstable?

Was he a danger to Daniel? To her?

A new surge of fear plunged through her, making her shake so hard she could scarcely gulp air into her lungs.

Could this man be the one who murdered her father? Were all of Daniel's efforts—all of her efforts—pointless? Had Chicago PD had the right guy all along?

She had to know.

Summoning every iota of courage she possessed, she loosened her seat belt and leaned forward. "Excuse me," she said, her gaze fixed on the man in the front passenger seat.

He turned to look at her, the movement so slow, so deliberate, that every instinct urged her to take back the words.

When those icy blue eyes stared into hers, she asked, "Can you tell me who killed my father?"

His lips curled into a derisive smile. "I can do better than that."

Her heart climbed into her throat during the pause before he continued.

"I can show you."

"Which way?"

Daniel's demand was sharp. Colby's attention shifted to him, as did Emily's.

"Just keep going," Colby snapped. "I'll tell you when to deviate from your current course."

Jim Colby turned back to Emily once more and smiled, a sinister gesture that was no smile at all. "Aren't field trips fun?"

Emily leaned back into her seat, tried her best not to let him see how very much he terrified her. That was his intent, she felt certain. She had to be strong. If Daniel saw how scared she was he would surely insist on taking her back to the agency to wait this out.

She couldn't do that. Her father was the one who'd been murdered. She had a right to be here.

Jim Colby directed Daniel to a modest neighborhood well out of town on the south side. Emily studied the area, tried to recall if she'd ever been here before.

It had started to rain and the overcast sky made it feel like dusk when night was still hours away. The perfect weather for cornering a killer.

She shuddered.

"Are you all right?"

She looked up to find Daniel watching her in the rearview mirror. Jim Colby's attention appeared to be riveted to the house across the street from where they had parked.

Emily nodded. She didn't trust her voice enough to make a verbal response. The last thing she needed was for Daniel to get wind of just how shaken she was.

"Let's go."

Both Emily's and Daniel's attention swung to the man who'd spoken and who had already opened his door.

"Hold on," Daniel said firmly. "Whose house is this? We need to inform Lucas of our change in plans before we proceed."

Jim Colby made a sound in his throat, a laugh that wasn't a laugh at all. Emily shivered before she could steel herself. She had to pull it together. They'd come too far for her to screw it up now. This could be the moment she'd waited for.

"We don't need that old man to do what we've gotta do," Colby growled.

This time Daniel grabbed Colby by the arm when he started to get out. "Don't play games with me. I asked you whose house this is."

Emily held her breath uncertain which of these two would prove superior if push came to shove.

Colby shook off Daniel's hand. "Don't get all bent out of shape, Marks," he snarled. "I've brought you right where you wanted to be. This—" he glanced at the small craftsman-style cottage "—is where my father, the great James Colby, lives." He turned back to Daniel and flashed one of those lethal grins. "Aren't you just dying to meet him?"

Daniel let go of Jim Colby's arm and met Emily's gaze. She was scared to death. He could see the extreme fear in her eyes. "You should stay in the car." He passed his cell phone to her. "Call Lucas now."

By the time he'd relayed these instructions, Jim was already across the street. He had to move.

"I should go in with you," Emily urged.

"There's no time to argue. Do it!" He shot her a look that he hoped relayed the urgency of his command.

"All right." She reluctantly shifted her focus to the cell phone.

Daniel hurried across the street, one hand beneath his jacket, ready to snag his weapon.

Jim Colby walked straight up to the front door and kicked it in.

Daniel swore. He had to get this guy back under control. Two seconds later, he crossed the threshold to find Colby waiting for him.

"You really shouldn't let a woman slow you down, Marks," he warned. "Distraction can get you killed."

Daniel wrapped his fingers around his weapon and withdrew it from his waistband. "Why are we here?"

"I told you." Jim waved his arms magnanimously. "You're looking for James Colby, right?"

"Your father is dead," Daniel reminded. "Our goal is to nail the person responsible for Carter Hastings's murder."

"Well." Jim set his hands on his hips. "I can tell you two things, Marks."

He moved closer to Daniel. Daniel's fingers tightened on his weapon. The dead last thing he wanted to do was have to disable Victoria's son.

"Dear old Dad didn't kill him, but he's the reason Hastings is dead."

"No more games and riddles," Daniel cautioned. "Tell me what you know."

Jim motioned for him to follow. "I'll show you."

Daniel took a moment to get his bearings before agreeing. The place was modestly furnished but looked neat and clean. No pictures on the walls. Nothing really that personalized the space.

"Let's go, Marks, before trouble arrives."

Daniel narrowed his gaze, scrutinized Jim Colby's posture and expression. Whatever the hell he was up to, there was no reading his intent.

Daniel followed him into the small kitchen.

Jim pointed to a door. "We have to go down there." He smirked. "Are you afraid of damp dark places, Marks?"

"Why don't you lead the way?" Daniel suggested impatiently.

"No problem." Jim reached for the door. "I'm right at home in places nightmares are made of."

Daniel knew he wasn't exaggerating.

The stairs that led downward were narrow and steep. About halfway down, Colby flipped a switch and a dim light filled the cavernous space.

Daniel assessed the situation in one cautious sweep of his gaze. As lacking in personal touches as the upstairs had been, the basement walls were lined with photographs and framed newspaper articles. Every square inch was covered with memorabilia except a small section of the far wall where drapes hung.

Unlit candles sat all around the room on every available surface. A single chair, overstuffed and upholstered, dominated the center of the space. A table with reading lamp sat next to it.

"This—" Jim Colby turned all the way around in the middle of the room "—is all for him."

As Daniel moved deeper into the space, he recognized the face in the photographs. Literally hundreds of pictures of James Colby were plastered on the walls. The newspaper articles were all ones touting the latest about him or his missing child.

As Daniel's instincts roared with warning, he watched an abrupt metamorphosis take place in Jim. The cocky attitude was replaced with fear and uncertainty.

The weaker emotions quickly turned to rage and that cocky alter ego reappeared. "Some people just don't know when to admit the game is over."

Daniel tensed as Colby strode straight over to him. "Ready for the finale?" he asked in a cruel, taunting tone. "You won't believe your eyes."

He led Daniel to the far side of the room and then whipped back the drapes covering that section of wall.

Daniel hadn't really expected a window, since the room was beneath ground level, but he definitely hadn't expected what he saw.

A massive chest-style freezer.

Colby pushed up the large lid as if he were raising a car hood, then waved to the interior. "I give you James Colby."

Daniel stared at the clearly dead, perfectly preserved body long enough to acknowledge that it was, in fact, James Colby. The temperature setting on the freezer had been set to ensure no frost formed on the skin.

"Who did this?" Daniel lifted his gaze to Jim Colby's. His eyes had lost their lethal gleam, had turned dull and listless.

"I did."

Daniel whipped around at the sound of the unfamiliar voice.

He recognized the woman midway down the stairs

from the newspaper spreads he and Emily had found on their first day of research. She was decades older, but he would know her anywhere.

Madelyn Rutland.

In the flesh.

And she wasn't dead or deep frozen.

"You understand what you've done here is against the law," Daniel said calmly. The last thing he wanted to do was antagonize her, considering the barrel of her handgun was aimed directly at him. But he had to say something.

"He belongs to me," she snarled, then moved down a few more steps. "I won't allow anyone to take him from me."

The picture cleared instantly for Daniel. "You love him," he suggested.

"More than life itself. I won't let you take him."

"That's why you gave up your life," Daniel went on, "to be with him."

"That's right." She descended the final step. "He was mine. I couldn't let her keep him from me, so I took him." She shrugged. "It was easy enough. Security isn't always what it should be."

He understood she meant the security at the funeral home.

"Hiring a street bum to do the heavy lifting was even simpler. Tying up that loose end was like taking out the city's trash. No one ever misses the trash."

Daniel resisted the impulse to tell her that murder was a crime no matter the identity or social standing of the victim. But then, she'd once been a homicide cop. She already knew all that.

"What's the matter, Mr. Marks? Overwhelmed?" she jeered.

He gave her a little shrug. "I guess I'm just confused as to why you would tip off the police that you had James Colby's body? Why use his prints the way you did?" There was no question now. She'd left those prints at the Hastings home specifically so they would be found.

"I had no choice." She looked past Daniel to Jim Colby. "I couldn't let the police try to pin Carter's murder on him. I knew James would want to do whatever he could to help his son. It was quite easy, you know. All you need is a transferable surface and you can implicate anyone you want at a crime scene."

"Are you telling me you did this to protect Jim Colby?" That didn't sit right with Daniel and keeping the disbelief out of his tone had been impossible. Daniel dared a glance in Colby's direction. He still stood by the freezer, staring down at his father. If Daniel were lucky, Jim would stay right there until this was done.

Daniel hoped like hell that Lucas was on his way. Otherwise he and Madelyn were just going to have to see who had the fastest trigger finger.

"Of course I did it to protect him. Why else?"

Daniel shook his head. "I'm not swallowing it," he said bluntly. "After all these years, why have Carter Hastings murdered? Did he figure out you were still alive?"

Her lips compressed into a thin line as she evidently weighed whether to answer.

"He saw me." She swore hotly, repeatedly. "I've always been so careful. But I screwed up." She glanced at Jim. "Ever since he's been back, I haven't been able to think straight. I finally had to contact him. I knew his father would want to see him." Her expression took on a look of yearning. "That's all I ever wanted. To make James happy."

"So you killed Carter because he figured out you were alive," Daniel said, snapping her back to the present. He could have taken her out twice already, but he needed answers. Victoria would want answers. So would Emily. The risk of keeping her talking was necessary.

"I killed the bastard because he let me believe he hadn't seen me. Then he started following me. Followed me here one day but didn't confront me. He waited until I'd gone out and then he came in." She glanced back to the freezer. "He found James and threatened to have me put away."

"But you killed him first," Daniel countered.

She smiled, something evil and cruel.

"It was so easy. The stupid bastard had always been a pushover for a sob story. He found out about me and James after—" her gaze went back to the freezer "—after James left his wife. He threatened to report me then, but I cried and made him feel sorry for me." She laughed. "It was just as easy this time. He told me to leave and never come back to Chicago. He would report the house but wouldn't tell anyone it was me who'd lived here."

"He gave you an out," Daniel offered, disgusted by her lack of compassion.

"He was a fool," she snarled. "Didn't he know that I could never leave James? So I killed him. I hadn't expected Jim to follow me. I'd only just managed to get to know him. I couldn't let Carter take him away from me. Or James. A boy should be able to spend time with his father."

"You killed my father."

Madelyn spun around, her aim landing on Emily at the same instant that Daniel's gaze did.

"You and your mother were through with him anyway. What do you care?"

Daniel barely resisted the urge to shoot the woman where she stood. But if he did, would she fire, ultimately hitting Emily?

Emily visibly faltered but didn't break down as Daniel feared she might.

"You're right, Madelyn—I wasn't much of a daughter."

Emily moved down a couple more steps.

"But you were the worst kind of partner. And now everyone will know."

Emily braced on the railing and glared at the woman.

"The police are on the way. You're going to pay for what you've done."

Daniel had no choice now. He made his move. He flung himself at Madelyn's back, slammed into her just as her weapon discharged. She fought him with more strength than he'd expected for a woman of fifty-two. She screamed and ranted. Tried to bite him, but he managed to subdue her.

"Emily!" He risked a glance toward the stairs. "You okay?"

She was running toward him. "We have to tie her up!"

Daniel had to smile at her ability to recover. "That would be good."

He watched as Emily ripped the electrical cord from

the lamp and brought it to him. When he'd tied Madelyn up tight, he pulled off one of her shoes and used her sock to gag her. He'd heard enough of her ugly threats. Emily didn't need to hear her hate-filled taunts.

"You called Lucas?" he asked as he stood and took stock of the room once more. Incredible. The woman's obsession was clearly documented.

"He should be here any second." Emily stared down at Madelyn. "But when I saw her get out of her car, I called Norton, too. I knew it was Madelyn."

Emily looked up at Daniel then. "It's over now, isn't it?" She looked ready to crumple.

He went to her, took her into his arms. "Yes, it is."

He held her that way for a while and then he reluctantly drew away. "I need to check on Jim."

She nodded her understanding.

Daniel approached the other man cautiously. "Are you all right?" he asked, uncertain who would greet him, Jim or Seth.

Jim closed the freezer lid and turned to face Daniel. "I finally remember what happened."

Daniel heard footsteps upstairs. Emily was right. It was over. The only question now was where did they go from here?

CHAPTER THIRTY-TWO

SUNDAY MORNING, Daniel knocked at the door of Victoria Colby-Camp's home. The air was brisk, but the sun had finally poked through the clouds.

For two days, it had rained. For those same two days Daniel had worked side by side with Detective Franko as the forensics techs sifted through Madelyn Rutland's lair.

She had lived under an assumed name since faking her death. She'd survived on savings and odd work here and there. In Daniel's opinion, the woman had been a nut of the highest order and should have been institutionalized years ago.

James Colby's body had been turned over to another funeral home for burial. Victoria wasn't trusting his security to Cortner again. Granted, knowing Madelyn Rutland, it wouldn't have mattered who had been in charge of the body all those years ago; she would have found a way to do what she did.

This morning, Daniel had something different to deliver to Victoria. A bit of good news.

She opened the door and managed a weary smile for him. "Good morning, Daniel, please come in."

He returned the smile but declined the generous invitation. "Forgive my hurry, but I have something else I have to do this morning."

Victoria gave him a knowing look. "I understand her flight leaves at noon. I suppose you will have to hurry, won't you?"

"Yes, but this will only take a moment."

Victoria had to be the strongest woman he had ever met. Despite all that life had thrown her way, she held her head high, carried on in spite of the tremendous burdens.

"I could have given you this tomorrow, when I report for my first official day of duty at the Colby Agency," he added with a grin, "but I knew you would want it right away. We only found it this morning and Detective Franko gave me authorization to bring it to you."

Daniel reached into his interior jacket pocket and removed the envelope. "This was found along with a number of other things belonging to James, all of which will eventually make their way to you."

Victoria accepted the envelope, looking confused and yet somehow ever hopeful. She gasped when she read her name on the front. But Daniel knew it wasn't her name that startled her; it was the handwriting.

This letter was from her late husband.

"Franko had to open it," Daniel explained when she noted the open flap. "It might have been evidence that needed processing."

She nodded. "I understand."

"Well, I'll leave you to it."

Victoria gifted him with another smile. "Good luck," she said mysteriously.

But there was no real mystery…he knew exactly what he had to do.

Victoria stood very still until Daniel Marks had climbed back into his rented car and driven away. His SUV was still in the shop having the damage from Madelyn's shooting rampage repaired.

Victoria closed the door and went into her private study. Lucas was busy in the kitchen cleaning up after the enormous breakfast he had prepared. She should have invited him to hear what Daniel Marks had come to say, should be sharing this with him right now. But she couldn't.

She had to do this alone.

Comfortable in her favorite chair she reached into the envelope and removed the folded document inside.

The letter was handwritten. From James, addressed to her. Her heart pounded furiously as she read the very first words.

My dearest Victoria…

She couldn't hold back the tears. They crowded into her throat, burned in the backs of her eyes. She blinked rapidly and focused on the page.

For a very long time now, our relationship has been tested. The loss of our beloved son has torn us apart in far too many ways.

I have searched for just the right words to tell you of my mistake. Finally, I believe I can say what must be said.

Victoria's heart stumbled. She had had time to come to terms with James's affair with Madelyn, but somehow she couldn't get past it…couldn't believe he would hurt her that way. She had loved him so very much. To have the worst confirmed in his own handwriting…

During our darkest hour, another woman took my hand and offered me the kind of consolation you could not. Please don't misunderstand me, I don't hold this against you. Like me, you were too overcome with grief to be able to offer anything to anyone else. You know this woman. Her name is Madelyn Rutland, one of the detectives who investigated Jimmy's disappearance.

Victoria turned away, unsure she could read the rest. Tears spilled down her cheeks and she wanted to sob out loud. This…this travesty had marred her life with James, had changed all that she had believed to be true.

Summoning all of her courage, Victoria read on.

Madelyn and I spent many hours together talking and enjoying each other's company for many, many months. She always managed to find a way to take my mind off the pain of losing our son.

Something Victoria hadn't been able to do. She squeezed her eyes shut a moment before continuing.

I know this was wrong. I should have found a way to comfort myself in your arms, but I was a fool. I was weak.

Victoria stopped. Lucas had been right. James had been only a man. One with faults and weaknesses, just like all others. She had them herself. How on earth could she hold this single mistake against the man she had loved so dearly?

She could not.

It didn't matter what James had done. She had loved him unconditionally…still did and always would.

She started to crumple the letter but forced herself to finish it. He'd written these words to her; the least she could do was read them.

I have made two mistakes, my darling. I have hurt you and I have hurt Madelyn. I perhaps allowed her to believe that this relationship was more than mere friend-

ship. For those two errors I will never forgive myself. But, please know that in the end, you were the only one who owned my heart. I could not permit mine and Madelyn's relationship to move beyond that of friends. She was kind to me and I will forever appreciate it. But I will never love anyone the way I love you, Victoria. I hope that you can forgive me for skating dangerously close to making the biggest mistake of my life. Your loving husband, James Colby.

The breath in Victoria's lungs rushed out in a single exhale.

James hadn't cheated on her.

She stared at the date on the letter and saw that he had written it the day he was murdered. Dear God, why hadn't she found it?

Madelyn, she realized. She'd probably found it in James's study when they searched the house after the murder.

Victoria touched the page, traced the elegant, bold lines of her husband's handwriting. How she missed him. She swiped at her tears and smiled. But he would be happy for her. Happy that she had found Jim and happy that she had found love again.

"Is everything all right, Victoria?"

She looked up to find the man she loved waiting in the door. She stood, set the letter aside.

"Yes. Everything is perfectly fine."

She rushed over to him then, put her arms around his neck and smiled up at him with all the love bursting in her heart.

"We have some making up to do," she said frankly. "Are you up to the task, Lucas?"

One strong hand moved down to caress her bottom while the other pulled her more tightly against him. "Have you ever known anything to stop me before?"

Victoria started to respond but understood that it was a rhetorical question, for he closed his mouth firmly over hers in a deep, loving kiss.

Yes, everything was finally perfect.

CHAPTER THIRTY-THREE

TASHA WATCHED Jim sleep. He'd had a hell of a weekend so far. She and the therapist had arrived at Madelyn Rutland's house even before the police. Thankfully, things were not as bad as she had worried they might be.

They had spent most of Saturday in session with the therapist, who had determined that Madelyn's influence was what had sent Jim spiraling backward.

He seemed completely himself again now, though, and she had thanked God over and over for keeping him safe. She'd thanked Daniel Marks, as well. When Marks had deviated from the plan on Friday afternoon, Tasha had all but gotten hysterical.

But it was over now and that was all that mattered.

She'd wanted to tell Jim about the baby last night but he'd been too exhausted after the lengthy session. She'd found him asleep on the sofa.

Now, she lay next to him, watching his chest rise and fall, and hoped that this beautiful man would never be lost to her again. Whatever it took, she had to keep him safe.

He was her lover, soon to be her husband. And the father of her child.

His eyes opened and the extraordinary blue color took her breath away.

"Good morning," he murmured.

"Good morning." She nipped his bottom lip. "I was thinking of preparing breakfast."

His arms went around her and pulled her close as he rolled onto his back, settling her atop him. "I was thinking of having you."

"Hmm. Sounds good to me." She kissed him, let the sensations overtake. God, she loved this man.

He rolled, tucking her beneath him, then peered down at her with a sly look in his eyes. "Maybe some syrup or whipped cream." He licked his lips. "I'll let you decide where I should start."

Heat shimmered through her at the idea of what he proposed. Jim liked getting creative…so did she.

"I need to tell you something first."

She had to do this now. It wasn't fair to make him wait any longer…even if every moment would be incredibly worth the wait.

"Make it fast," he murmured between kisses along her jawline. "I'm starved."

He was right. They hadn't made love once since the night she'd had dinner with Martin. Both of them had been afraid of what would happen.

But she wasn't afraid any more.

"We may want to move up the date of the wedding," she suggested nonchalantly.

He stopped in his sensuous progress down her throat, looked her straight in the eye. "We can do it today if you want." He grinned. "Mom might have a stroke, considering all the plans the two of you have made."

The church, wedding gown, invitations…too many things to list. "You have a point there," she said, trac-

ing a path along the masculine contours of his amazing
chest. "But I'm afraid this won't wait."

"Okay, spill it," he ordered, his face going all serious.

She had to smile at that look, especially considering
his generous and hard-as-a-rock sex was pressing insist-
ently against her. It was all she could do not to arch into
the feel of him, but that would end any possibility of a
conversation for at least an hour.

"I just thought you would want to know that we're
having a baby."

For several seconds, he just looked at her as if he
were still waiting for her to say what she had to say.

"Well, say something!" She bopped him on the
shoulder.

He kissed her so softly tears welled in her eyes. On
and on, he let his lips show hers how much he treasured
her, how much he wanted her. Then he pulled away just
far enough to look into her eyes.

"I hope we have a girl so she can be just like you."

She blinked, promised herself she wouldn't cry. "I
love you, Jim."

He smiled the sweetest smile she'd ever seen. "I love
you." He kissed his way down to her belly, then whispered, "I love you, too."

And then he made love to her every bit as slowly as
he'd kissed her, making her feel cherished and utterly
complete.

CHAPTER THIRTY-FOUR

DANIEL PARKED the rental at the curb in front of the Hastings home. He jumped out and hoped he hadn't missed her. With the security requirements, early arrival at the airport was crucial for all flights these days.

Just don't let her be one of the ones who err on the side of caution.

He took the steps two at a time, not slowing until he'd reached the door. A firm knock followed by two rings of the bell should bring her to the door...if she hadn't left already.

The house sounded empty. His hopes fell to somewhere in the vicinity of his feet. Anticipation had his heart galloping like a wild horse.

Glancing at his watch, he weighed whether he still had time to make it to the airport before her flight boarded. Most likely.

Just as he'd decided she must have gone already and turned to go, the door suddenly opened.

"Daniel?"

She held a small bag, carry-on size, in her hand, while another, larger one sat at her feet.

"I was afraid you'd left already." Anticipation or maybe just plain old nerves made his voice a little shaky.

She glanced past him. "My cab should be here any minute." Then she lifted her face toward him and gifted him with the most amazing smile. "I'm glad you came to see me off. I would have hated not getting to say goodbye."

How did he begin? They were practically strangers.

"That's part of the reason I came," he said, not sure where to take it from there.

She chewed her lower lip, looked toward the street again. "You'll have to talk fast, Daniel. That's my cab."

He held up a hand for her to hold on. "Let me talk to him—see if he can give us a few minutes."

Looking uncertain, she relented. "Okay. But I can't be late."

A grin stretched across his face. "Don't worry."

Confused and sure she would never get through the next few minutes without breaking down, Emily watched Daniel bound over to the taxi. He ducked down to peer inside the window and said something, then reached into his pocket and withdrew a couple of bills.

Did the guy require a deposit for waiting?

"He doesn't mind waiting?" she asked when Daniel rejoined her at the door.

"It's taken care of." He looked around anxiously. What was wrong with him? "Do you mind if we talk inside?"

Worry twisted through her. Had he learned something new about the insane woman who had killed her father? Emily wasn't sure she wanted to hear any more. She wanted to put this nightmare behind her.

Her father's killer would be behind bars or in an institution soon, James Colby's body would be returned to his final resting place and Jim Colby was doing well once more.

Everyone had gotten what they wanted.

Well, at least part of what she'd wanted. The ball of nerves in her tummy roiled again.

"Sure, we can go inside." Emily opened the door wider and stepped back for Daniel to come inside. She worked hard to keep her composure in place.

She had spent most of last night closing things up around here. She'd cleaned out the fridge and donated the canned and dry goods to a local charity. She'd done about all she could do unless she decided to sell the place. But she had no plans to do that just now.

Coming back to check on things would give her a chance—excuse, actually—to see Daniel.

As much as she hadn't wanted to leave without saying goodbye, she had dreaded this moment.

She'd taken a real tumble for this handsome guy in the past week. And he liked her. She'd felt it in his kiss. But liking her and wanting to pursue a relationship with her were two very different things.

"What did you want to talk about?" she asked, taking a moment to admire how good he looked. Today he wore a pale blue shirt and a pair of softly faded jeans. He looked relaxed and entirely gorgeous.

Those dark brown eyes mated fully with hers and she abruptly understood how just looking into the right man's eyes could bring one immense satisfaction. Her body temperature shot up at least ten degrees.

"Let me take that." He took the bag she'd been holding and set it aside.

"Is something wrong?" Was he behaving nervously or was it her imagination? She was the one who was nervous.

He exhaled a big breath. "Just one thing, actually."

A frown pulled out her brows. "What?"

"I can't let you just leave like this, Emily." He held his hands palms up in a gesture of exasperation or desperation. "We've hardly gotten to know each other. There's too much that hasn't been said."

Her heart did one of those crazy acrobatic things. "What're you saying, Daniel?"

"That I want to get to know you better. I want…" He took her hands in his. "I'd like you to stay a while longer. See where this takes us."

A warm, dizzy feeling made her sway, but his strong hands steadied her.

"But what if it doesn't work out? What if what we've felt was only related to the adrenaline of the moment?" she asked, then shrugged. "Maybe all the time we spent together?"

He silenced her with his mouth. Kissed her on and on, urging her to surrender completely to him.

When she could no longer bear the yearning inside her, she leaned fully into him.

He was right. They should explore this…see where it took them. She could get another week off from work.

Who knew? Maybe she'd stay. She had her father's house. Being a secretary—a damned good one, at that— would ensure she found work quickly. And maybe she'd try her hand at writing again.

She had to be crazy, insane with the temptation of his kisses.

"Wait." She pulled away, looked deeply into his eyes. "Are you sure you'll have time for me? Don't you start working for the Colby Agency soon?"

"I can put that off a few days." He brushed his lips to hers, teasing the flesh he'd already tortured.

"But what if it doesn't work out?" She'd never taken a chance like this. Not once.

"And what if it does?" He pulled her closer, wrapped his arms tightly around her. "I want you here with me, Emily. You don't have to make a lifetime decision right now. We'll take it one day at a time."

How could she say no? She'd already fallen head over heels for him. He was one of those rare men whom every woman dreamed of finding. Hadn't she been looking for him her whole life?

She would be out of her mind to let fear keep her from going after the chance at complete happiness.

She sighed a mighty breath. "All right, then. Let me tell the taxi driver I won't be needing his services."

Daniel grinned. "I already did. Gave him a hefty tip, too."

Her mouth gaped. "You were certainly sure of yourself, Mr. Marks."

He shook his head. "Sure of us."

"Well, then. I guess we should get started. What do you want to know first?" she asked, infusing all the lusty invitation she could into her words.

"How about what you'd like for brunch?" He stole another quick kiss. "You're going to need your strength."

Before she could summon a proper answer to the unexpected question, he'd ushered her out the door and down the street to the little diner she'd loved as a child. They shared pancakes coated with syrup, fruit and the special house blend coffee. With each bite he fed her, and he insisted on feeding her, he whispered sweet things to her, made promises she prayed he would keep. She did the same for him, loving the feel of his lips as they brushed her fingers whenever she placed a strawberry against his lips.

By the time they'd walked back home, she was ready to tear his clothes off. But Daniel had other plans...plans that included making every nuance of every moment special.

He undressed her slowly, so very slowly and kissed each new expanse of skin he uncovered...paid special attention to all the right places.

When he'd deposited her onto the canopy bed she'd slept in the first half of her life, he took off his clothes, with the same infinite slowness, making each movement a choreographed part of foreplay.

By the time he moved over her, she was well beyond ready. She needed him now...no more waiting.

He kissed her once, tenderly, with that same slow-motion, heartrending finesse, and then he entered her in one smooth but urgent thrust.

She cried out at the feel of him inside her, but the sound was muffled by his sweet kisses.

The intensity of their lovemaking built until their movements reached a fever pitch.

Release came simultaneously and in that final burst of sensations, Emily knew that there was no way she could ever leave. Her heart belonged here. With this man and all that he so selflessly offered.

She was finally home.

CHAPTER THIRTY-FIVE

"THANK YOU, LUCAS." Victoria accepted the glass of wine he offered.

He sat down in the chair next to her.

"The moon is lovely tonight," he said after taking a sip of the special vintage she'd been saving for just such a moment.

"Yes, it is."

Though the night air was a little brisk, Lucas had built a glorious fire in the patio fireplace. The flames dancing in the darkness were hypnotic. She could sit here like this all night. Sipping exquisite wine and enjoying the company of the man she loved.

"I'm thinking if the baby's a girl, she should be named after you," he said, lavishing her with a charming smile.

"I believe Tasha and Jim will be deciding on the name for their baby." Her heart leapt with joy at the idea of becoming a grandmother. "But we'll give him or her everything else he or she needs."

Lucas chuckled. "That I don't doubt." He sighed and slipped one strong arm over her shoulders. "James would be very proud, Victoria."

A flicker of sadness went through her. "Yes, he would."

"We'll make sure this child knows all about her grandfather," Lucas assured her.

Victoria looked deep into his kind eyes. "Yes, Lucas, we'll make sure she or he knows everything about Jim's father, but *you* will be this child's grandfather."

Lucas kissed her temple. "That means a great deal to me, Victoria."

"You mean a great deal to me."

They sat in comfortable silence for a minute, perhaps two. Victoria considered that life truly was good now. Her son was healthy again and a grandchild was on the way.

The future looked very bright.

"Daniel called a little while ago," she said, only then thinking of her newest investigator's request. "He's asked to take a few days more before he comes on board."

Lucas smiled knowingly. "I'll bet Miss Emily Hastings delayed her flight, as well."

"Your instincts have always been uncanny, Lucas."

"Right now, they're telling me I should freshen your drink."

She laughed softly. "If I didn't know better, I'd say you were trying to seduce me."

He leaned forward and retrieved the bottle. "To my way of thinking, we haven't finished making up for lost time just yet."

She tipped her glass to his in an impromptu toast. "Agreed."

"Does that mean you'd consider taking off a few days with your neglected husband?"

A smile curled her lips. "Absolutely." She snuggled closer to him. "A break would be nice before the storm."

"Storm?" He peered down at her. "What storm?"

She shrugged as if she weren't quite sure, but the plan had already taken form. "I'm thinking I need to up the agency's ranks. Bring in some more new blood."

"Really? A recruitment?"

The concept fueled the excitement already growing. The more she thought about the idea, the more she liked it. "That's exactly what I need. A Colby Agency recruitment."

"The various government agencies have done that for years. You can't go wrong."

"I'll call a staff meeting first thing in the morning and make the announcement." She couldn't wait!

"So much for taking a few days off," Lucas said glumly.

Victoria nuzzled up to him again. "Who says I can't take off after I set this thing in motion?"

"I'll hold you to that, my dear."

She traced a path down his shirt front with her fingertips. "Would you like a down payment on that promise?"

He tipped up her chin and brushed his lips to hers. "A good negotiator always gets something up front."

She stood, pulled him to his feet and led him inside. Tonight was theirs.

And tomorrow, well tomorrow was whatever she wanted to make it. After all, she was Victoria Colby-Camp. She never gave up...never surrendered. Not with a man like Lucas at her side and her son where he belonged…and a grandchild on the way.

Oh, yes. The Colby future was full of promise.

* * * * *

Look for COLBY AGENCY: NEW RECRUITS
*coming in April and May of 2006
from Harlequin Intrigue.*

Everything you love about romance...
and more!

Please turn the page for Signature Select™
Bonus Features.

Bonus Features:

Signature Select™

BONUS FEATURES

COLBY CONSPIRACY

AUTHOR'S JOURNAL
The Colby Agency:
Where Are They Now?

Have you wondered what happened to your favorite COLBY AGENCY characters? Debra Webb gives an update on all the characters you have grown to love.

4   I want to thank all of those loyal readers who come back to the Colby Agency time and time again, and all those new folks who join in with each newly released book. As I wrote the Colby Conspiracy, I wondered what special thing I could do to show my appreciation. As an avid series fan myself, I knew immediately that I would want an update on all those characters from previous stories. So, here it is! A quick look into the lives of characters, past and present, from the Colby Agency. Enjoy!

Safe by His Side featuring Katherine Robertson and Jack Raine: This is the story where the Colby Agency began in Harlequin Intrigue. Raine is still advising various government entities from time to time, but mostly he spends time with his two children, the oldest of which will start school next year. Katherine is absolutely satisfied being a stay-at-home mom and a loving wife to Raine. Her father recently moved into a small cabin next door and loves being a full-time grandfather.

The Bodyguard's Baby featuring Nick Foster and Laura Proctor: Nick decided to leave the agency in order to pursue a quiet life with Laura and their son, Robby. Since leaving the Colby Agency, Nick has pursued a career in developing security systems for residential use. He and Laura are expecting their second child.

Protective Custody featuring Ian Michaels and Nicole Reed: Ian and Nicole remain at the Colby Agency as two of Victoria's top investigators. They have two beautiful children.

Solitary Soldier featuring Trevor Sloan and Rachel Larson: Sloan is completely retired these days. He and Rachel homeschool their two children. They hope to add a third child to their family one of these days.

Personal Protector featuring Ric Martinez and Piper Ryan: Ric is still a mover and shaker at the Colby Agency (with those Latin good looks, who could help but shimmy in his presence?). He and Piper have tied the knot but won't be starting a family for a while. Piper has become a household name in Chicago as the princess of investigative journalism.

Physical Evidence featuring Mitch Hayden and Alexandra Preston: Long-distance relationships often don't work out as planned. Alex and Mitch decided they wanted to settle together in Tennessee. The two recently married. Mitch remains sheriff and Alex is doing a little selective private investigations work locally in Raleigh County. At Alex's recent visit to the doctor she learned that their first child would be a baby girl!

The Marriage Prescription featuring Zach Ashton and Beth McCormick: Zach and Beth married, as you know, and went on to have two beautiful children. They found the perfect house in the suburbs near Chicago. Beth is practicing medicine at Chicago General and Zach is a stay-at-home dad, advising on cases at the Colby Agency once in a great while, like when Victoria's son was in trouble. Zach and Beth moved both their mothers to Chicago to be near the children. The two women still bicker over who will hold which child first.

Contract Bride featuring Ethan Delaney and Jennifer Ballard: Ethan is still on board at the Colby Agency, and his lovely wife Jennifer works side by side with her father at the family pharmaceutical business. The couple recently welcomed the birth of twin boys. Mildred, Victoria's secretary at the Colby Agency, plays surrogate grandmother for the boys since she and Jennifer's father are a couple (there may be a wedding in their future very soon).

Her Secret Alibi featuring Simon Ruhl and Jolie Randolph: Simon and Jolie are living happily in Chicago. Simon is still one of Victoria's right-hand men. Jolie is working for an investment firm near the agency. The two are making ambitious plans for a family.

Keeping Baby Safe featuring Scout Jackson and Pierce Maxwell: Scout and Max both work at the Colby Agency part-time. They spend the rest of their time with their child and are working on child number two.

Guarding the Heiress featuring Doug Cooper and Eddi Harper: Doug and Eddi are happily married with a beautiful baby girl. Doug left the Colby Agency to work with Eddi in the D'Martine jewel business. Eddi's father sold his hardware business and he and Eddi's mom are very involved in the D'Martine ventures, as well, making for one big happy family.

Cries in the Night featuring Melany Jackson and Ryan Braxton: Melany and Ryan are married and living happily in Chicago. Their daughter, Katlin, is thriving. Ryan is still with the Colby Agency.

Melany plans to start working in the Colby Agency's research department part-time after Katlin begins school.

Romancing the Tycoon featuring Amy Wells and John Calhoun: Amy and John had a big Texas wedding. The two commute aboard John's private jet between Dallas and Chicago. Amy loves being a Colby Agency investigator and John is still running his ranch and the family oil business. John's father is campaigning for a grandchild, but for now Amy and John are happy with things just the way they are.

Agent Cowboy featuring Kelly Pruitt and Trent Tucker: The happily married couple lives in Texas on the Pruitt family ranch. Trent helps out the Colby Agency whenever they need him for backup in the Lonestar state. The first Tucker child will be born this Christmas.

Situation: Out of Control featuring Heath Murphy and Jayne Stephens: Heath and Jayne are still living above the Altitude Bar and Grill in Aspen. Heath works side by side with Jayne giving guided tours to the thousands of tourists who flock to the snow-laden city each winter. Jayne's friends and teammates have accepted Heath as one of their own. Jayne and Heath plan to start a family soon.

Full Exposure featuring Cole Danes and Angel Parker: Cole still works for unnamed agencies of the government in an advisory capacity, but never strays far from the small home he and Angel share outside Chicago. Cole loves Mia as if she were his own child. He and Angel recently learned that they are expecting. Cole is equally thrilled and terrified. (Can you imagine a man like Cole Danes being afraid of anything?)

Watch for the *COLBY AGENCY: NEW RECRUITS* coming next spring from Harlequin Intrigue. You'll meet lots of newcomers to the agency who will take you on one thrilling, edge-of-your-seat ride after the other.

Cheers!
Debra Webb

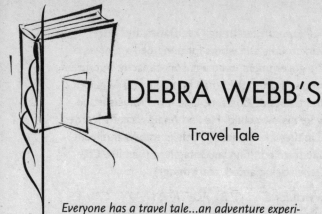

DEBRA WEBB'S

Travel Tale

Everyone has a travel tale...an adventure experienced while on vacation or while on a business trip. Debra Webb shares one of her favorite stories about Chicago, the city that is the setting of her COLBY AGENCY stories.

Chicago: Home of the Colby Agency
Chicago is the third largest city in the U.S. The thing I love most about Chicago is the magnificent architecture and the equally turbulent and colorful history. Imagine Chicago during the time of Al Capone and John Dillinger. This city, with all its character and characters, teems with inspiration.

Some of the world's finest museums can be found in Chicago and there is no end to the diversity of the culture. The famous citizens of Chicago range from athletes to gangsters. But, personally, I'll take the shopping (well, I could go for a virile cop or fireman, as well). The sheer number of shops available makes this city a world-class shopping stop.

Still, there is one thing for which I will always remember Chicago (other than the Colby Agency of course): Chicago is where I met Hugh Grant. True story! I swear! My friends Rhonda Nelson, Sabe Agee and I were traipsing the Magnificent Mile one hot July day (actually we were AWOL from a conference) and decided we might just wilt if we didn't get back to the hotel. Before going back, I insisted that we have pizza in "the" pizza place (you know the one I mean). Rhonda and Sabe didn't want to walk that far out of our way, but I forced the issue so they went along.

Once we reached the restaurant we had to wait forty-five minutes to get inside the door (there was a really long line). The whole time Rhonda

> *Chicago is where I met Hugh Grant.*

complained loudly, something to the effect that if it wasn't the best pizza she'd ever eaten...well, you get the idea.

After making it through the doors, we had to wait even longer for a table. Finally, finally we were served the best pizza I've ever eaten in my entire life. As I was devouring said pizza, my two cohorts suddenly fell into trances staring, seemingly, at me. When I demanded to know if I had something in my teeth they eventually sputtered that I should look behind me. And what did I see? Hugh Grant! He was standing right behind me as the waiter cleared a table for him and the two unidentified people accompanying him (one looked sort of like a model, but who had time to attempt to identify her).

To this day I tell everyone I had pizza with Hugh Grant. And I did, actually. He was only three or four tables away. I did stare at him while he ate and we virtually breathed the same air.

Oh yeah, and my friend Rhonda owes me big-time. You see, Hugh Grant is her favorite actor. Lesson learned: walking can be good for your heart in more ways than one.

Chicago...one of my favorite cities.

THE BEGINNING
by Debra Webb

Go back to where it all began.
One pivotal night was all it took to align
three lives toward a single, unforgettable
destiny. Read on and discover how Victoria
met the one and only James Colby and the
unstoppable Lucas Camp in this brand-new
short story.

THE BEGINNING

VICTORIA DREISER held her breath a moment before opening her eyes. Then she gasped.

"You're beautiful, Victoria."

Victoria turned to smile at her friend. "Thanks to you," she offered before shifting back to the mirror and the unexpectedly elegant reflection there. Victoria had never been one to focus on fashion or vanity of any sort. She was far too practical for such things. Gowns that cost hundreds of dollars. She touched the necklace at her throat. Diamonds and emeralds. Just not her style.

She took a deep breath. But tonight was different.

Tonight she wanted to be the belle of the ball. She wanted to be the princess in the fairy tale. If only Prince Charming would appear…

A deep yearning curled inside her. She was only twenty-two—it wasn't like she was an old maid. But Victoria wanted desperately to get on with the rest of her life.

"You know," Marsha Winton, her dearest friend in the world, whispered as she leaned closer, "Father has invited several of the young gentlemen who work at his Washington office."

Victoria felt a flurry of anticipation in her tummy. Her friend's father didn't work at a mere office. He held a position of tremendous authority within the government's enigmatic intelligence field. No one, perhaps not even Marsha, knew exactly for whom he worked or precisely what that work consisted of. Spying on the country's enemies, foreign and domestic, perhaps. Helping to keep the country safe. She shivered at the idea that the very man she'd waited for her whole life might be here tonight. Strong, loyal, kind and, of course, handsome.

"You're certain this color is right for me?" Victoria asked, doubt creeping into the mix of emotions churning wildly inside her.

Marsha gave Victoria's shoulders a hug. "Far better than it looked on me."

The dress had never been worn, in fact. Marsha had dragged it from her massive closet where a dozen others of similar quality and beauty hung.

Victoria smoothed her palms over the beaded bodice of the lovely emerald gown created from the most exquisite silk. "Well, I suppose I'll do, then."

Marsha laughed. "Yes, Victoria, you'll do quite well."

Victoria followed her friend from the room. The

sapphire-colored gown Marsha had chosen to wear looked amazing with her fiery red hair and creamy complexion. Victoria appreciated the way the color of her own gown complemented her dark hair and eyes. She felt exactly like a princess. Her mother would approve.

Marsha hesitated at the top of the staircase. Victoria didn't dare peek beyond the sweeping stairs to the entry hall below. Her pulse started to thud as her excitement built even higher. This would be her first official foray into the world of glamour and glitz.

"Is my hair okay?" Marsha patted her carefully constructed French twist.

"Perfect," Victoria assured. She'd fashioned her own hair in a similar manner, leaving a few curled strands to drape down her neck.

Marsha coiled her arm around Victoria's. "Let's not waste any more time, then."

The two descended the staircase together. The entry hall buzzed with the steady flow of new arrivals. Men dressed in elegant tuxedoes. Women floating across the gleaming marble floor in stylish formal gowns. It was the party of the decade. Victoria doubted Chicago had ever seen such a crowd of socially elite gathered in one place. Everyone who was anyone had been invited. Many had come all the way from Washington, D.C., which was where Marsha's father spent most of the workweek.

Classical music wafted through the air from the

small orchestra holding court in the ballroom. Victoria couldn't help thinking that every home should have a ballroom. She did so love to dance. Her mother had instilled that longing in her from the time she was able to walk.

"There's Father." Marsha pointed through the crowd to a group of gentlemen standing near one of the bars that had been prepared to serve the numerous guests. "Let's go say hello. Maybe he'll introduce us to someone important."

Her nerves jangling, Victoria hurried after her friend. She couldn't catch her breath. She couldn't recall ever being this excited before. Not even at graduation from the stuffy women's finishing school her parents had insisted she attend. But Victoria understood that she would appreciate the fine education she'd received when she moved forward into the rest of her life, which would not happen until the end of summer. Her father had insisted she take the summer off after graduation. *It's your last chance to relax and enjoy complete freedom, little girl,* he'd said. No matter how old she got, Victoria understood without doubt that she would always be her father's little girl. Since her mother was gone, she was all he had now. In all likelihood this "freedom" summer was more about him not wanting to let go than anything else.

She so wished her mother had lived to see her in this dress. Victoria's lips quirked. Ruth Dreiser could never understand why her only daughter, only child for that matter, didn't care to do all the girly, feminine things her mother had taken such pride in accomplishing. That nagging question, Victoria mused, was still a mystery.

There simply was no explanation for why a proper young woman, such as her, would read every political and law book she could scrounge up every night with a flashlight under the blankets, while studying fine arts and proper etiquette by day at a strict women's college. Or that she would chose to ignore her social life and focus on her education so intently. Her friends hadn't understood Victoria's burning need to accomplish all she could, to be certain she was well prepared. She wanted more than just a career. She wanted to make her mark, to stand out among the crowd.

Yet, here she was, dressed exactly the way her mother would have wanted and fully anticipating a night she would never forget.

She couldn't remember actually making a decision to do this. She'd certainly been invited to dozens upon dozens of parties before. Maybe her latent hormones had simply kicked in. Most women her age had participated in at least one or two romantic relationships.

Not Victoria. She'd been concentrating on her education and saving her heart for…something. The perfect man? Did such an animal even exist?

Victoria abruptly crashed into a solid object.

Her breath stalled in her throat when her gaze collided with silvery gray eyes that instantly drew her in and held her helpless to do anything but stare.

"Pardon me, madam," the man said, his voice deep and husky and utterly titillating.

Victoria's heart skipped a foolish beat. "I'm..." She drew in a shaky breath, told herself to stop staring at him, but it didn't work. "I'm terribly sorry, sir," she managed to say past the hopeful tightening in her throat. His hair was raven-black, and those eyes...so intense...as if he could see right into her thoughts.

20

"May I get you a drink, Miss...?" He looked at her expectantly, the slightest hint of a grin tugging at one corner of his nicely shaped mouth.

"Victoria!"

Victoria blinked, felt as if she'd suddenly emerged from some sort of daydream. "Yes?" She looked toward the sound of her friend's voice.

"Come!" Marsha grabbed her by the arm and tugged. "There's someone Father wants you to meet."

"Excuse me, sir," Victoria said to the handsome gentleman still eyeing her with blatant masculine approval. There was something about him that made her feel strangely comfortable and entirely intrigued.

"I trust you'll save a dance for me?" he challenged as Marsha pulled her away.

Victoria didn't get to answer, but she did flash him a smile and hoped he recognized a *yes* when he saw one.

Marsha dragged Victoria to where Mr. Winton stood amid several elegantly dressed men.

Before any formal introductions were made, someone to the right of her said, "You must be Victoria."

Victoria angled away from her friend and stared at the gentleman who'd addressed her.

"And you are?" she asked without confirming his assumption. She prided herself on caution when it came to strangers. Especially tall, good-looking male strangers.

"James Colby," he said with just a dash of arrogance. He took her hand and lifted it to meet his lips. "You're even lovelier than your friend suggested."

Victoria resisted the urge to shoot Marsha a warning look. Who was this man? Victoria did not like being caught off guard like this. From the corner of her eye she could see that her friend and several gentlemen, including Mr. Winton, were deep in conversation less than three feet away, and yet Victoria felt as if she were inexplicably alone with the man staring at her just now.

"That's very nice of you to say, Mr. Colby." Victoria quickly reclaimed her hand as well as her full composure.

"Nice has nothing to do with it, Miss Dreiser." He smiled and when he did those eyes sparkled like the bluest sea glittering beneath the tropical sun. "I'm a man who recognizes when he meets someone special."

Before Victoria could decide how to respond to that remark, the eloquent Mr. Colby had ushered her out onto the dance floor and the orchestra had begun to play something slow and sensuous.

His palm flattened against the small of her back and in the same smooth move he drew her in close. The fingers of his other hand folded around hers at the same time as he began to move with the rhythm of the wistful melody.

"I understand you've just graduated from Mary Margaret's," he said, those blue eyes watching her as if anything she said would surely be of the utmost importance.

She tried not to be flattered that a man so incredibly handsome would ignore the rest of the gorgeous women in the room and center his attentions solely on her. "You appear to know a great deal about me, Mr. Colby," she said, opting once again not to answer his question. What had her sneaky friend been up to? Matchmaking? She and Marsha would need to have a long talk very soon. Victoria had a plan that included careful selection of the man with whom she wanted to spend time. She would choose the terms and the timing.

"James," he recommended. "I'd like it very much if you called me James."

James. It fit his charming personality, she decided. "All right, James."

"May I call you Victoria?"

"I believe you already have, haven't you?" she teased good-naturedly, her tension easing into something much more pleasant.

The grin that spread across his lips just then did unexpected things to the pattern of her heartbeat. Victoria closed her eyes and tried to stop the slight spinning that had started for reasons she couldn't quite name. Maybe the dress and the music…the man certainly.

Perhaps it was the enticing way he smelled or the strength she felt in his arms. Whatever it was, she was keenly aware of the need to lean into him and that was certainly a first.

"Do you know what you are, Victoria?"

Her eyes fluttered open. "Pardon me?" Was the man going to dance with her or analyze her? Perhaps his charm only went so far.

"You're the kind of woman who knows what she wants and goes after it."

Another tendril of tension vibrated through her. How could he read her so easily? Her mother had told her for the first seventeen years of her life that she was determined to have her cake and eat it, too. Victoria had known what she meant. She wanted to be a properly educated woman who could pursue whatever career avenue she chose and still she wanted the fairy-tale love life, in that order. Was it possible to have both? She'd made up her mind long ago that it very definitely was. Nothing should get in her way. Male-female stereotypes never entered Victoria's reasoning. A woman could surely do anything a man could.

She had no intention of changing that firmly entrenched attitude whether men like James Colby liked it or not.

"I suppose you believe a woman's place is somewhat different from that of a man's," she returned crisply.

He chuckled. "Now what kind of fool would I be if I believed that?"

The sincerity in his eyes told her that there was a great deal more to this man than charm.

They danced for what felt like mere moments, but was in reality hours. And they talked. Talked endlessly. About everything and nothing in particular.

He couldn't tell her about his work due to its sensitive nature, of course, but he could tell her about himself and his past career. He'd served as a special forces officer in Vietnam and ended up a prisoner of war. He told her about the horrible weeks and months he'd spent at the hands of the enemy. Her heart ached as she listened to him speak of that time and how his closest friend had saved his life.

Victoria was very glad for that friend. She couldn't say for certain what it was, but the connection between her and this man felt stronger than any she'd ever experienced before. The memory of the first gentleman she'd met tonight—or bumped into, rather—surfaced briefly, but James said something that made her laugh and she forgot all about everyone else in the room for the second time that night.

When the dance floor no longer felt intimate enough they moved to the terrace. Victoria shivered as the cool night air brushed over her heated skin. She couldn't help admiring James's profile in the moonlight. This night was moving way too fast, but she couldn't seem to slow it down.

James sighed. "It's not every night that you see a sky like this."

Victoria smiled at the reverence in his voice. "You have to get away from the city's downtown lights to see its full beauty," she said quietly. She couldn't imagine any other place on earth being as beautiful as Chicago.

He inclined his head and appeared to listen. "Do you hear that?"

Victoria recognized the melodic notes of "Love Is Blue" floating on the air. "One of my favorites," she admitted, wondering vaguely if it was possible that they shared an interest in the same sort of music.

"Mine, too."

James turned to the woman at his side. If he had ever seen a more beautiful woman the memory escaped him just then. Yet, as beautiful as she was, her intelligence and strong will were her most compelling assets and intrigued him as nothing else ever had.

Since his return stateside he hadn't felt as compelled to reach out to anyone as he felt just now. What was it about this beautiful young woman that made him want to know all there was to know about her?

He suddenly wished this night would not end, and that tomorrow wouldn't take him back to D.C. and so far away from this jewel he'd just discovered.

"One last dance?" He found himself holding his breath as he waited for her answer.

The smile that trembled over her lips made his chest tighten with anticipation.

"I suppose we shouldn't change our evening's strategy now."

As she stepped into his arms once more, James experienced that intense feeling of belonging he'd felt from the moment he first touched her. How was that possible? They'd scarcely known each other a few hours. And yet he couldn't deny the sensation.

James had never believed in fate. He'd always made his own destiny. Even as a POW, he and his loyal friend had survived by sheer willpower. Neither would give up or allow the other to waiver.

They had both survived that harrowing time. Had a second chance to really live.

Why waste another second of that second chance?

"Victoria, I know we've just met—"

Victoria's heart leaped. This couldn't be that moment…it was too soon. As he said, they'd only just met. This wasn't fantasy. This was real life.

"I have to return to D.C. tomorrow, but I would very much like to see you again. May I call you, Victoria?"

Perhaps it was the way he looked at her. Or maybe the gentle, protective way he held her. But somehow she recognized that if she let this man slip away from her, her life would somehow be less than it should be.

Victoria Dreiser refused to take that risk.

"I would like that very much."

She watched his mouth lower toward hers and she caught her breath. His lips brushed hers, and in that infinitesimal space in time before he made the seal complete she felt a completeness she had never known before.

He kissed her with the same gentle intensity with which he held her. He tasted exactly as she had known he would, warm and exciting. She melted into his arms with the knowledge that this was where she wanted to be for more than just this night.

Drawing away just far enough to rest his forehead against hers, James murmured to her, "I'm of the opinion that a bargain is far better sealed with a kiss than a handshake."

"I wasn't aware that we'd negotiated any sort of deal, Mr. Colby," she teased.

He cupped her face with his hand, traced the pad of his thumb across her cheek. "My work can be very dangerous, Victoria. I've come too close to death too many times to take a single moment of life for granted, including this one. Once I've set a course, I rarely deviate."

"So we've gone from negotiations to a set course, have we?" She loved the way her retorts affected him, made him wonder, second-guess himself. She had the distinct impression that this was something James Colby rarely experienced.

He took her hand in his. "We have." He glanced toward the French doors and the ballroom beyond. The music continued to coast on the night air like a summer breeze swelling and receding. "I suppose we should return to the party before a search team is sent for us."

Victoria had no idea how long they'd been outside but she felt certain her friend would be looking for her if for no other reason than to drill her about James Colby.

The furor of the ballroom felt jarring compared to the relative quiet of the terrace. A giddiness wrought with possibilities shivered over her as she considered the man who stayed at her side for the too-fleeting remainder of the evening. Charming, handsome, brilliant. What else could a woman ask for?

And he wanted to call her.

Her father would say that she shouldn't be surprised since she possessed those same qualities. But then, fathers were supposed to say that.

Whatever the future held for them, Victoria wanted to see where it led. She didn't want to risk that he was the one and she let him get away.

She resisted the urge to shake her head. Had she really just thought that?

Evidently she could be love-struck like all the other silly girls she'd chastised in the far-too-recent past for that same behavior.

"Expect my call," he promised one last time before leaving a chaste kiss upon her cheek.

She nodded, then watched him walk away. She didn't wonder if he would call—she understood with complete certainty that he would do just that.

"Tell me everything!"

Victoria jolted from her thoughts as Marsha

popped up alongside her. "What happened to you?" she demanded of her sneaky friend.

"The better question," Marsha said knowingly, "is what happened to you?"

Victoria blushed, couldn't help herself. "We danced. We talked. We…" She sighed. "He has to return to D.C. tomorrow, but he's going to call."

Marsha rolled her eyes and heaved a woebegone sigh. "Finally."

Victoria frowned. "What do you mean *finally*?"

"My father has been talking about the great man James Colby for months. I—" she tapped herself on the chest "—was certain he would be perfect for you."

"Speaking of which, why didn't you warn me that you were setting me up, *friend*? And I use the term in its loosest form."

Marsha curled her arm around Victoria's and started across the swiftly emptying room. "Because I know you. You would have resisted."

"So what did you tell Mr. Colby?" Victoria had a feeling that whatever it was, it was more than she would have preferred.

Her friend grinned mischievously. "That you were destined for greatness and that he should lay claim before someone else did."

If Victoria hadn't known her friend so well she would have been mortified. "Since I know you're lying, I'll assume you provided the usual background information."

Marsha shrugged. "You can't grow up in a family headed up by an ex-superspy without playing by the rules."

"I'd thank you but I don't want this to go to your head. Playing Cupid can be risky business."

Her unrepentant friend grinned. "Another maneuver I learned from my father."

Victoria pulled Marsha to an abrupt stop as they neared the entry hall. "Who is that man?" she asked, covertly pointing to the gentleman shaking hands with Marsha's father.

Though Victoria didn't know his name, she remembered him quite well. Silvery gray eyes that radiated such intensity. She shivered at the memory of his decadent voice. What on earth was wrong with her tonight? She never behaved so…impetuously.

"That's Lucas Camp," Marsha said, drawing Victoria's attention back to her. "He and James are like brothers. Where you see one, you see the other. They're inseparable."

Victoria felt oddly startled. "Is he the one who saved James's life while they were POWs?" Her pulse had started to pound. It was the strangest thing.

"Yes, that's him. See—" she urged with a nod of

her head rather than pointing, "—he walks with a slight limp. Some sort of injury from the war."

Victoria watched as he made his way toward the front door. The limp was scarcely noticeable unless one paid close attention. Her chest constricted ever so slightly as she fought the urge to run after him and make good on her earlier promise.

"Do you know him from somewhere?" Marsha asked, clearly confused.

Victoria almost shook her head then nodded. "In a way," she said. She'd heard so much about him from James she felt as if she knew him quite well. "I owe him a dance, that's all."

"I don't know about you," Marsha said, dragging Victoria's attention away from the door closing behind the enigmatic man, "but I'm exhausted."

Upstairs, as they stored away their lovely dresses and prepared for bed, Victoria made the occasional agreeable sound as her friend rambled on about all the gentlemen she'd danced with and the interesting stories she'd heard. But Victoria's mind was on the two men she'd met tonight. James Colby and Lucas Camp. Somehow they had both made a tremendous impact on her in those few hours. James through hours and hours of getting to know each other, and Lucas through James's stories and that one moment of direct interaction.

As Victoria closed her eyes and drifted off to sleep she dreamed of both men, but in her wildest dreams she could not have imagined just how important to her each would become in his own right. She dreamed of love and adventure and extreme happiness.

She had no way of knowing that this night would forever change her life. This was the beginning of so many things, good, bad and all things in between. For that night three destinies collided and one unalterable force was born—the Colby Agency.

THE END

THE FORTUNES OF TEXAS: Reunion

Coming in October...

The Good Doctor

by *USA TODAY* bestselling author

KAREN ROSE SMITH

Peter Clark would never describe himself as a jaw-dropping catch, despite being one of San Antonio's most respected neurosurgeons. So why is beautiful New York neurologist Violet Fortune looking at him as if she would like to show him her bedside manner?

Silhouette®
Where love comes alive™

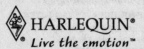

Starting over is sweeter when shared.

What else could editor Elisha Reed do when
she suddenly goes from single workaholic
to mother of two teens?

Starting from Scratch

Marie Ferrarella

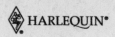
HARLEQUIN®

INTRIGUE

brings you an exciting new

3 IN ONE

collection from three of your favorite authors

EPIPHANY

by

RITA HERRON,
DEBRA WEBB
AND MALLORY KANE

**Christmas—a time for family, love and
celebrating new beginnings....**

With crime running rampant through the city of
Atlanta, Georgia, quickly destroying the holiday
spirit, only three hard-edged and jaded cops can save
Christmas and protect the citizens from danger. And
this holiday brings each detective face-to-face with
their own epiphany, and their worst fears—falling in love.

You'll never look at Christmas the same way again....

Available November 2005 at your favorite retail outlet.

www.eHarlequin.com